Following the Love

By
Lewis Pennington

Silver Lining
PUBLISHING

Silver Lining

PUBLISHING

159 Waightstill Dr.
Arden, NC 28740

ISBN: 979-8-9923401-1-2

Disclaimer

This is a work of Christian fiction. All characters, names, businesses, organizations, events, and situations portrayed in this novel are either products of the author's imagination or are used fictitiously. Any resemblance to actual persons, living or deceased, or to real companies, churches, ministries, institutions, or organizations is purely coincidental. While some locations, historical references, cultural details, or public places may be inspired by or based on real-world settings, they are used for storytelling purposes only and should not be interpreted as factual representations. Scripture references, spiritual themes, and expressions of faith are included as part of the fictional narrative and are not intended to replace personal study, pastoral counsel, or biblical teaching.

Dedication

For MBH
Thank you for six of the best years of my life.

Chapter One

A dozen students stood gazing up at a painting hanging beside the NC State University logo. Some scribbled quietly on small notepads while others spoke with practiced enthusiasm, parroting the adjectives and insights they'd memorized from that morning's lecture on the piece's artistic significance. A moment later, having absorbed all the painting had to offer, the crowd shuffled down the hall to the next piece of art. Charlie Carraway, a skinny boy clad in an oversized NC State sweatshirt and matching baseball cap remained. His green eyes narrowed on the imagery before him, two men standing on a mountainous cliff—one forlorn, distress etched across his face, the other reaching out for him in a dramatic moment of aid.

"Extraordinary how much pain can be depicted with just watercolors," floated a young girl's voice from behind him.

Charlie nodded without looking back, his focus growing more intense on the artwork, his eyes jumping back and forth between the two men on the canvas. His chest tightened. "What's it about?" he replied, his gaze unwavering.

"It's called *Manfred on the Jungfrau*, painted by Ford

Brown in the 1800s," the girl said. A bead of sweat inched down Charlie's temple. "But what's it mean?"

"It represents a scene from a poem with the same name. The man at the edge—that's Manfred. He's contemplating suicide."

Charlie grimaced as he leaned toward the painting, his gaze locking onto Manfred's distressed face, closing in on the lines of anguish running across his brow.

"What about the man coming up behind him?"

"He's a hunter who's going to attempt to rescue him from leaping to his death." The girl's voice was followed by a sigh. "So much tension—so much despair."

Charlie turned to the image of the hunter, studying the urgency in his face. He leaned closer, tilting his head as he struggled to appreciate the art for what it was—just art, not a representation of what had haunted him through the years. He turned away, shaking his head, then glanced up at the girl he had neglected to acknowledge. "Do you like this?"

She smiled. Her eyes were tender and warm with an innocence that rejected any attempts at glamor yet radiated the softness of a beauty from within. Petite in a bright yellow sundress, she brightened the beige backdrop of the gallery's dull walls. She brushed back her hair and answered, her confidence steady and assured. "Yes. In fact, I love it!"

Charlie gave her a curious look, struck by the conviction in her response. "Why?"

Her smile widened. "Simple…the potential for salvation."

He stared at her for a moment, intrigued by her answer yet still caught in the painting's lingering grip. Sweat gathered beneath his hairline, and his breath came heavy and uneven.

"Are you okay?" she asked.

He wiped his forehead. "I was when I came in here."

"I think you might be dehydrated."

"I-I'm sure I'm okay, it's just…" His voice trailed off as he looked at her again, and this time it hit him—she was beautiful. He blinked, caught off guard by the realization. "I'm, uh…I'm Charlie. Charlie Carraway."

She tucked a notebook under her arm then stretched her hand to him. "I'm Bree. Nice to meet you Mr. Charlie Carraway."

"Thanks for the insight into the painting. You must be an art major."

"Nope…paper science and engineering."

Charlie blinked. "Excuse me?"

Bree chuckled. "Yeah, I know. Not real glamorous but it's my ticket back to the hills."

"The hills?"

She brightened. "The Smoky Mountains." Her lips skewed. "You know—those big lumpy things in Western North Carolina. I'm going to work at the paper mill in Canton. It's just outside—"

"Asheville." He smiled. "I know it well. I grew up in Brevard and kayaked around Nantahala. I even know the paper mill. Heck, everybody knows about that thing."

"So what's *your* major, Charlie Carraway?"

"Just Charlie…and it's computer programming."

"Ah! You put all those ones and zeros together and make stuff happen on our computers. Very interesting."

Charlie shook his head, "Mmmm…no not really but I'll give you a pass."

"But you're a nerd—right?" she said.

"Profiling, are we?"

She laughed.

Charlie looked back at the painting. His smile faded but reappeared as he turned back to her.

"I think you were right. I believe I am a little dehydrated. Would you like to grab a soda at the snack bar?"

"Sure… that'd be nice."

As they turned to leave, Charlie asked, "So what's your specialty going to be when you make it back to Canton?"

She held her chin high. "Sustainable packaging."

"Boxes…you're going to make boxes?"

"Su-stain-a-ble boxes!" she said, drawing out each syllable for maximum impact. "The ones that are good for the environment."

"Boxes…" he said with a definitive air. "You're going to make boxes."

She tilted her head in a childlike admission. "Yes…I'm gonna make boxes."

They walked on, smiling, comfortable in the easy rhythm of their conversation.

She chuckled. "Maybe I'll make you one, and you can stuff all those ones and zeros inside it."

A cardboard box, the size of a Kleenex container, sat beside a glowing computer monitor. Scrawled on the side in bold black marker: *For all the ones and zeros – Love, Bree.* Next to it was an NC State wolf mascot bobblehead and a framed picture of Charlie and Bree standing in front of a church in a tux and wedding gown.

Charlie reached into the box and pulled out a peppermint, popped it into his mouth, and started typing.

Clickety-click. Clickety-click. Faster and faster his fingers flew until coming to an abrupt halt, his hands hovering over the keys as he leaned back in his chair and studied the screen like a maestro admiring his final note, as if he'd just composed the digital equivalent of Beethoven's Fifth. Instead of music, the monitor pulsed with an endless stream of cryptic code. Next to it, a second screen showed a fan of poker cards spread across a green felt table. Above them glowed the neon-styled logo, *Dealer's Choice Gaming.*

Charlie nudged his mouse. The cursor drifted across to the screen to a button that said, *Place Your Bet.*

Just as he was about to click, his phone buzzed. *Paper Princess,* the screen read. He glanced at it, hesitated, then silenced the call.

Back to the site. Click. He was in.

By six thirty that evening Charlie was still bouncing back and forth between his lines of code and the gambling site. For his efforts he had created eight new pages of code, lost $500 on the gambling site and missed a half dozen calls from Bree.

At seven o'clock the back door slammed shut. He scrambled to shut down *Dealer's Choice Gaming* then stretched his coding pages to fill both screens.

"Charlie!" Bree's voice came from the kitchen. "Charlie! Are you here?"

"Hello, beautiful," Charlie exclaimed, bounding down the stairs. His jovial entrance followed him over to her as he planted a kiss on her cheek. "How was your day?"

"My day was fine," came an icy reply. "I got to see Ashley perform an incredible piano recital. What happened to you? I called and called and it kept going to voicemail. I can't believe—"

"I'm soooo sorry. I forgot. I-I got so caught up in the final coding for the app and just zoned everything out."

Bree stood, lips pursed. "You and that coding." The words came out frosty but thawed by the last syllable. "You missed a good show. She was incredible. She even got a standing ovation when she played 'Für Elise.'"

"Is she mad at me?"

"That's for you to find out." She motioned him toward the hallway. "Go on. I'm sure she's waiting."

"Can I just tell you about the app first and what I've got—"

A quick wag of Bree's index finger stopped him cold.

Charlie tiptoed down the hall to a door with a pale blue light flickering underneath it. He raised his hand, pausing it over the sign pinned to its center—*Girls Rule*. He took a deep breath and gave it a two-knuckle tap. No answer. He knocked again.

"Come on in!" came his daughter's singsong greeting.

Charlie poked his head inside. The room was dim, the only light coming from the computer monitor sitting on a tiny desk at the foot of a single bed. Instead of the typical music, movie, and TV posters that plastered most teenage girls' walls, hers were lined with NASCAR memorabilia, most of it featuring a handsome young blond driver clad in a black-and-gold racing suit.

With his eyes downcast Charlie crept in. A moment passed as he stood in the middle of the room, his tail tucked between his legs. A host of cuddly plush animals sprawled across the bed's ruffled comforter eyed him, all judging—most of them gifts he had carried home over the years.

Expecting to be the recipient of his daughter's disapproving glare; instead, he found her sitting in the wheelchair she had known since birth, gleefully lost in the website on her screen. The soft glow painted her face, the same face that used to light up the moment he walked through the door.

"Honey?" he said with a tender smile, lingering there like he wasn't sure he deserved to come any closer.

She moved the mouse around the screen with a soft giggle, an easy sound—one of those small, lovely laughs that made her impossible not to love.

"Ashley? Honey?"

She angled her head and exhaled with a drawn-out "aww," her fingers absentmindedly reaching to tug at the frayed cuff of the old sweatshirt she wore—the one that used to be his.

"Ashley, dear, I'm so—"

She snapped her head at him, eyes bright, wounded more than angry. "I'm not talking to you!"

But the words came out thinner than she meant them to, her voice catching just slightly before she jerked her gaze back to the computer and resumed her session as if he had never entered.

"But you see, I've got the conference tomorrow and I was behind. I couldn't just—"

She pushed the mouse to the side and, with one quick heave on the chair's wheels, whipped around to him. Her blue eyes turned dark as she glared at him, gripping the armrests. "You don't think I know what you do at that computer all day long—do you?"

Charlie's jaw dropped.

"You think you're pretty clever."

"Honey, you don't—"

"You're my dad most of the time and then you're—"

"Ashley, please, I can—"

She bent forward, her eyes narrowing.

Charlie swallowed, prepared for the inevitable.

In an instant, the erupting volcano stopped cold as a Cheshire grin replaced his daughter's scowl. "And then," she continued, "you're a WIZARD—conjuring up digital worlds, creating algorithms from dust, and weaving spells in gibberish that magically make things happen online." She stopped, her smile growing larger. "No, Dad, I'm not mad."

"You're not?"

"No. I hate those recitals. I only do them 'cause Mom likes them. So, how's the grocery app coming?"

"It's done! I'll see it in action tomorrow at the trade show and then," he crossed his fingers, "I should be getting a signed deal."

"And then we'll be able to plug in our grocery list on our phones at any supermarket and voila…we get a map where everything is?"

"That's right!"

She laughed. "You created this for yourself, didn't you?"

"Well, kinda. I mean, who likes spending all their time wandering around a store looking for the Crustables or that special protein drink that should be in the drink section when it's in the pharmacy section?"

Ashley's eyes crinkled at the edges as she looked at him. "My daddio—the wizard."

He looked past her to the computer screen. "Whatcha looking at?"

She spun back to her computer. "One of those reels that shows random acts of kindness."

He studied it for a minute, then blinked. "Oh, before I forget, Mom mentioned you needed forty dollars for your trip this weekend. He reached into his pocket and pulled out two twenties. Along with them came a poker chip that plopped onto the floor.

"What's that?" she said.

He held it up, admiring it. "It's a neat marketing gimmick from the hotel I'm staying at for the conference. On one side is their logo," he flipped it over, "and on the other side is their website and QR code." He bounced his eyebrows. "And the good part is it's worth ten bucks."

"Coooool."

He handed it to her. "Keep it for luck this weekend."

"Dad, it's a church retreat. Why would I need luck?"

"I don't know, maybe for all those Bible trivia games you guys play."

She grabbed a purple magic marker and drew a heart on it, then handed it back. "Better yet…why don't you take it on your trip and give it to somebody who needs it."

His lips curled up. "Will that help get me into heaven?"

She looked up as if staring through the ceiling, then back to him with a hint of a smile and shrugged.

Charlie stood at the bottom of the stairs smiling at the purple heart Ashley had drawn on his poker chip. Beside him, a group of photos lined the walls. One in particular caught his eye—a picture of two young boys standing in a lake, their arms draped over each other's shoulders. The shorter boy beamed up at the taller one who was holding a tiny

American flag and sporting a toothy grin. For a few seconds his mind drifted back to the day he met Bree, the day he had also laid eyes on the *Manfred on the Jungfrau* painting. He shook his head, vanquishing the image. The boys in the picture remained, smiling up at him. He touched two fingers to his lips, pressed them to the image of the bigger boy, then proceeded up the stairs.

The door swung open to reveal Bree sitting cross-legged on their bed, piles of paper and folders strewn around her. A candle burned on the bedside table as Frank Sinatra crooned from her cell phone.

"I'm liking the vibe," Charlie said.

"Vibe?" she replied, giving him a quizzical glance over the top of the reading glasses that hung from the tip of her nose. "I'm not sure what vibe there is doing bills but if you're wanting to partake, grab yourself a crying towel 'cause that's the real vibe."

"Maybe you want to change your playlist then?"

"I can't. Frank's the one thing keeping me sane." She took off her glasses and rubbed her eyes then looked at him with a pitiful frown. "The paper mill shutting down has put us in a real bind."

"I know."

"I should've been out looking for another job as soon as I heard rumors about its closing. Now every job I'm qualified for is taken." She glanced up at him and whimpered, "Not a lot of companies are looking for a box maker."

Charlie chuckled then sat down beside her. "Don't worry, hon. My app's rock solid. It'll get us out of this, wait and see."

Bree returned a thin smile, but her eyes said she was less than convinced.

"You don't believe me?"

"I-I do. It's well, you know…"

Charlie's brow drew tight. "No, I don't know."

"Honey, you're a coding genius—you are. But…"

"Go on. I'm a genius but…"

She shook her head. "Nothing. I'm sure it'll work."

Charlie stood up. "But you don't think it's going to be any good."

"I didn't say that. I'm sure it is—it's going to be great! What I meant was that, well, you've built great programs before, and they all were awesome but then—"

"It's not my fault those other guys had the same ideas as me but were backed by major corporations. This time's different. I've got one of the largest grocery store chains interested in us. They've even soft tested it and it was working just like we hoped." He laid a hand on her knee. "This time tomorrow I'll be sitting with them at the conference signing a deal. Trust me."

Bree nodded. "You're right. I should trust. Faith…that's what we need. It's all in God's hands." She took him by the hand. "Can we pray?"

Charlie's lips tightened. He sat tense, his face lacking expression. "Bree, you know I—"

She swung her head, cutting him off.

He sighed and shut his eyes.

"Dear Lord, please hear our prayers this evening. Thank you for all the blessings you've bestowed upon us. Forgive us of our sins and trespasses. We thank you for your grace and mercy. Above all we thank you for your son Jesus Christ, thankful for his sacrifice…"

As she continued, Charlie cracked his eyes open, searching the room for any distraction to keep him occupied as he waited for her to finish.

"…in Jesus' name we pray, Amen." Bree raised her eyes to him, a sparkle now in them where fear had been before.

Chapter Two

The dinging of slot machines. The tinkling of roulette balls dancing around their wheels. Shouts of joyous winners and groans of dejected losers. Charlie walked through the noisy casino, his head on a swivel, taking in the chaos. He passed a sign that read, "Welcome to the 8th Annual Vegas Food and Beverage Digital Conference." He looked at his watch then down the hall to his destination, a pair of double doors leading into a great hall. The trade show booths loomed inside, blurred and indistinct. Somewhere among them was the one that would decide his family's financial future.

A sudden rush came over him. The trade show booth was just ahead, waiting for him, but it blurred at the edges as another path pulled at him. Just a few spins of the wheel of fortune and he would be on his way, he told himself. Bree's prayer the night before was no match for the quiet, insistent superstition threaded through his bones. The table—that was where it had to begin. A win there would settle everything, carry him clean into the moment that mattered, where his app would sit under the scrutiny of his potential benefactor—National Grocery Enterprises.

He turned, almost without deciding, and rushed to a roulette table, tossing down a chip on black.

The wheel spun.

"Black!" announced the solemn-faced croupier pushing a chip to him.

Charlie beamed. His first sign. He looked back to the double doors then turned and placed a stack of five chips on red.

The wheel spun.

"Red!" said the croupier, sliding five more chips to him.

"Beginner's luck," he said with a modest tone, not wanting to offend the hands of fate already smiling down on him. He stacked all his chips back on red while still checking the double doors.

The croupier scanned the betters at the table. "Final bets!"

Charlie glanced toward the double doors, then back again. The wheel was already in motion, the tiny white ball ticking and clinking along the rim before settling into an odd number—red.

"Yes," he breathed, his fist curling at his side in a small, trembling triumph.

The croupier maintained his stoicism until breaking character with a snort.

Charlie jerked his head back to the conference hall. Two men had started to close the doors. He scooped up all his chips and raced down the hall. As he ran, he passed a man slumped into a corner. His clothes were tattered, and his hair was dull and matted, suggesting he hadn't showered in a while. Once the casino's security saw him, they would certainly help him back to the streets. Charlie turned and ran back to him. His good fortune felt like more than luck, it felt like direction. If the course had been set, he would see it through, sealing it with an act of kindness. He reached into his pocket and drew out Ashley's heart-marked chip, turning toward the stranger with quiet resolve.

"Here you go, sir."

The man tilted his head, examining it. "But I don't gamble."

"It's worth ten dollars. You can cash it in."

"But—"

Before he could finish, Charlie was handing him a twenty-dollar bill. "Here—and keep the chip. It's good luck."

Like the casino, the trade show floor pulsed with noise and motion, only here the chaos was dressed in polish and purpose. In place of tables and slot machines stretched an endless maze of booths, some no larger than closets, others sprawling like miniature city blocks. Everywhere he looked, logo-clad pitchmen and pitchwomen leaned into their rehearsed enthusiasm, voices rising above the hubbub as they hawked the next must-have gadget or service, each one promising, in its own way, to help grocery stores squeeze a little more profit from the everyday.

For several minutes Charlie wandered through the maze searching for booth 1123. Just as he was about to turn a corner, a voice rang out from down the aisle. A young girl was waving at him. Above her a huge sign hung from the ceiling trusses that read, "National Grocery Enterprises."

Charlie feigned exhaustion as he walked up to her. "This place is like New York City. How are you, Betty?"

"Great! How've you been?" Her voice came full of the obligatory excitement NGE's management had instructed all its employees to adopt while working the booth. "I assume you're here to meet Travis." She rubbed her hands together and conjured up a hopeful grin. "We're all pulling for your app!"

"Thanks! I heard the soft test went well."

"Man, did it ever! We had the focus group using it in an actual store." She grabbed his arm. "Charlie, there was one guy with a list of thirty items on it. He was in and out the front door within twenty minutes! A list like that takes at least forty-five to accomplish! This thing works! Nobody even had questions about how to use it. I watched them enter their lists and off they went. Not one wandered off course. "I'm telling ya, that app's going to change your life!"

Charlie felt his toes curl inside his sneakers as he tried to maintain his composure. "Mind if I sit over in the corner until Travis comes in?"

"Sure. He should be here in the next ten minutes."

Charlie sat down at a table on the far side of the booth and pulled out his phone. His hands shook as he texted Bree. "I'm at the booth now. They LOVE it!!! Will call U soon."

Several minutes later a tall, angular man wearing a blazer, a bow tie and a fedora walked in. He went straight to Betty. Charlie watched as she pointed at him. The man nodded at him then walked off, disappearing into the maze of booths. The girl trotted over to him.

"He said he'd be back in a minute." She bounced, clasping her hands together. "Are you excited?"

Charlie nodded rapidly, unable to hide his excitement.

"Well, hang tight. He should be back soon."

Charlie pulled out his phone, swiped open his grocery app and smiled. The time at the top read 9:42 a.m. He crossed his fingers and shut his eyes. "Please, please please," he whispered.

At 10:16 a.m. he checked his phone again, shifted in

his chair, and tapped his foot in time with his fingers. At 11:01 a.m. he craned his neck, searching the aisles for signs of Travis. From a distance Betty leaned out of a group of fellow booth workers and raised her hands, commiserating from a distance and seeking his patience.

"I'm so sorry for your wait, Mr. Carraway," came a voice from behind him.

Charlie turned to find a short man in a tweed coat and thick-rimmed glasses standing behind him.

The man pointed to the table. "I'm Giles Pendleton. Mind if I join you?"

"Uh, no, of course not."

"I'm afraid Travis was called away for an impromptu meeting. It appears it will be lasting most of the afternoon."

"Should I come back?"

"No, that won't be necessary as he sent me to discuss your app. I'm the chief marketing officer, so I was going to be coming along with him anyway."

"Oh! Nice to meet you, Mr. Pendleton."

"Likewise." He cleared his throat. "So, your app, Mr. Carraway…" He cleared it again. "Your app tested through the roof with our focus group."

Charlie lit up. "I heard!"

"Very well done, sir. Not a glitch or bug to be found and a beautiful interface as well. Kudos."

"Thank you."

"So, here's the short of it. The bloody thing performs so well it actually cannibalizes business."

Charlie's lips parted but nothing came out.

"You see, Mr. Carraway—" he chuckled, "—and this is on us…we didn't factor in grazing or any secondary search time which results in additional sales."

Charlie stood silent for a moment. "I-I don't understand."

"Mr. Carraway, your app makes it so easy for customers to buy their groceries they don't spend any time looking for anything else."

"Which is the point!" Charlie replied.

"Not really. It's that additional time they spend in the aisles that leads to them buying other things. We thought the time they would save would allow for upselling and cross-selling opportunities. That's what we were after. Our research department estimated we could lose 12 to 15 percent of additional sales."

Charlie staggered back. "But—"

"Without a doubt, you've built a better mouse trap. It's just we don't want to catch our mouse that quick." He patted Charlie on the shoulder. "I'm sorry, Mr. Carraway. I'm afraid we won't be able to purchase the software."

Charlie could only nod, the gesture small and hollow against the weight settling in his chest. He turned and stepped out of the booth.

The noise didn't stop so much as slip away—voices thinning, then dissolving into something distant and unrecognizable. The bright banners and polished displays dulled as he passed, color draining from them until the whole floor felt washed in gray. The carnival energy, the easy promise of it all, receded with each step—taking with it the fragile hope that he might still find a way to pull his family back from the edge.

He paused at the exit where a doorman waited to offer him a way out. What would he tell Bree? How would he explain to Ashley all his magic was gone? The doorman reached for the handle and pulled. A wave of the casino's chaos, sights and sounds hit him like a tsunami, coupled with the impact of his app's rejection drowned his soul in despair.

Charlie sat at the end of a bar staring into a drink as his cell phone buzzed. "Paper Princess" appeared across the screen. Another two buzzes and it went silent, but his stare remained.

"Hey buddy!" A voice came to him from the other end of the bar.

Charlie looked up. A cheerful, dough-faced man with a mess of shaggy dark hair and that same crooked, slanty grin he hadn't seen in years stood wedged between two scantily dressed, bleached blondes, both draped over him with a familiarity that looked freshly claimed.

"I thought I might see you out here," he shouted, like they'd just missed each other yesterday instead of somewhere further back. "How you been?"

"Xander?" The name came out half-laugh, half-disbelief. "What're you doing here?"

"I've got a couple side hacks I've invested in since we last worked together," Xander said, the words rolling easy, like picking up an old rhythm. "Figured I'd come out, make some noise, help promote 'em. No luck though." He pulled the blondes in tighter with a grin that hadn't changed a bit. "But hey—it's Vegas, baby." His eyes flicked between them, then back to Charlie, motioning with a covert nod for him to come over.

Charlie answered with a tight smile and a glance down to his finger tapping his wedding ring.

Xander caught it, read it just as easily as he always

had, and gave a shrug that said *fair enough* without making it a thing.

Charlie looked down, pulling out his phone more for something to do than anything else. He scrolled through his messages—two from Bree, one from Ashley, marked with a purple heart. *How's my chip doing?*

He stared at it a beat longer than he meant to.

A hand clapped down on his shoulder, solid and familiar enough to make him jump anyway.

"I can't believe you're out here. This is great!"

Charlie turned. Xander stood there again, this time alone, drink in hand—like he'd shed the noise and distraction just as easily as he used to, dropping back into place beside him as if no time had passed at all.

"Where're your friends? Let me guess…not your type."

"Not my price range," he snickered. "Say, I heard you had a killer app you were working on. How's that going?"

Charlie's head dropped. "Nowhere."

"Sorry to hear that," he said, jerking his head to the side. "Hey, bartender, a couple bourbons straight up, please."

"Thanks, but my beer's fine."

"Nah…when you're licking your wounds, bourbon's always the best medicine."

Two drinks slid up to them. "That'll be—"

"Put'r on my tab," said Xander. He handed Charlie his drink and slapped him on the shoulder again. "Man, it's good to see you again."

An hour later, six empty shot glasses and a couple mugs were scattered across Charlie and Xander's table.

"Would you gentlemen like another round?" a young waiter asked from the next table over.

Xander looked at Charlie with a lazy eye. "Whatcha think? One more for the road?"

"Ohhhhhh…I don't see why not." Charlie turned to the waiter. "Two shots and two beers, please."

Xander held up his hand and counted out the drink order on his fingers. "Two shots plus two beers…Hey! That makes four."

Charlie snickered.

A moment later the drinks arrived. "Okay, fellas, this'll have to be your last round."

"Goooood," said Xander, "'cause I'm pretty drunk." He slapped the table. "Drunk as a skunk I am."

Charlie sat, eyes fixed somewhere past the noise, past the bar, the corners of his mouth turned down.

Xander reached over and rested his hand on his forearm. "Man, I'm sorry about the app."

Charlie let out a breath that didn't quite make it all the way out. "I don't know what I'm gonna tell Bree. She already thinks I'm a loser."

"Phhht—no she doesn't," Xander said, quick and certain. "That's just you talking." He gave a small shake of his head, a faint smile appearing. "Bree? She's the one who used to make sure you didn't tank those late demos, remember? Always cheering you on. And praying for you. Boy how that girl loves to pray. She didn't do all that for a loser."

Charlie hesitated. "She's a great cheerleader alright. Not so sure about the need for all the prayers.

"Bottom line is you got a good girl with that one Charlie Carraway."

"You don't understand," he said after a moment, quieter

now. "We're flat-out broke. Since Bree's been out of work, we've had to borrow from relatives just to cover rent while I've been building the app. My brother even paid for my trip out here. The only money I've got is what I won at the roulette table yesterday. And even that's going straight to the electric company when I get back."

He let out a hollow chuckle. "Best part? I'm still fifty bucks short."

"How much did you win?"

"Twelve hundred."

Xander's eyes lit up. "There's your answer!"

"What?"

"Your mojo. If you won that big, you can do it again and make enough for your rent and then some."

"Ah…I don't know…"

"You gotta believe." He stood, pulled out a wad of bills and threw them onto the table. "I got all this. Now come on. Let's go tap into that luck of yours. I could use some myself."

Charlie and Xander squeezed in beside a couple at a roulette table.

"Place your bets," announced the croupier.

"Is this the table?" Xander asked.

Charlie nodded as he placed a single chip on black.

"That's all you're betting?"

"For now."

Xander tossed a chip of his own next to it.

The wheel spun, and the ball clinked around until dropping onto a black slot.

"Winner to the black," the croupier said.

"Nice!" said Xander. "Now what?"

Charlie stacked five chips on red.

Xander smiled and did the same.

The croupier waved his hand. "No more bets."

The wheel spun.

The ball plunked down into a red tray. Xander slapped Charlie on the back. "I told you. You got it, man!"

Charlie remained stoned-faced, eyes fixated on the wheel.

The croupier slid both Charlie's and Xander's winning chips on red. "Place your bets, gentlemen."

"Let 'em ride," Charlie said.

Xander looked at him, a bead of sweat running down his forehead. "You sure?"

Charlie's eyes didn't leave the wheel.

"No more bets," said the croupier. With a flick of his wrist, he sent the wheel in motion.

Xander's eyes followed the ball as more sweat beaded on his forehead.

Around and around it went, clinking along on its journey until landing on another red slot.

Xander jumped, grabbed Charlie by the shoulders and planted a sloppy kiss to his cheek. "Holy smokes, man, you're on fire!"

Charlie began collecting his chips.

"What're you doing?"

"By my calculations I just made enough for the rest of the electric bill and most of next month's rent. I'm going to my room."

"You can't. You got the magic! You can't stop now."

"I'm sorry," he said, stuffing chips into his pocket. He looked at his phone. "It's almost midnight anyway."

"Midnight? It's Vegas! Midnight's the start of the evening. Come on…please? Just a few more spins. I need some of the Carraway mojo. Please!" He bent over, looking up at Charlie with pleading eyes. "And I'll get us another bourbon."

"No! No more bourbon." Charlie looked around the casino. "Oh, alright, just a few more."

Charlie stared at his phone. The time was 3:29 a.m. Xander sat next to him, slumped in his chair at the roulette table, passed out, clutching a half-empty bourbon.

"Will you be placing a bet?" asked the croupier.

Charlie stared at the empty section of the table in front of him then reached into his pockets and turned them out. "I guess not." He placed his face in his hands.

"Sir?"

Charlie sat shaking his head.

"Sir, I'm afraid you and your friend will need to vacate your seats if you're no longer betting."

He grabbed Xander by the shoulder, jostling him. "Wake up."

"Wha…"

"We gotta go."

Xander slid out of his chair, stumbling backwards. "Did ju turn it awound?" he slurred.

Charlie took him by the shoulders and aimed him toward a bank of elevators, patted him on the head and gave him a nudge forward. "Go to bed."

Xander staggered forward, waving over his shoulders and mumbling, "Yeah, beddy bye. Sounds good…"

Charlie watched him disappear past a row of slot machines then turned to the wall and banged his head against it until a security guard threw his hand in front of his face. "Sir, one more thump and you'll be spending the night in one of my less than luxurious suites. Do you have a room here?"

Charlie nodded.

"Then I suggest you go find it."

"Yes sir." His voice was low and broken. "I'm sorry, sir." With the weight of the day's losses pressing down on him, he turned and sulked away. As he neared the elevator, an unexpected scene unfolded a few steps away between an elderly man and a younger one.

The elderly man sobbed openly, his shoulders shaking. The other man—the one Charlie had given Ashley's heart chip to the day before—held the chip out to him with both hands and whispered something only they could hear. Whatever he said broke the man, causing his weeping to deepen.

Charlie stepped into the elevator. As the doors slid shut behind him, a trembling voice slipped through the narrowing gap. "God bless you, sir…God bless you."

Chapter Three

The gate attendant cleared her throat. "Ladies and gentlemen, at this time we'd like to inform you that there's been a slight delay in flight 303 to Asheville along with a gate change. Boarding time is now 10:02 at gate twelve."

Charlie rubbed his temples. The four Tylenol had done little to reduce the hangover brought on by the devastating amounts of bourbon from the night before. With a groan he swung his backpack over his shoulder and headed for the new gate assignment. The dinging of the airport's slot machines along the way—a painful gauntlet reminding him of his financial collapse at the casino— churned his stomach. By the time he got to gate twelve, sweat was pouring down his forehead. Across from the gate, next to the restrooms was Xander, slouched in the same position as the night before when he had sent him stumbling back to his room. Charlie plopped down beside him.

"You on this flight?" he said.

Xander cracked one eye open, pausing to clear the haze. "Oh hey, buddy," came his beleaguered response. He straightened in his chair, blinking himself out of the painful catnap. "Yep."

Charlie sighed. "I'm so ready to get out of this place. All I want to do is get home."

Xander managed a crooked smile. "That was a good time last night," he snickered, "right up until we lost our shirts."

Charlie shook his head. "I don't know what I'm going to tell Bree. I came out here with a guarantee that I'd be coming back with a signed contract and now—no contract and even less in our bank account."

"What're you going to do?"

"I don't know. I'm all out of ideas."

Xander reached in his pocket, pulled out a poker chip and handed it to him.

Charlie backed away as if being handed a dead rodent. "Oh no! I'm done with that whole thing."

"No, it's not a real chip. It's my business card."

Charlie rotated it. It was just like the one Ashley had drawn the heart on. One side was a company logo, TS Enterprises, on the other side, Xander Whitman, Marketing Director, along with his contact information and a QR code.

"You wouldn't believe how much retention we get with this type of business cards. And the QR code makes it easy for us to capture their information when they visit our site."

"Ladies and gentlemen," came the gate attendant over the speaker, "we'd like to announce flight 303 to Asheville is ready for boarding. Passengers in rows twenty-five to thirty-eight may now board."

"That's me," Xander groaned as he eased out of his seat. "This is gonna be one painful flight." He took two steps forward then stopped. "You should use the chip if you have any more ideas. My boss is looking for some additional revenue streams and he's into technology. Bitcoin—you name it, he's into it. Hope to see you back in AshVegas!"

Charlie shoved the chip in his pocket and followed the cattle call of passengers toward the gate. As he waited for his row to be called, the attendant came on the PA stating that the flight was full and asking if anyone was willing to give up their seat for another passenger. Standing next to the attendant was a woman with an infant strapped to her chest. The plea-filled look on her face indicated the seat being requested was for her.

Several minutes passed with no one coming forward. Charlie turned around and saw the crowd standing resolute, unflinching, all avoiding eye contact with the mother in need. Her eyes welled with tears as she stroked her little one's head.

"Excuse me, sir. Excuse me, ma'am. Pardon me…" One by one Charlie maneuvered through the line, rebuked several times for line jumping. By the time he reached the counter, the attendant was back on the microphone requesting the seat exchange again.

"I'll do it," Charlie said, holding out his boarding pass.

"You're wanting to give up your seat?"

"Yes ma'am."

She smiled at the woman with the child, then turned back to him. "Thank you, sir," the attendant said. "On behalf of the airlines, we'll be offering you a round-trip ticket good for any flight to and from Las Vegas."

"I appreciate that but that won't be necessary."

The mother shifted her baby to her hip and with her free arm gave him as much of a hug as she could. "Thank you so much," she said, wiping her eyes. "You'll never know what you just did for us." She reached into her purse and pulled out a hundred-dollar bill.

"That's quite alright, you keep it."

The attendant handed Charlie a slip of paper. "If you'll come back in twenty minutes, I'll have information about getting you back to Asheville."

Just as he was about to turn around, he looked up to find Xander at the gate door, his cell phone in hand snapping picture of him standing next to the attendant.

Bree paced around the kitchen island, her shaking hands twisted in frustration, sometimes dragging through her hair as she groaned, then stopping to glare at Charlie, who sat knees together, head lowered like a child weathering the storm from a disapproving parent..

"I can understand not getting the contract but to go gambling!"

"I'm sorry. I-I thought I could at least bring something back. I started out so lucky with all the mojo going for me but then it all—"

"Luck?" she said. "We don't rely on luck! We rely on our faith—in Him—not superstition, not lucky rabbits' feet, and not that mojo thing." She clasped her hands tightly, as if trying to steady herself. "Lord Jesus, give me the words." She glanced at him. "Help my husband lean into You, not false hope and idolatry."

"I did *not* commit adultery!"

She snapped her head toward him, eyes widening in disbelief. "You're not even paying attention, Charlie. I said, 'i-dol-a-try.' You're putting all your hope in other things rather than God."

Bree took a stool across from him and rested her chin in her hands with a look of exasperation. "National Grocery isn't the only grocery chain in America. What about some of the others?"

"Almost all of them were at the show and they all knew about NGE's focus group test and agreed that it would eat into profits." He tapped his fingers together and smiled. "But…I do have another idea for another app that—"

Bree threw her hands over her face. "Oh no!"

"Wait—before you say anything, just listen."

"Charlie, I love you, but this *has* to stop. Isn't it time to get a real job, one with a salary and benefits? We need the security now more than ever. My COBRA benefits are ending soon but Ashley's medical bills are going to keep coming. And the gambling…" She squeezed her eyes shut. All she could do was shake her head.

"Kindness!" Charlie blurted.

"Wha…"

"I've got a way to spread kindness! Isn't that what the Bible says to do?"

"That's one thing. But what're you talking about?"

"My idea is to track random acts of kindness. I came up with it on my trip."

Bree narrowed her eyes on him, her tirade softening into curiosity. "Don't random acts of kindness websites already exist?"

"Yeah, Ashley showed me one. But here's the thing— none of them track the impact or pass-along effect of the individual acts. With this app, I've got a way for people to see how their kindness generates other acts of kindness. It'll show where the next act occurs and with whom and where it goes from there."

"I LOVE it!"

Bree and Charlie spun around to find Ashley sitting in her wheelchair in the doorway.

"Dad, that's awesome! Giving people a way to see what impact their kindness had will make other people want to do it!"

Bree drew a long, deep breath. "I get what you're saying, but we still have bills. Couldn't you find something steady for now and work on your stuff at night?"

"Like what?"

"My friend Stephanie said there's an entry-level IT job open at MB HAYNES."

"The construction company?"

"Yeah…they do just about everything…industrial stuff, commercial and residential. I don't know all the details, but she said they've been around for over 100 years, so you know they're solid."

"But I don't know anything about construction. And all those guys look like Vikings. I'm a scrawny nerd."

"You'd be in IT, not swinging a hammer, silly."

"Still." He rubbed the back of his neck. "I really want to do my own thing. You know that. It's my dream."

"I know." Her voice softened. "But dreams are a lot easier to chase when the lights stay on."

He looked away.

"Oh," she said, as if remembering. "And Stephanie said they're employee-owned, too."

He gave her a look.

"What?" Bree said. "Technically, that kind of makes it your business."

"I don't know. Seems like a stretch for me."

"I know," Ashley chimed in. "You could charge people for using the site!"

Charlie nodded, thankful for his daughter's redirect away from Bree's MB HAYNES pitch. "Yeah, we could do that," he said, looking hopefully at Bree.

"Noooo, you can't charge people for doing something good!"

Ashley sighed. "Yeah, Mom's right."

"What's not right about it? It's a service like anything else. Of course we could charge."

Bree motioned to Ashley to follow up on her comment.

"It just wouldn't be right is all," Ashley said. "We're taught to do acts of kindness out of love—"

"NOT to profit from it," Bree added.

"Where's that written?"

Ashley and Bree glanced to one another with a knowing look, then turned to him and together said, "The Bible!"

Charlie pursed his lips, knowing his argument could go no further. "Well then, I guess I'll just have to figure out another way."

Bree's eyes brightened. "You mean of getting a full-time job?"

The room fell silent. "Yes…. I'll look for a nine-to-five gig."

Bree jumped up and hugged him. "That's my man!"

Ashley wheeled up next to him and said with a smile, "And you can work on *Following the Love* at night!"

"Hmmm, that's kinda catchy," he said. "I kinda like that."

Charlie sat in his office, his hand resting on the mouse. He inched the cursor up and to the right until it found the browser's incognito option. He looked over his shoulder, making sure the door was shut, then turned back and opened a new window. In the search bar, he typed *Dealers Choice Gaming.* There it stayed, blinking back at him, the words hanging there like a shot glass set too close to a recovering alcoholic's hand. His fingers curled into a fist, then slowly opened again. With a quick head shake, he dragged the cursor across the words, erased them, and typed something else.

A moment later he was putting his credit card back into his wallet. He stared at the screen and smiled.

"Daddy, are you in there?" came Ashley's voice from the hallway.

The door creaked open.

"Come on in, honey," he said.

Ashley wheeled to him. "Whatcha doin'?"

He slid his chair to the side, his screen glowing bright, revealing his new purchase. On screen, in bold letters under the *GoDaddy.com* logo, was a single line: *Congratulation, you now own Followingthelove.com.*

"You've started!" she squealed.

"Yep," he said, a grin stretching across his face.

"How long before you can get it going?"

"I don't know. There's some special coding needed that I'm not very familiar with so I may have to find some-one to help."

"Wait'll Mom finds out!"

"Ash…maybe we should wait on that a bit."

"Oh, yeah, you're probably right." Her eyes crinkled at the edges. "This is so exciting!" She spun her chair in circles. "*Following the Love*…It's perfect. My dad…doing good!" She stopped. "Just remember though…no—"

"Profiting from it." He sighed.

"Right." She leaned forward. "Just leave that part to God."

"Deal." He bent over and kissed her on the cheek. "Run off to bed now."

As soon as the door closed behind her, Charlie turned back to his computer, closed his GoDaddy account and proceeded to PinnacleLoans.com. The site's animated headline, *10 MINUTE LOAN APPLICATION*, changed from black to green text then exploded into tiny hundred-dollar bills floating down the screen like confetti. A click of his mouse and the money was gone, replaced by an online form. He pulled his license and a credit card from his wallet and laid them next to the keyboard, then glanced down to his computer's clock—10:11 p.m. He rubbed his hands together and began typing.

At 10:20 he sat back in his chair, crossed his fingers then clicked the submit button and watched the progress bar churn in circles as the Pinnacle Loans' system evaluated his worthiness. It stopped. He took a deep breath and watched two simple words pop up that sent the same wave of despair his last spins of the roulette wheel had. *Loan Denied.*

Chapter Four

The foyer of TS Enterprises was a chrome and marble masterpiece fit for display in the Guggenheim. Charlie sat squirming on a sleek black leather sofa, its shiny angular metal frame providing the perfect accent to the Picasso-style painting hanging behind it. In his lap he cradled his laptop. His knee bounced in rhythm to a distant jackhammer from the construction work being done twenty stories below.

Just then the elevator doors slid open and two men walked out together. One was broad and beefy. He wore a T-shirt and jeans and had a fearsome scowl and a tattoo of Thor's hammer on his neck. The other was sleek and sophisticated in a crisp dark suit, his blonde hair pulled back into a short ponytail. The more sophisticated of the two stepped toward Charlie, paused a minute, then with a raised eyebrow and crisp Scottish accent said, "Mr. Donavan, I'm Murdock. Mr. Sinclair asked that—"

"I'm sorry, my name's Carraway."

The man stared at him a half second, a puzzled look on his face.

"Charlie! My man," came a voice from the elevators.

He turned to find Xander walking up with a big smile.

Charlie glanced back to the two men, but they were gone. He turned around reaching out to shake Xander's hand. "Thank you for letting me drop in like this so soon. I-I was going to wait but, you see, I'm kinda in a bind. Like I was telling you in Vegas, things have been tight and with the app not selling and not being able to get a loan I was—"

Xander put his hand on his shoulder. "Listen, I meant what I said—if you had any other ideas, my boss would love to hear about them. I just remember how creative that brain of yours operates, so I'm sure whatever you have will bowl him over. Not to get all mushy but I really missed working with you. So whatcha got?"

"It came to me on my way back from the conference. The premise on how it works is based—"

"Before we go in, let's get a pic of you and Pablo for posterity. You know, in case you become rich and famous I want to have proof I was around when it happened." Xander led him back to the sofa where he pulled out his cell phone. "Ready?"

Charlie smiled.

"Got it."

"So, as I was saying," Charlie continued, "the concept—"

"Oh shoot! We gotta go. I'm sorry, buddy. I had to get a meeting with him at the last minute and that last minute's right now. I'll wait to hear the pitch the same time you give it to Sinclair."

"I hope he's into kindness," Charlie said.

"What he's into is making money," Xander replied.

The marble and chrome motif followed them on their walk to Thomas Sinclair's office through a maze of modern, shiny, organized cubicles. A dull hum could be heard along the way with minimal office chatter. Peppered between the outer offices, the walls were hung with pictures of automobile dealerships, restaurants, and cargo ships, all of which Xander explained were either partially or wholly owned by TS Enterprises. As they came to the end of a hall, a large glass-walled conference room occupied most of that side of the building. Inside was an enormous table with more than twenty high-back leather chairs wrapped around it. As they passed, Xander pointed to a large gold plaque with the Bitcoin logo etched into it. "See, I told you he was into tech." A few more feet and they were standing in front of a door with a silver plate in the center, the name "Thomas Sinclair" engraved on it.

"Get your game face on," Xander said. He raised his hand to knock but before he could strike, the door eased open. Xander gave Charlie a quick smile. "He likes doing that."

Charlie looked up. Wedged in the corner of the ceiling and wall, above the door, was a tiny spy camera angled down on them. Charlie began to smile at it but thought best not to.

Sitting behind another marble desk was the striking figure of a man in a tailored vest, crisp white shirt, and tie. Without uttering a word, he exuded power and money. His chin was square and firm, almost military, marked by a small scar to the right of a deep cleft. Dark, discerning eyes studied everything with quiet precision beneath closely cropped black hair. There was a restraint to him—an economy of movement and expression—that suggested discipline rather than display.

"Good morning, Mr. Carraway. I'm Thomas Sinclair."

At five feet ten inches, Charlie somehow felt smaller than he ever had before. Standing in front of a massive wall of floor-to-ceiling windows, Sinclair's backdrop was a panoramic view overlooking the Asheville skyline out to the Great Smoky Mountains.

Charlie's voice faltered. "G-good to meet you, sir."

"Xander tells me you're into technology and that when you and he worked together in a past life, you showed a great deal of creativity."

Charlie stood mesmerized, eerily drawn in to every syllable of Sinclair's compliment.

"He went on to say that you've developed a lot of software that—for whatever reasons—never took off."

"That's right."

Sinclair waved his hand to a wall covered with logos of all the companies he controlled. "Here at TS Enterprises, we value technology. It's been key to our success. As such, I'm always open to new ideas and opportunities, anything to grow the business and set us apart from the competition." He clasped his hands together in front of him. "So, Mr. Carraway, what monumental idea do you have for me today?"

Charlie set his laptop down and wiped a bead of sweat from his forehead before it had a chance to show itself. He understood the man in front of him most likely didn't suffer the weak. He cleared his throat, raised his chin and began his pitch. "Kindness—"

Sinclair turned his right ear to him, leaning in as if unable to hear. "Excuse me. Did you say 'kindness'?"

Charlie was taken aback by Sinclair's immediate reaction. His practiced intro was already in jeopardy. The bead of sweat returned, multiplying along his entire brow. He cleared his throat again.

"Yes sir. Kindness. The software, which is in an app platform, is based on it."

"Kindness? And this helps business how?"

"If you'd just…" Charlie balked at completing his sentence. The man in front of him had probably never been on the receiving end of any type of rebuke.

To his surprise, Sinclair owned up to his impatience. "I'm sorry, Mr. Carraway. I'm such a busy man I often jump into questioning mode to move things along so I can tackle the next agenda item. My apologies. Please proceed."

"No worries, sir. So, imagine a way to actually *see* kindness spreading around the world—that's what the app is all about. It's a simple idea—you give someone a token when either you do something kind for them or they do something kind for you. Each token has a unique code that can be logged on our website so you, and they, can track where it goes next, who receives it, and how it impacts lives along the way. What's even more special is that there will be an interactive map to follow tokens in real time as they create a ripple effect of good deeds." Charlie ended with a smile and a quick glance at Xander who was standing with a quizzical look on his face.

"How would it be monetized?" Sinclair began. "Would you sell the tokens?"

"We couldn't do that. Since it's based on doing good, that would come across as being opportunistic."

"What about advertising?" Xander asked. "I'm sure sidebar ads from charities or other downstream companies in this space would want that type of association."

"I'm afraid that could come off in the same ways as token sales."

Sinclair let out a gasp, his tone taking an edge. "Seriously, how do you make money with this?" He looked to Xander. "What do you think?"

Xander shrugged with an apologetic look.

Sinclair's jaw dropped, his eyes growing wider. "Ahhh! You're thinking a 501C. This is a nonprofit play, isn't it?"

"I-I'm not sure yet," Charlie said. "I just set it up online last night as an LLC."

Sinclair rocked back on his heels, his face drawn up as if he had smelled something foul. "I'm sorry, but I'm not interested. I'll admit the concept is unique but you're obviously not a businessman." He turned to Xander. "Your friend's creative but I only invest in opportunities and solutions that have a clear path to generating revenue. Now, if you'll excuse me, I have a meeting to attend. Xander can walk you out." Without a handshake or goodbye, he turned and headed out the door.

Xander walked behind Charlie out to his car. They stopped when they got to a sickly minivan with a back bumper hanging off and rusty wheel wells drawing attention to the bald tires.

"This is yours?" Xander said.

Charlie's head dropped. "Yep."

"Buddy, I'm sorry how that went. He's…well, he's—"

"No apologies needed. He's right. I'm not a businessman. I'm just…I…I'm not sure what I am anymore." He took Xander's hand. "I appreciate you at least getting me in to see him. If there's anything I can ever do for you, please let me know."

Xander nodded. "You got it, buddy."

Charlie got into the van and sat watching as his friend walked back inside. He pulled out his cell phone and sent a text to Bree. *Please send cell number of your friend with the IT job at MB HAYNES - Love C.*

The TS Enterprise conference room sat silent except for the occasional shuffling and flipping of papers between Sinclair and an older, balding man in horn-rimmed glasses. Sinclair alternated between scratching out something on a page and scribbling his signature on a check. In an assembly-line fashion, the older man would flip a page over from a stack of papers and slide it to him, followed by a check to be signed. When there were no more papers or checks for Sinclair to put pen to, he sat back in his chair with his hands clasped behind his head. The older man examined him without a word then reached into a manila folder. His hand shaking, he slid one more document to him.

"This is what we're looking at, sir."

Sinclair examined the page left to right until settling on the lower right corner. He closed his eyes. His breathing grew heavy. He stood, walked to the window and looked down at the streets below. The sounds of the construction workers' jackhammers grew louder.

The older man fidgeted with his glasses. "What're we going to do, sir?"

A moment passed. Sinclair took his time turning back to him. The whisper of a smile appeared on his face.

The following morning Charlie walked out of his front door wearing a short-sleeved button-down and a tie that had yet to be pulled into place. Bree ran up, pulling him back around to her. "Here, let's fix this thing." She took his tie in both hands and shimmied the knot snug up to his chin.

"Ahhrrrgg, yur chok'n' me, Mom!"

"There you go, little fella." She gave him a peck on the cheek. "Sharp as a tack." A final jostle to his collar, a pat on his shoulder and she was all smiles. He, on the other hand, struggled to muster a sliver of enthusiasm.

"I know this isn't your dream but it's times like this, that make me fall in love with you all over again."

"What if I don't get it?"

She tugged on his collar. "I'll still love you." She grabbed his hands. "Let's pray."

Charlie looked out to the road and around the neighborhood. "What, right here?"

"Of course. It doesn't matter when or where. Here, I'll say it." She closed her eyes, leaving him staring down at the cracks in the cement. "Dear Lord, please be with Charlie today. Guide him in his meeting and give him confidence and wisdom. Whatever is your will may it be done. Amen."

"That's it?"

"Yeah, they don't all have to be long, just to the point. Besides, *He* already knows what we need anyway. Now go shine!"

Charlie forced a smile, turned and walked to his van. He closed his eyes again, not to pray but to gather himself for a trip to interview for a job he already hated.

Just as he reached for the ignition, his cell phone buzzed. Without looking at the screen, he answered it.

"Hey buddy," came the voice on the other end.

"Xander?"

"Yeah, who'd you think it was?"

"Sorry, I didn't check my caller ID and…what's up?"

"Remember what you said about doing me a favor if I ever needed one?"

"Yeah."

"Well, I need one."

"Okay, what is it?"

"I need you to come back in. The man wants to see you again."

Charlie reared back from the phone. "What for? To tell me how stupid I am again?"

Xander chuckled. "Noooo, he wants to talk about following the kindness."

"You mean *Following the Love*?"

"Yeah, yeah...*Following the Love*. When can you be here?"

"Are you sure, because I've got a job interview in forty-five minutes and—"

"Cancel it. Cancel whatever it is and get to Asheville."

"But Bree lined up it up with a friend and it's—"

"Trust me, Charlie. You need to get your butt over here."

"What's it about?"

"He didn't elaborate. In fact, he told me not to say anything else."

Charlie looked back at his house. "I-I don't know. Bree's counting on me. I can't let her down again."

"Carraway, if you don't ever listen to me again, you have to now. Trust me. Get in your car—"

"I'm already in it."

"Good! Now turn it on, press the accelerator and get that hunk of junk here now!"

Charlie continued staring at the house.

"Charlie?"

He chewed at his lower lip.

"You still there? Hello?"
Charlie turned the ignition. "I'll see you in thirty minutes."

Chapter Five

Charlie walked through the revolving doors of the TS Enterprise building; his phone held in front of his lips like a slice of pizza.

"Please tell me you're here." Xander's voice came from it.

"I'm in the lobby just outside the elevators."

A minute later the metal doors slid open. Xander stepped halfway out and waved him in. "Hurry." He said pulling Charlie inside.

"Why such a rush?"

"He's got another meeting in fifteen minutes."

"Are you okay?" Charlie asked.

"I'm fine. It's just a man like Sinclair doesn't like to be left hanging and we're already ten minutes late."

"Hey, he's the one who called this last-minute get-together—"

Ding. The elevator stopped on the twentieth floor. Xander bounced on his toes, waiting for the doors to open as he fumbled with his phone.

"What're you doing now?" Charlie asked.

"Going to record mode."

"You're going to document this?"

"Absolutely," he said as he rushed him back through the cubicle jungle. "I record everything. You never know when you can get some dialogue or image for something promotional…I'm in advertising, remember?"

They stopped in front of Sinclair's office. "Plus," he said with a toothy grin, "I'm kinda addicted to it." He took Charlie by the shoulders. "Are you ready?"

"I-I guess so, but can you tell me—"

"Great," he said, spinning him around while nudging him inside.

Behind his desk, Sinclair sat rigid, his fingers tapping out an impatient drumroll on its marble top. He looked at a clock on the wall then turned his gaze to Xander.

Charlie suddenly felt a pang of sympathy for his friend.

As if a switch had flipped, Sinclair's eyes lit up and a megawatt smile replaced the dower expression. With his hand stretched out, Sinclair surrendered his throne and walked out from behind his desk to greet Charlie with a bear of a handshake. "I'm sorry about all the rush, Mr. Carraway." Still holding Charlie's hand, he placed his other one on top of it. "May I call you Charlie?"

"Yes sir, of course."

"I'm afraid I came across a tad less than polite yesterday. In fact, I was just downright rude. I was hoping you could forgive me."

Charlie gave Xander a sideways glance. "No apologies necessary, sir. I understand. Xander told me how busy you are."

Sinclair released his grip on him. "Indeed, but that still doesn't give me the right to be such a jerk. It's something I'm working on." He chuckled. "Three wives have tried to reform me but…" he sighed, "to no avail." He started to drift off in thought then snapped his head to the clock. "Therefore, I remain a work in progress and as such, I'll get right to the point of why I wanted to see you again…I'd like to fund you. Indirectly, that is."

Charlie stood thunderstruck. "Fund me?"

"I would like to fund your venture—*Following the Love*—your kindness website."

Charlie glanced at Xander then back to him. "But why? Yesterday you seemed so opposed to it."

"Sometimes things are simpler than they appear. In this case I just had a change of heart." He motioned to the logos covering his walls. "All those companies make me a lot of money, more than you can imagine, but not one of them does anything for our fellow man…Oh, their mission statements paint a pretty picture of doing what's right and Xander's a master at marketing us as being the guys in the white hats." He turned to Xander. "What do you call it?"

Xander straightened up. "It's called creating a halo effect. We strategically position ourselves with other companies who are already well respected for their charitable giving or are known for doing good works which in turn is projected on us. It's when—"

Sinclair waved him off. "Yes, yes, he gets it. Anyway, back to your idea. Having thought about it, I feel it's high time we started doing the right thing on our own. And what's more perfect than using technology to spread love and kindness?"

"I'm speechless," said Charlie, a smile beginning to form but wavering a moment. "What about your objection about monetizing it?"

"We don't! Not in a direct sense anyway. It will basically be a charity structure, but I still want to accept donations.

All the other do-gooder sites allow them, so I see no harm in it being done here."

Xander poked Charlie's shoulder, giving him a smile. "What do you think?"

Charlie stood looking back and forth between the two men.

"So, here's the funding aspect," Sinclair began. "We're going to pay you $50,000 to get it running—$20,000 up front which will be a gift, so you won't get taxed, and the remainder in cash installments of $10,000 a month for three months. This way you won't get taxed on that amount either."

Charlie's jaw dropped.

"I'm not finished…If you complete it within two months, you'll get a bonus of $20,000, also in $10,000 installments. By the time all the installments are complete, I'm sure you'll be clearing enough from the donations to fund yourself."

"This is great but there's some serious coding involved that—"

"No worries. I know you'll need help." Sinclair continued, smiling. "I have someone that I'm going to hire to work with you. You're okay with that aren't you?"

"Uh, okay. Sure, that sounds reasonable."

"So, do we have a deal?"

"Yes sir! Absolutely!" Charlie held his hand to the top of his head, his smile growing larger by the second. "So, what do we do now? Is there a contract to sign or some other paperwork?"

Sinclair thrust out his hand. "No need for that, just your hand and your word are enough."

Charlie grabbed it, shaking it rapidly. "Thank you, Mr. Sinclair, thank you. Thank you!"

Sinclair nodded, then looked to the door. "Ah, my balance-sheet banshee, right on time."

Charlie turned to find the older man Sinclair had been working with in the conference room the day before.

"Allow me to introduce Jerold Drummond, chief accounting officer for TS Enterprises. Jerold, this is the young man I told you about, Mr. Charlie Carraway. He's the gentleman who's going to put us on the right track to a kinder future."

Without a word, Drummond nodded in the manner a butler would upon greeting the master of the house.

"Charlie," Sinclair continued, motioning to the door, "if you would, follow Jerold. He's going to go over some of the infrastructure items on how this will all work. And if you're still okay with everything, you can begin work as soon as tomorrow afternoon. How's that sound?"

"Great!" Charlie grabbed his hand and shook it again. "Thank you, sir. I appreciate this more than you can imagine."

Sinclair gave a glancing directive to Drummond, who immediately placed a hand on Charlie's elbow. "Come, Mr. Carraway. Follow me to the conference room."

Xander winked at him as the two walked out the door.

As they vanished around the corner, Sinclair sat down and lit up a cigar. Taking a long drag, he arched his head back and blew the perfect smoke ring.

Bree sat next to Ashley on the sofa, her ever-present wheelchair in front of her. Both leaned forward, mouths agape. Charlie stood in front of them, arms raised and hands out, as if he'd just completed a magic trick. "What do you think?"

Ashley pressed her fingers to her lips. "I think it's a miracle!"

All of Charlie's attention fell to Bree. "Hon?"

She slowly moved her head side to side.

"Well…" he coaxed. "Do you think it's a miracle too?"

"I…I don't know what I think. I'm in shock."

"Good shock—right?"

"Give me a minute…I've got to make sure I'm not dreaming."

Ashley reached over and pinched her forearm.

"Ouch!" she said, swatting Ashley's hand away with a smile.

Ashley giggled. "No dreaming here!"

"Let me get this straight," Bree said. "You're going to get paid more than both of us combined in any given year, you're getting a bonus, and you've already got a staff—"

"I wouldn't exactly call one co-programmer a staff," Charlie said.

"And on top of everything, you're getting a ridiculous salary and probably great benefits."

"This is where it gets even better. There aren't any benefits per se but—"

"How's that make it better? It's a huge company. I'm sure you'd get benefits."

"Since I've already applied for an LLC, he's going to let the company remain in my name. It'll be *my* company! All that up-front money, salary and bonus are set up so that I can create my own benefits package as well as deal with the operational expenses."

Bree's eyes narrowed. "So, all of a sudden what you're making isn't what you're *really* making."

"Well…yes, but I sat with his accountant, and we went through all the numbers and it's still a lot. I'm telling you, hon, the guy's a genius. If he can run the financing for a billion-dollar enterprise, I'm sure he's right about this."

"Yeah, I guess so." She skewed her lips. "But Charlie, you don't know anything about bookkeeping."

"But he's a computer wizard!" Ashley said. "That's the most important thing."

"You're right, honey. Dad's the best at that but there's more to a business than just the service or products you make. You have to know numbers." She tilted her head at Charlie. "And let's face it, all dad's numbers are zeroes and ones."

Charlie shook his head and chuckled. "You and your zeros and ones."

"I'm serious, honey. That's just not you're strong suit."

"I know," he said with a growing smile. "That's why Mr. Drummond has set everything up for me. Since our main income will come from donations, we'll need a separate *media fund* for marketing."

"To keep things organized?" Bree asked.

"Exactly. It'll track what we spend on travel, equipment, and advertising without mixing it into everything else. A portion of each donation will automatically go into that account, so we always have money for promotion."

"That does seem helpful."

"He even lined up a company to manage it all so I can focus on the coding and tech side—which I love. I just sign off on the bills. Honestly, it couldn't get any better." He took her by the hands. "This is it, Bree! An opportunity of a lifetime is at my feet. I'll have my own company without any risks. It's a no-brainer!"

"So, if it's your company…" She hesitated. "I hate asking this because, well…what's in it for him? He's doling out all this money and resources and giving away a company—I know I should have faith, but it doesn't make sense."

Charlie picked up Bree's Bible from the end table, gently

laying his palm on the cover. "He only wants to do good… nothing in return. In fact, he doesn't want to be mentioned in association with it."

"Mom—that's straight out of Matthew chapter six! It's the scripture that says—"

"I know," she said softly. "'Be careful not to practice your righteousness in front of others to be seen by them. If you do, you'll have no reward from your Father in heaven.'" Her eyes welled with tears. She placed her hands to Charlie's cheeks and smiled. "Okay…go…go spread the love."

Charlie bumbled into his office banging the doorjambs with a tiny desk he purchased at a yard sale. Once inside he slid it into the opposite corner from his workstation.

Bree followed him in with a vase of flowers she had grabbed from the kitchen. "Where do you want them?"

"On her desk will be fine."

Bree looked at his huge workspace with its two wrap-around monitors and oversized laptop then turned and frowned as she placed the flowers onto the almost doll-sized desk.

"Don't worry, it's just temporary," he said.

Just then the doorbell chimed.

"I'll get it!" Ashley called from down the hall.

"Shoot, she's early! Quick, grab a kitchen chair for the desk while I finish cleaning up in here."

A minute later Bree and Charlie were standing in the middle of his office, hands folded in front of them, facing the door and waiting as the sounds of Ashley's wheelchair clunked down the hallway. A moment later she appeared in the doorway. "Mom and Dad, this is Lydia Phelps," she said, spinning around to a young girl in an earth-tone skirt and a crocheted crop top she likely got at a consignment shop. She wore strands of beads and trinkets in her long, slightly disheveled black hair that framing a face that was undeniably cute, if a touch sour.

Bohemian to the bone—and, Charlie guessed, a programmer's natural-born introversion.

An awkward moment passed as Lydia looked over the space. Her eyebrow rose as she took in the diminutive desk.

"It's just for this week." Charlie said.

"No need."

Charlie glanced at Bree then back to her. "You're okay with it? I've got a much nicer one in mind that I'm sure you'll—"

"No, I won't need anything. I'll be working from my home too."

"Oh! I-I just figured that during the start-up we could—"

"Seriously, I'm good in my own space. Besides, Sinclair only wants me to check in with you once a day."

"But if we're going to meet the deadline, there'll be a lot of back-and-forth, and most of it needs to happen in real time. By the way," he added, a sharper edge creeping into his voice, "what programming skills do you have? The platform's going to require a heavy load, including—"

She sighed. "All the basics. C++, Rust, Python, JavaScript, yadda yadda."

"Okay, but given the tracking aspect of the platform… anything there?"

"Ohhhh, that stuff," she said with a smirk. "So, we're talking geospatial programming, right?"

"Exactly."

"In that case how about geographic data work using

Geopandas and Shapely along with all the mapping frame-works and if you want real-time location services then how about I throw in experience with WebSockets, MQTT and Kafka. Not my favorite pastime but still rock-solid on scalable backend systems and database design and query optimization. Oh, and what about analytics and machine learning? Will my experience in those come in handy?"

Charlie stood speechless. Bree and Ashley eyed him, both looking as if they were about to burst.

"Okay then…" he finally said. "Working from home's probably good. Yeah, I think it'll work out fine."

"Great, then I'll be on my way." She turned to walk out but stopped at the door. "Since Sinclair wants me to call in at least once a day, how about noon?"

"Uh, sure."

"Okay then, I'll talk to you tomorrow." She hesitated. "And don't worry, I'm also good with email and texting."

Chapter Six

Over the next few months Ashley and Bree went about their days with Ashley going to school, practicing her piano and chatting with friends online while Bree gradually began living her life apart from Charlie as he worked nonstop to meet his deadline and the $20,000 bonus. Every day he was up before dawn at his desk, tapping out code. In the evenings Bree would bring his dinner and set it beside his keyboard. At bedtime she went to sleep alone while he worked until midnight. Head down into his programming, he only came up for air for his daily noon-time calls with Lydia.

"Charlie, how much longer are you going to work at this pace?" Bree would say. "It's bad for your health—more importantly you're not spending any time with God like you've been saying you would."

"I'm sorry, dear. I just want to make this work. One more month and we'll be launched and I promise every Sunday, rain or shine, I'll…"

"You'll what?"

"Just one more month. Everything will be different. I promise."

Charlie and Ashley stared at the refrigerator calendar and the purple heart she had drawn on the twenty-eighth day of the month. Charlie handed her a marker. "Here, you do the honors."

She hovered the marker tip over the twenty-eighth then moved it two days to the left and drew a smiley face. She smiled at him. "The wizard strikes again!"

"Hey, mister wizard, "Bree said, coming from the living room, "mind waving your wand to help set the table? Your peeps will be here any minute."

He picked up a spoon and tapped Ashley on the head. "Pit stop?"

"Let's ride, Daddio!" In a flash she whipped her chair next to the kitchen cabinet.

A split second behind her Charlie was opening drawers, slinging out plates, saucers and utensils and stacking them onto her lap.

"Oh no," she laughed, "we're losing one."

Charlie, quick as a cat, reached down and snagged a plate before it crashed to the floor.

Bree chuckled. "You guys break my plates, and I'll be sidelining that NASCAR of yours."

Charlie craned his neck to the window. "He's here!"

Bree opened the door just as Xander was about to knock.

Xander smiled. "Security cameras?"

"No…windows."

Squeezed between his elbow and forearm were two small vases, each with a single purple rose in it. He handed her one. "For our gracious host."

"Ah, thank you, Xander." She eyed the second vase. "Why the reserve?"

A moment later a yellow vintage VW bug pulled to the

curb. The custom-painted eyelashes over the headlights were a dead giveaway that Lydia had arrived.

Bree studied a sudden air of excitement on Xander's face as he watched her getting out of the car. Lydia's eyes drifted downward the closer she came. By the time she was at the stoop, all her attention was at her feet. "I'm not late, am I?" she muttered.

"No," Xander said, "I just got here too." He held the vase out to her. "I, um, I got you this. I mean I got both you and Bree one. See?" He pointed to Bree who followed along in the awkward moment by holding her vase up for display.

"What's it for?" Lydia asked.

"For meeting the deadline of course!"

"Mom," Ashley said as she nudged her wheelchair up behind her in the doorway, "Dad said we're ready."

"Lydia, Xander, this is our daughter, Ashley."

Ashley looked past Lydia, her eyes growing wide. "Is that your yellow bug?"

"Sure is."

"Ohhh wow! I love, love, love it! Did you paint the eyelashes?"

"A friend did those."

"Soooo cool!"

Xander tilted his head toward the back of Ashley's wheelchair. "Wait... is that Dusty Harmon's number eighty-two back there?"

"Sure is! Do you like NASCAR?"

"Like it? I love it! We've got VIP box seats at Bristol Speedway."

"What? You're kidding me."

"Nope. Would you like to go sometime?"

"What's going on out here?" Charlie said, coming up behind Ashley. "The party's inside."

"I just invited your daughter to a race at Bristol," Xander said. "And if she says yes, we might even get a chance for her to meet Dusty."

Ashley grabbed Bree's blouse, pulling her in. "Mom, what did he just say? Am I dreaming?"

They all laughed.

"Dusty Harmon," she swooned. "He's sooooo cute."

"Xander, do you know this guy?" Charlie said.

"We're not buddies or anything but he's done some promo spots for us in the past. Good kid. The fans—especially the young ladies—absolutely love him."

Lydia rolled her eyes.

"No, Lydia, you don't understand," Ashley said, "he's perfect."

"You know what's perfect?" Charlie said. "The lasagna Mom made. Come on everybody, let's celebrate!"

Charlie paced in front of his desk; phone pressed to his ear.

"I don't know, boss," Lydia said from the other end. "Everything's running perfectly on my end. Has anyone used it today?"

Charlie dropped into his chair and pulled up the admin page for the *Following the Love* website. His eyes narrowed as the screen loaded. "Well… that's interesting."

"What is it?" Lydia asked.

"Three tokens just went through, but something's off."

"I'm not at my computer—what do you see?"

"They look valid," Charlie replied, scanning the entries. "But they all originated weeks ago… from the same person."

He paused, reading. "One went to Beth Ann—she did something kind for someone with the initials T.J. Another moved from Tony to Aunt Mami, then to Sister Suzie. And the last one went to someone named Caleb… but it hasn't been passed on yet."

Lydia was quiet for a beat. Then, "What about the location feature? Is it still working?"

"Yeah, they're all around here—Sylva, Asheville, Arden and Candler. The one that was passed to TJ is in Raleigh."

"Any comments?"

"Yep! In fact, they all included a sentence or two describing the act of kindness."

"Nice! So, who's our good Samaritan dishing out all the love?"

"There's no name. They just put #82 as their ID tag." A moment passed as Charlie calculated. "So, counting these three, that's a whopping twelve tokens passed in our first three weeks. Not a raving success."

"I'm sure Sinclair's not happy with it," Lydia said.

"Have you talked to him?"

"No, remember, he wants you to fly solo."

Charlie dragged his hand down his face. "The problem isn't the app—it's that no one's using the darn thing. And you can't really fault people for not donating to something they're not even using."

"Maybe it's time to bring Xander back in," Lydia said.

"I don't know. We launched with the goal of letting word of mouth build the user base."

"Maybe there's another way, something less salesy. He's pretty good at promotions. Want me to give him a call?"

Charlie hesitated. "Sure, let's see what he can come up with."

Charlie peeked his head into his bedroom. Bree was fast asleep. He turned and tiptoed to his office and booted up his computer to find Xander already on a Zoom screen holding a cocktail.

"I thought you'd forgotten our call."

Charlie glanced back at the door; his ear turned for any movement from his bedroom. "Just making sure Bree was asleep."

"So, you're ready for a little promo mojo?"

"I guess…but not anything too overt. You know what I mean?"

"Yeah, I actually have your whole 'want to keep it low-key' speech to Sinclair recorded."

Charlie smiled. "So, any thoughts?"

Absolutely. I just need to know how low-key you want to be because it'll affect the results not to mention the cost."

"I don't know. What do you think?"

Xander sighed. "Typical non-committal response from a programmer." He scratched his chin. "How about we go at it this way. We hire a local influencer with a small following—"

"An internet influencer?"

"Uh, yeah."

"Sorry, keep going."

"So, we hire them for a one-month test run and gauge the bumps they generate, then determine if we want to scale up or down with their exposure. How's that sound?"

"Do it!"

"Dad, do you have some more tokens?"

Charlie turned from his computer screen to find Ashley sitting in the doorway.

"How many do you want?"

"Can I have ten?"

He reached into a box, counted out ten and handed them to her. "Feel free to use them all. We need as many out as possible."

"Will do!" she called over her shoulder, already turning toward the door.

"Thank you," he replied, watching her go—the makeshift #82 paper logo fluttering against the back of her chair as she disappeared around the corner.

He turned back to his computer. The screen flickered once, then brightened as the *Following the Love* dashboard came to life.

"Hmm." His eyes narrowed at an oval link in the top-right corner labeled *Newbies: 7*. He clicked it. A subpage popped open, listing the newest token recipients, those now officially part of the kindness train. He selected the filter marked *Originator*.

In an instant, the list rearranged itself. The top seven entries all bore the same name: Karstin Taylor.

"Cha-ching." The sound effect had come from his computer and startled him. He was moving his cursor to investigate when— "Ding"—another sound effect came. There, next to a new entry was the name Karstin Taylor again, the source of yet another token recipient.

Charlie jumped at the more familiar sound of his cell phone buzzing. He picked it up while still staring at his screen.

"You at your computer?" came Lydia's voice.

"Yeah."

"Then what do you think?"

"What do you mean what do I… Wait…did-did you add sound effects?"

"Sure did! Every time we get a newbie we'll hear about it."

"I love it! Great job, young lady."

"Aaaannd…"

"And what?"

"What about the cha-ching?" She said.

"That was you too?"

"Yep!"

"What's it mean?"

"Come on, boss. Think about it."

"We got a donation!"

Lydia chuckled as Charlie rushed to pop up the "donations" page. In the center in bold text it read, *"Congratulations! You have received a donation of $10. Click for donor details."*

Chapter Seven

Lydia sat in the coffee shop across from Charlie, her hands folded, resting in her lap while he held his out to her—pleading.

"But it's only been three months since the launch!" His voice resonated with restrained anger. "Sites like this take time to develop a following."

"I agree but Sinclair's an impatient man."

"Maybe I should talk to him."

"That won't help."

"Why? I can show him the analytics. I know it's not much, but we do have some momentum."

"He's already seen the numbers."

"But pulling the plug now is just…just stupid! I'm gonna talk to him!"

"No, Charlie—you know the deal."

"So, I can't talk to him?"

Lydia's taut lips and lack of a response were his answer. He arched his head back and groaned. A moment passed. "I can't keep doing this. One failure after another…"

"He doesn't want you to fail. He just wants a different strategy, one that he knows you're opposed to."

The ambient chatter of the barista taking orders, of coffee dripping and the murmur of customers faded.

"Which is…"

"To push harder."

"I am pushing harder and so are you."

"It's the marketing strategy that needs to be harder. He wants it to be more…" She looked around, searching for the word.

"Stronger," Charlie said, "more in your face…more sales focused?"

"Exactly, but he knows you're totally against it."

Charlie stared out a window for a moment then turned back with gritted teeth, chewing on a thought that had his chest tightening. As if turning state's evidence, he said, "The only one against it is Bree."

Charlie's eyes were glued to his computer screen. Without looking away he reached over and picked up his cell phone. For a split second his gaze glanced down, and he swiped his finger across the instant dial button.

Xander's voice came quickly. "What took you so long?"

Still locked onto the screen, Charlie replied. "Are these numbers right?"

"I don't know. I'm away from my computer. What do you see?"

Charlie leaned toward the monitor. "969 visitors!"

"Hit your refresh button and let me know," said Xander.

"Holy cow! Now it's 989! That's twenty new visitors in less than…" He clicked the refresh button again. "Now it's over 1,000!"

"Move on to the purchase page and let me know what you see."

No response.

"Charlie, you still there?"

"Uh-huh."

"How many tokens have been purchased in the past twenty-four hours?"

Charlie gasped, "Over 1,400!"

"Now brace yourself."

"For what?"

"Go to the donations page."

A second later…

"WHAT? You gotta be kidding me! $5,250!"

Xander laughed. "Who's your favorite marketing man?"

"You're a genius!"

"Dusty's the perfect influencer for this. Charlie, can you imagine what would happen if we had video associated with each act of kindness? Social media would eat this up. Oh, and before I forget, there's a bonus in it for Ashley. Dusty wants to meet her."

"Dad! Dad!" Ashley's voice rang out.

"I gotta go—it's Ashley." He chuckled. "I think she heard you!" Charlie trotted down to her room where he found her sitting beside her bed, staring at her phone, her mouth hanging open.

"Is something wrong?"

She held out her cell phone to him. "It's Dusty Harmon."

"And…"

"He's handing out tokens at the Martinsville Speed-way today."

Charlie took her phone, smiling down on the social media reel as it looped the image of the race car driver hugging fans and handing out *Following the Love* tokens. The caption read, *Dusty Harmon races to spread kindness at www.FollowingTheLove.com.*

The sound of rushed footsteps came clamoring down the hallway. "Is everything okay?" Bree panted as she staggered into the room. "I heard you all the way out back."

Charlie dropped the phone by his side. "Everything's fine. She was just telling me how well Dusty Harmon's doing in the NASCAR Cup Series this year."

"Not the series, Dad, it's what he's doing in Martinsville with the—"

"Everything's fine, dear. Ashley was just excited. Say, would you like some help in the garden? I'm taking a break right now if you'd like some help."

"Are you sure?" she said with a suspicious tilt of the head. "You never take breaks."

"Things are going pretty well so I think I can manage a half hour or so."

"Okay then. Come on out whenever. You can help me plant the new rose bushes."

Charlie held his smile until she walked out.

"What was that?" Ashley said. "You just lied to Mom."

"Yehhh, but just a little white one—"

"A lie's a lie, Dad." Her eyes dug into him.

The shame of his actions left him speechless.

Her gaze softened. "But I understand. It's about how you're going about building the following, isn't it?"

He nodded.

"How'd you manage to get Dusty Harmon to help?"

He shrugged. "I don't know. I left everything up to Xander."

"Are you going to keep having him give out tokens?"

"I'm not sure what Xander contracted him for."

"Did you meet him?"

"No, but he wants to meet *you*."

"Shut up!" She threw her hands over her mouth. "I-I'm sorry. I didn't mean that. I was just—"

"Excited? I would be too." He looked to the door then back. He lowered his voice. "Can we keep this between you and me though…you know, because—"

"I know, I know…" Her eyes suddenly lit up. "He really wants to meet me?"

"Yes. I'm going with Xander to next week's race at Bristol. You wanna come with us?"

"Wha…" the word failed to make it past her lips. She stared at him, unable to comprehend meeting the young man that covered the walls of her room. "Okay," she whispered, then she snatched a pillow from her bed and squealed into it.

Charlie laughed aloud. "I'll take that as a yes."

Charlie stood behind Ashley's wheelchair alongside Xander at the edge of the Bristol Motor Speedway straightaway. Generators hummed, and engines rumbled, idling like thoroughbreds waiting to be released from their gates. Crew members rushed about shouting over radios. In the distance the sounds of the incoming crowd, thousands of voices, rose in anticipation of the race to come. He took a deep breath. "You guys smell that?" Xander said.

Charlie and Ashley looked at each other, curious as to what smell he was referring to.

"That smell," he said, "that's burnt rubber, fuel, motor oil and churned-up asphalt—that's racing!"

"Heck yeah, it is!" Ashley shouted. She threw her arms in the air. "Bristol baby!"

Xander bent down to her. "And what day is it, missy?"

"Race day!"

Charlie smiled at him. "Thanks for getting these pit passes."

"Is this your first race too?"

"It's never been on my bucket list of to-dos, but now that I'm here, this is beyond exciting." He twirled Ashley around in her chair. "What do you say we take a spin around the track before the flag drops?"

"Let's do it, Daddio!"

Xander began waving his hand, working to get the attention of a pit crew member down the line. "I've got a better idea. How about we meet number 82 before he takes his own spin?"

Ashley attempted to push herself up for a look around. "Dusty! Where?"

Xander pointed to a young man, the same one in the black and gold racing suit adorning her bedroom walls, walking toward them. A woman followed along, a camera swinging from her neck.

"Oh my gosh…Dad, he's coming this way!"

Charlie chuckled. "Yes, I see, honey…just be calm." He turned to Xander and mouthed, "Thank you for this."

A moment later, the man in the black and gold racing suit was reaching out his hand to Ashley. "Hi, my name's Dusty…and you must be Ashley Carraway."

"Uh-huh," she replied.

Dusty slipped a quick grin at Charlie then back to her. His smile, almost too perfect, held her in a trance. The small cleft in his chin accented a squared-off jawline, balancing out deep yet soft blue eyes that crinkled around the edges when he spoke. "I hear you've been doing me the honor of displaying my vehicle's number 82 on your own vehicle. Is that true?"

Still spellbound, she nodded and pointed over her shoulder.

Dusty leaned around her chair as if inspecting a rear tire on his own race car. "Hmmm, I'm afraid we might be in violation here. My sponsors have a strict policy regarding the usage of our car's number which prohibits the use of black and white paper copies."

Ashley's mouth dropped.

"So, I'm afraid I'm going to have to ask you to replace it with this." The lady with the camera handed her a ten-inch black and gold embroidered patch with the number 82 stitched across it. "If you'll be kind enough to switch it out, I think we'll all be good." He turned to Charlie. "Dad, you think that's possible?"

"I think we can comply with that," Charlie said with a grin.

"Would you mind holding the number up, Ashley?" the lady with the camera said.

"Sure!" she beamed.

As the camera clicked away, Dusty bent down. "Ashley, I just want you to know that I think what your dad is doing is incredible." He pulled out a *Following the Love* token. He glanced up at Charlie and smiled. "Doing whatever we can to make this world a better place is something we all need to work toward. I'm sure you're as proud of him as we all are."

"I am."

Xander whipped out his cell phone. "Dusty, can I get a pic of you with Ashley?"

"Absolutely! Where do you want me?"

"How about you handing her the token?"

"Sure." He bent over and held it out to her. The smile on her face couldn't have been any bigger as she reached up and pretended to take it from him.

"Got it!" Xander said.

Dusty shook Charlie's hand. "Seriously, Mr. Carraway, I'm truly honored to be a part of what you're doing." He turned back to Ashley. "Before I go, do you think I could get a hug?"

Ashley's eyes bugged out. "Uh, yeah!"

Xander gave Charlie a wink after snapping the pic. "That one's worth a million bucks," he smiled.

Ashley waved Dusty goodbye until he disappeared into the sea of pit crew members prepping his car.

"He's soooo dreamy," she swooned.

"Dreamy?" Xander chortled. "What decade are you from, missy?"

"Dad," she said, "whatever you and Xander are doing to promote the website, you need to keep doing it!" She continued eyeing the pit area for signs of the black and gold race suit.

Xander shot Charlie a knowing look. "We need to listen to her. NASCAR's got some of the most loyal fans in sports. You hook a race car fan, and you got 'em for life."

"And they're good people too," she added.

"She's right again…perfect for spreading kindness."

"Tell that to my wife."

The next morning Charlie sat at the kitchen table hunched

over a bowl of cereal when Bree's cell phone landed in front of him with a clunk. "What's this?" she demanded.

Not yet fully awake, he eyed her through blurry eyes. "Uh, your phone."

"Look at the Facebook reels…go on—look!"

Charlie picked it up. He squinted, unable to make out the screen. He put on a pair of reading glasses. "What the…" He dropped his spoon.

On screen was Dusty Harmon bending over to hand Ashley the *Following the Love* token. He read the caption. "NASCAR favorite Dusty Harmon takes time out to share the love with a fan. Click to see how racing's number 82 is spreading kindness through new website and app called *Following the Love*."

"Seriously, Charlie, you're using our daughter to promote this?"

"I didn't know about it. This wasn't me! I swear."

"Don't swear, Carraway, don't you even…" She turned away then jerked back to him. "And it's a lie, a bold-faced lie. You used her like some pawn."

"I didn't. I'm telling you, I swe…I mean, I honestly didn't have anything to do with it."

"And how's that?" she said, jamming her index finger down onto the image of him standing beside Ashley's wheelchair, his face beaming. "Look at you, right there! How could you not know what was going on?"

"Xander took that picture. How it got posted, I don't know."

"Of course you know. He's a marketing maniac. He posted it. He exploited our daughter, and you let it happen." She stood fuming, the only sounds of the house coming from the clock ticking down the hall.

Charlie's eyes narrowed. His chest rose and fell heavy

as a deep-rooted anger emerged, his hand rising above his head, his finger pointing straight up. "A God you call merciful and just, loving and kind put our girl in a wheelchair…to somehow show his glory. How about *that* for exploitation!"

Bree shook her head. She parted her lips but said nothing.

"And Samuel? I guess there wasn't any exploitation happening at the courthouse that day either. Just another one of God's little messages to me that it's his way or no way!"

Bree inched to the door, fighting to keep the tears back as she shrunk down the hallway, back into her room.

Charlie collapsed into his chair and buried his face in his hands, overwhelmed by the hidden emotions that had just erupted. A moment later the back door slammed shut. He looked out to the driveway and watched Bree speed out of the driveway.

Chapter Eight

The midday sun peeked through Charlie's office blinds, the ticking of the hallway clock still the only sound filtering through the house. He parted the blinds and looked out to the vacant driveway while his cell phone sat buzzing on his desk. An email alert chimed. The phone buzzed again. With a quiet, irritated breath, he grabbed it and pressed it to his ear. "What?" he said flatly.

"Where've you been, boss?" came Lydia's voice. "Xander and I wanted to see if you were up for a celebration."

"To celebrate what?"

"You're joking, right?"

"No, what's going on?"

"Wow! I can't believe you haven't…never mind. Just open up the analytics dashboard."

Charlie blinked as the screen's progress bar crept along. A few seconds later he was scanning the page, his gaze frozen in disbelief.

"This is…"

"Pretty cool, huh?"

"Yeah!"

Just then the back door slammed shut.

"Sorry, Lydia, I've gotta go. I'll call you in just a bit." He tossed the phone to the side and rushed out, almost running into Bree pushing Ashley down the hall in her wheelchair.

"Excuse me," she said politely but with a fringe of indifference.

Charlie stepped to the side. "Is everything alright? Ashley?"

"She was feeling a little peaked, so the school called me to come pick her up."

"Are you okay?"

"I'm good, just kinda queasy."

He looked up to Bree with eyes begging for forgiveness. "I'm sorry."

"I'm going to get her situated. I'll meet you in the living room in ten minutes."

"Honey, I just want to say—"

Bree turned her head with raised eyebrows. "Ten minutes."

Charlie sat on the sofa, his hands tucked under his legs, rocking back and forth. When he heard Bree's footsteps, he pulled them out and began wringing them. In all their years of marriage, he could recall only one time she had walked away from him like she had earlier—the day he took the Lord's name in vain after discovering that yet another of his ventures had failed. This time was different. He had directly attacked her Lord and Savior—an act of sacrilege he was sure he was about to pay for.

When she entered, she walked past him to the front door.

"You're not leaving again are you?"

She spun around. "No. Of course not." Her voice was light, almost whimsical. She opened the door then reached behind the sofa to open the blinds, filling the room with a warm glow. "Just letting some of the gloominess out is all."

Charlie stood up and took her by the hands, leading her down beside him. His eyes were tender, bearing the remorse of his words that came pouring out. "I'm sorry I said those things. I'm a stupid, ignorant, wretched, selfish person. Honey, I just…"

Her lips pressed into a broad smile and her eyes brightened.

"Why are you smiling? Don't you hate me? You should hate me. I hate me—"

"Well, I don't."

He reared back. "You don't?"

"Of course not. I love you. But *I am* concerned."

"Why? Everything's fine. In fact, it's great! Since yesterday, our website traffic has grown more than 500 percent, almost 6,000 tokens have been purchased from all over the country and a third of those have already been passed. And half actually include comments!"

"That's fantastic, Charlie, but—"

"And donations are coming in right and left! In just one day we've reached almost $26,000! Bree, it's working—it's really working!"

The app's sudden success shocked her causing her to momentarily get caught up in Charlie's excitement. "Wow. That-that's pretty amazing. What's making it work?"

"Not what, but who. All this is because of how Dusty Harmon is promoting it for us. Xander said these race car fans are crazy loyal, but I never imagined this."

"So, you're giving all the credit to who…Dusty or Xander?"

"I guess Xander for the idea but Dusty for the effort."

She leaned forward. "Anybody else you can think of?"

He looked out the window, scratching his chin. "The fans! Of course, the fans!"

"What about God?"

Charlie's focus immediately fell to his feet, where it remained for a long moment as he worked through his reply. "Yes, God. Of course. He had to be at the track yesterday." He stared at her nodding emphatically. "Yep, I know it."

"You can stop now," she said.

"What? I'm sure he was."

"That's it?" She shook her head. "You think God got a ticket to Bristol, showed up and helped hand out tokens or something? That's the way you made it sound. Charlie, do you not know how powerful our God is?"

"Of course I do. He made everything."

"And what did his Son do?"

"Jesus?"

"Oh my gosh! Yes, Jesus!"

Charlie smiled. "Just playing…Hmmm, let's see. He turned water to wine, made a blind man see, forgave…" He tapped his fingers together as he struggled for more.

"Come on, Charlie, what else?"

"He, um…he turned over tables at the mall—I mean marketplace."

Bree's lips drew tight as lines in her forehead deepened. "You don't know. All these years and I thought something would stick. My conversations with Ashley over dinner, our prayers, and my Wednesday night connection group… did you ever listen in or eavesdrop, even out of curiosity?"

"I didn't want to intrude."

"You know you were always welcome. I must've tried a hundred times to get you to come to group but you've always had an excuse. Are you still so mad at God that you won't give him a chance?"

Charlie's head dropped as he contemplated his answer. Ever so slowly it rose. His tone of voice struck a chord rooted in a past that he had managed to live with but had yet to overcome. "Bree, you knew when we married where I stood with religion and why. You've been faithful in your promise to never try and push me where I wasn't comfortable going, but I'm asking you now, with so much at stake, will you continue to let me focus on this?"

"Yes," she said softly. "But would you at least consider coming to church with me every now and then? Please?"

He took a breath. "I'll think about it."

Lydia and Charlie stood in a quiet corner near the edge of the TV studio's glowing lights. Charlie, dressed in a neatly pressed suit, rolled his shoulders, trying to shake away his stiffness. He flipped through a set of note cards, mumbling some of the prepared lines.

"I wish Xander was here," Lydia said. "This is his type of rodeo."

"Me too, then he could be the one being interviewed. So how do you think I should bring up Sinclair?"

"You don't! Whatever you do, don't mention him, okay?"

"I really don't understand why he's so opposed to sharing the limelight. If it wasn't for him, we wouldn't even be here."

"This is *your* moment, boss. Now go shine." She eased him onto the set floor where a young female handler guided him to a chair next to the show's host, a tall black gentleman in a bow tie. His smile was as bright as the LEDs shining in on them.

From off set a man's voice filled the space. "And ready in…five, four, three, two, one…"

"Good afternoon, western North Carolina," the host began. "Welcome to another segment of *In the Spotlight*. I'm your host Tim Musgrove and today we have the pleasure of speaking with local tech guru Charlie Carraway, the founder and CEO of the popular website and app *Following the Love*. How are you, Mr. Carraway?"

Charlie produced a plastic smile. "I'm good, thank you."

"I'm sure you are," the host chuckled. "For our viewing audience, Mr. Carraway's website, which launched several months ago, is dedicated to the sole purpose of generating random acts of kindness and it's been quite the success. Tell me, Mr. Carraway, what makes your site and its associated app different from other sites dedicated to spreading kindness?"

Charlie's eyes darted to Lydia who stood tugging her blouse, smiling and nodding for him to produce an answer.

He swallowed. "Well, you see…um, it-it's more about tracking the kindness." He glanced back at Lydia who motioned him to keep going. "Other sites and apps simply show snippets or video clips of acts of kindness. *Following the Love* has a tracking aspect to it."

"How so?" asked the host.

Charlie struggled to pull a token from inside his suit's breast pocket. Halfway out it slipped through his finger, clinked to the floor and rolled off set.

Charlie jumped from his seat in pursuit of it until an anonymous hand appeared off camera holding another token out to him. Charlie grabbed it and slunk back to his seat, his face bright red. "Sorry about that."

"That's quite alright," the host said, skillfully navigating them out of the awkward moment. "Your fingers are probably a little fatigued from all the tokens you've given out, which has been how many to date?"

Charlie clutched the token tightly. "Just over 80,000."

"Eighty thousand! That would mean the majority of everyone in Asheville could have one."

"That's right. However, they're now being spread all over the country." He cleared his throat. "In fact, some are already showing up in Australia, Alaska, Spain and England."

"And you track them by the QR code on the back?"

Charlie held up the token with both hands, determined to keep it in his grip. He flipped it over to show the QR code. "That's correct. Once an act of kindness is performed, the person who received it logs it in at the website or through the app using this code."

"Then you can see where it's at?" the host said.

"Correct." The monitor next to Charlie switched to a Google map with thousands of tiny hearts spread out all over the U.S. "From there, if anyone clicks on a heart, they can see where it's been." He touched one heart which expanded to a drop-down list of different towns and cities.

"That's incredible! So, you really are following the love."

Charlie nodded.

"This is just incredible. I imagine there's a lot of interest in this from not only individuals wanting to do good but businesses and organizations in general."

"That's right—we're getting requests from all kinds of groups, nonprofits and charities, community organizations like Rotary and Kiwanis, schools and universities, even government and civic agencies. They're coming from just about everywhere."

"And churches, of course?"

"Some, yes."

"I bet the folks in your congregation are thrilled by this."

Charlie's brow glistened with sweat. Unable to provide an affirmative response he redirected. "We definitely welcome all faith-based organizations."

Three neckties were laid out on his bed. Charlie stared at them, giving each one careful consideration. He picked up one and held it against his shirt, tossed it down, picked up another, held it against his shirt then tossed it down and did the same for the third. "I can't decide which looks best."

Bree stood in front of a mirror adjusting her blouse.

He turned to her and held out the three ties. "Which one should I wear?"

"None of them," she said with a smile.

"But I don't have another one."

She kissed him on the cheek. "You don't need a tie, honey."

"Don't you want me to look good?"

"Charlie, there are close to three hundred men in our church and only two wear ties." She straightened his collar. "God doesn't care what you look like. He just wants you to show up."

He snorted. "This might be okay after all."

Bree eyed him. "You're not just going because that show host cornered you with that comment about your church, are you?"

He squinched up his face. "Nooooo."

"Well, just wait and see. You're going to enjoy it more than you think. And don't forget, no cell phone during the sermon."

"Yes ma'am." He started for the door. "Is Ashley ready?"

"No, she's staying home today. She's not feeling well."

"What's wrong?"

"She's just tired."

"That's the third day in the past two weeks she's missed out on something because she was tired. Maybe I should stay home with her. You know, just to make sure she's okay."

"Ohhhhh no you don't!"

Charlie and Bree turned back to the door. Ashley sat in her wheelchair holding a handful of *Following the Love* tokens. "No backing out, Daddio. Besides, you might come across some folks who'd enjoy a token or two."

"Ashley…" Bree said, shaking her head, "that's not a good idea."

Charlie scooped up the tokens and stuffed them in his pocket. "Of course it is."

Bree held out her hand to him, flipping her fingers back into her palm "Anywhere else but *not* in the Lord's house— now give 'em up."

Charlie deposited the tokens into her hand. "Killjoy."

Nestled on a ridge against a line of century-old oak trees was Bree's church. With a backdrop of the Great Smoky Mountains, the building sat with its white clapboard siding softened by weather and time. A modest steeple rose above the roofline. Topped with a small cross, the sunlight gleamed off it like a beacon welcoming its congregation. As Charlie and Bree drove up the gravel road to the parking lot, Bree reached over and took Charlie by the hand. "Thank you."

"Howdy, Mrs. C," an elderly man in overalls said as he eased out of a rusty old pickup truck. "Who's the new-comer?" he said with a wink.

"This is my husband, Charlie. Honey, this is Nathan Fields. He's one of our deacons."

"Glad to meet you, sir," Charlie said.

"Where's Mary Beth?" Bree asked.

"Home, she was feeling a little puny this morning, so she'll be watching online."

"Must be something in the air. Ashley's home for the same reason."

"That's one precious child you have. We'll be praying for her."

"We'll be praying for Mary Beth as well. Give her our regards."

"I will. Nice meeting you, Charlie. By the way," he said, digging into his pocket, "I just got one of your chips." He held up a *Following the Love* token. "Came with a letter signed by Dusty Harmon."

Charlie beamed.

"I hope to be passing it along this week."

Charlie turned to Bree, his smile and raised eyebrows letting her know his position on promoting his new venture just took a giant leap.

Chapter Nine

The pastor, a stocky man built more like a former pro line-backer than a clergyman, stood just outside the church doors greeting his congregation as they filed out into the noonday sun. Slaps on the backs and fist bumps for the men and cordial, gentlemanly hugs for the ladies with an occasional hand on the shoulder with a quick prayer for others. Bree hung tight to Charlie, preventing him from bolting to the car, making sure she could make an introduction.

"Don't worry, I'm not going anywhere," Charlie said.

A minute later Bree was receiving a hug from the pastor. "Good to see you, Bree. Nathan just told me Ashley's under the weather. I hope it's nothing serious."

"Just a little fatigue," she said. "Pastor Dan, I'd like you to meet my husband, Charlie."

He took Charlie's hand into his bear-size palm and shook it. "Nice to meet a local celebrity, especially one with your credentials."

Charlie angled his head. "Celebrity?"

"*In the Spotlight*," Pastor Dan said. "My buddies and I saw you on the show that aired just before the Alabama-Auburn game."

"Pastor Dan actually played football for Alabama," Bree said.

"I don't know if you could call being on the practice squad 'playing,' but hey, I always had good seats to the games. So, Charlie, what did you think of the sermon—or more specifically, the part about how doing good matters, not just for the person you're helping, but for you and for God?"

"I thought it was spot-on!" Charlie said, pulling out a folded church bulletin with scribbling across it. "I even wrote down the scripture you mentioned…Matthew 5:16, where Jesus said, 'Let your light shine before others, that they may see your good deeds and glorify your Father in heaven.'"

Bree stood mesmerized at Charlie's sudden biblical acumen.

Pastor Dan continued, "The Bible also says, 'Do not forget to do good and to share with others, for with such sacrifices God is pleased' Hebrews 13:16. Think about that Charlie—when you do good, God is pleased with you. Can I get a big AMEN for *Following the Love*?"

"What's going on here?" Bree said.

Charlie gave her a wink. "We need to listen to the good pastor."

"Will you do me a favor, Bree?" Pastor Dan said.

"What kind of favor?"

"Do you think you could bring this young man back a little more often?"

Bree turned to him. "What do you say?"

Charlie pursed his lips, the request landing heavy on him. "Well…"

Pastor Dan laid a hand on his shoulder. "Charlie," he said softly, "I understand the reluctance."

"You do?" Charlie said.

"I was part of the recovery team that day."

"So, you…you were there?"

He nodded with a look that was more apologetic than a straight acknowledgment.

The chatter of the departing congregation faded as the moment stretched out.

"Won't you just give God a chance?"

Charlie turned away, searching the sky, his focus on a single dark cloud on the horizon. "Bree, we'd better get going. It looks like a storm's coming up."

Bree looked to Pastor Dan, her lips stretching downward.

On the way home Charlie sat in the passenger seat staring out the window. Bree occasionally looked over, checking his mood, concern etched across her face. Unable to bear the silence, she blurted, "You at least enjoyed the sermon, right?"

"Yeah, I guess," he muttered.

Another minute passed. "So, you think you'll be back?"

"Bree, I think it would—" His phone buzzed. Welcoming the interruption, he quickly reached down and answered it. "Hey, Xander, what's up?"

Bree glanced between him and the road ahead, watching, only hearing his part of the conversation.

"They what? Are you sure? Why would they… Yeah, I-I guess…what time?" His voice took on an air of disbelief. "And you're sure about this?" He turned to Bree, his eyes wide, somewhere between excitement and panic. "Okay, I'll meet you there."

He eased the phone into his lap and turned to her, still trying to process it. "*Good Morning America* contacted

Xander. They saw the *In the Spotlight* segment… they want to interview me!" He ran his hands through his hair.

"When?" she asked.

"Day after tomorrow."

"Where?"

He drew a long breath. "Where else, New York!"

The overhead lights of the plane's cabin burned soft across Charlie's fluttering eyes. His head gently swayed as the steady thrum of engines began to lull him to sleep.

His breathing slowed, shoulders relaxed. In a moment he drifted away, carried by the hush of the flight. His face, serene and peaceful, began to twitch as a darkness gathered from his subconscious. Shapes formed—at first only shadows, then a ledge carved against a stormy, steel-gray sky. The blurred vision of a boy stood, arm outstretched, straining toward another just beyond reach. Lightning flashed and the ground gave way, crumbling into a black abyss.

Charlie jolted upright, a sharp gasp tearing loose, his eyes darting wildly about. The cabin remained unchanged, indifferent, its hum unbroken.

"You okay there, buddy?" Xander said from beside him. He closed the laptop he had been working on.

Charlie cleared his throat while straightening up in his seat. "Yeah, I'm good." He rubbed his eyes. "How long was I out?"

"I don't know. Am I my brother's keeper?" He grinned. "Sorry, I've always wanted to say that. So, what do you wanna do tonight?"

"Eat a good meal and then have a good night's sleep."

"Ah, come on! Let's celebrate. Besides the interview's not until 10 a.m."

"I know and if you'll recall, I tanked the first one. I don't intend to do it again."

"Mmmm, I wouldn't call it 'tanked,' maybe…well… no, 'tanked' is a good word for it." He slapped Charlie's shoulder. "Seriously, you were a little nervous was all. Now that you've got the first set of butterflies out of the way, you're going to do great. And besides, that's what they liked about you."

"What, that I flop-sweated and stuttered my way through a little local TV station's entertainment segment?"

"No, it's because you're relatable. You're not polished. You're just a good guy trying to do good things." He batted his eye lashes at him. "And to top it off…you're rather adorable."

Charlie swiped his hand over Xander's face. "Get outta here."

A moment passed as Xander hailed an attendant for a cocktail. "You want one?" he asked Charlie.

"Nope."

"You're seriously going to teetotal it in the city that never sleeps?"

"You act like you've never been here before."

"To be honest, I've only been twice. Once in college and once last year for a wedding."

"With all that Sinclair's into he doesn't do business up here?"

"I'm sure he does. It's just that he's never asked me to accompany him or send me on my own. He likes to keep a lot of stuff on the down-low."

"Yeah, like our app. You'd never know he has any part in it."

"Because he doesn't—not on paper anyway."

"He funded the thing, Xander! Without him we'd never have gotten off the ground."

"You know that—but no one else does. Buddy, all that start-up money's been washed clean. Between the donations and the actual sale of the tokens, your salary and even that bonus came in organically. And once the advertising revenue starts rolling in, this puppy's all yours!"

"Don't get me wrong—I'm grateful but it still doesn't make sense."

"All great businessmen know that it's to their advantage to keep your cards secret, so I stay in my marketing lane. Probably best that you stay in yours too. By the way, he heard you went to church this past Sunday."

"And…"

"He loved it."

Charlie turned and looked out the window at the approaching Manhattan skyline 30,000 feet below. "So, he's a good man?"

"He's a very good businessman," Xander replied.

Lydia pressed the doorbell, then stepped back, bouncing on her toes. It had become a habit over the past few weeks—swinging by to grab Charlie before meetings. The door swung open.... Bree appeared, wearing rubber gloves and holding a dirty rag. Her smile was broad and welcoming with a degree of relief from the domestic chores she'd just abandoned.

"Hey Lydia. You just missed Charlie."

"What?"

"He's not here. Was he expecting you?"

"I called him last night to confirm a chamber of commerce meeting we're supposed to be at in thirty minutes."

"I'm sorry, he must have forgotten he double booked himself because as soon as he got up he grabbed a biscuit and headed out to some celebrity golf tournament."

"Dad blame it, now I gotta go it alone and explain the whole website to a bunch of suits." She arched her head back and groaned. "I absolutely hate speaking in public." She swung her head. "You know what? I'm not going. Nope. I'm not doing it. I was hired to be a programmer and to keep him—" She bit her lip, halting mid-sentence. "Sorry, Bree, I'm just a little miffed right now."

Bree pulled off her gloves. "It's quite alright. Why don't you come in? I just brewed some coffee and was about to take a break from cleaning toilets. Would you like a cup?"

"I'd actually love some."

A few minutes later they were sitting at the kitchen table, steaming mugs in hand, chattering away about Charlie's little nuances they found both lovable yet annoying.

"He's always complimenting me on the littlest things even when I don't deserve it," Lydia said. "It's nice and all but I don't always feel deserving of it. You know what I mean?"

"I totally get it. Sometimes it's a little much but after a while you get used to it. My pet peeve is that he's so darn hard on himself. Even now with all this success, he's still so…I guess paranoid or something, like he's always—"

"Waiting for the other shoe to drop?"

"Exactly."

"I do enjoy having him as a boss."

"Me too." Bree chuckled. "Having him as a husband, that is."

A moment passed as they sat silently enjoying their coffee.

"There is one thing I've noticed, though, if you don't mind me bringing it up," Lydia said.

"No, go ahead."

"On a few occasions I've noticed a little bit of a distance in him. Like there's something weighing on him. He's wicked smart so I just figure it's him thinking about some big idea or working out a line of code or maybe it's that other-shoe-dropping thought, but it's just his expression… it's…it's almost sad. Does that make sense?"

Bree stared into her mug. "Yes. I know that look."

The moment dragged on without her offering anything more until finally Lydia added, "And of course, as we've seen, he can be a little absent-minded sometimes, but I just chalk that up to how much he has going on. This is the second time he's double-booked himself."

"I'm not surprised. Ever since that *Good Morning America* segment a month ago, he's been bouncing from one engagement to the next. Funny thing is, he used to hate the limelight and couldn't stand doing interviews. Even funnier is that he's actually gotten pretty good at it…" Her tone drifted downward for a moment. "I think he's starting to enjoy it."

"I get that too," Lydia said. "He's pretty much left the running of the site to me. You know Xander told me there's even discussions about him doing a TED Talk."

"Hold that thought!" Bree said, jumping to her feet and running to the window. She slid her fingers through the blinds, pulling them apart and peeking through. "I think that's one of them."

"One of who?"

She shook her head, returning to the table. "One of those popper…poppa—"

"Paparazzi?" Lydia said.

"Yeah…but I think that was just a delivery guy next door."

"You're telling me that Charlie Carraway has paparazzi following him now?"

"Just a few times. And I'll be honest; that's a few times too many. All this success. It's just so different. Don't get me wrong, the success has helped us with finances but there's a lot of little things that I see happening that don't…well, suffice it to say there're other things he needs to prioritize. He's actually been to church with me some. I'm just not sure he's going for the right reasons though."

Lydia smiled politely.

"Do you have a church?" Bree asked.

"No. I mean, I guess…what I'm trying to say is…"

"You're not a believer?"

Lydia shrugged, looking away as if embarrassed.

"Do you mind me asking why?"

Lydia gave her a sideways glance. "You're not going to try and save me are you?"

"No, just asking. Besides, that's not my job."

Lydia stared into her mug. "You got a shot of liquor for this?"

Bree shot her a look.

"Just kidding."

Bree leaned to her, looking up with concerned eyes. "Would you like to come to church with us tomorrow? I think you'd enjoy it."

She shook her head vigorously and turned away again.

Bree leaned around her. "Now who's looking sad?"

"I'm sorry, I don't think that's a good idea."

"Why?"

"It's just not for me. For others, I'm sure, but no…not for me." She turned up her coffee mug and with a long gulp finished it off, then pushed back from the table. "Thank you for the chat but I've gotta get back in front of the ole laptop. While some of us play golf, the others have to work."

With a quick handshake she was out the door.

Chapter Ten

The Sunday morning sun, warm and inviting, stretched across the church steps as Charlie and Bree made their way up to greet Pastor Dan.

"There's the man!" the pastor said, throwing out his hand for a hearty handshake. "A computer whiz with a mean drive. I ask you, Mrs. C, is there anything this man can't do?"

Bree gave him a crooked smile. "Were you playing golf yesterday too?"

Charlie beamed. "I forgot to tell you. Dan and I were paired up together."

"That's right. Me and your hubby managed to take home the coveted last-place honors."

Charlie slapped him on the shoulder. "Let's just call it leading from the rear."

Bree threw up a hand, waving away the comment in disbelief. "I'm not sure what that meant but seriously, you two…on a golf course…together?"

"Sure," Charlie said, "the pastor and the programmer."

Pastor Dan laughed. "Sounds like an eighties sitcom."

"I'll say," Bree added. She smiled at him as she pulled

Charlie inside. Looking back, she said loud enough for the pastor to hear. "Let's just pray he brought his A game to church today."

As they made their way down the center aisle, a ripple moved along with them through the congregation. Heads turned, smiles widened, and waves were offered as they passed while others nodded as if acknowledging a hometown hero.

Bree leaned into him and whispered, "Am I seeing correctly? Is this church warming up to you?"

Charlie smiled. "Can't you just feel the love?"

On their way home from church, Charlie and Bree pulled into a McDonald's only to find the drive-through was a dozen cars long.

"We'll be in line for an hour. Can we go somewhere else?" Charlie asked.

"Ashley wants a fish sandwich." She peered inside. "There's only a couple people at the counter. If you'll park, I'll go in."

"Deal!"

As Bree scampered across the parking lot, a man in a weathered red parka stood holding the door open for her. An equally worn backpack hung from one arm. His thin, wiry frame was the build of someone who had missed many meals, and while his skin was dark and leathery, his eyes, even from a distance, reflected youth—a youth that had apparently been advanced from years on the streets.

Rather than rushing in, Bree stopped and began talking with him. Charlie watched as the man's demeanor suddenly changed from one of a dutiful doorman providing a simple gesture of civility to an engaged conversationalist. The more they talked, the more animated both became, then suddenly she vanished inside. For several minutes he remained, his weight shifting from one foot to the other. Twice he looked over at Charlie and smiled.

Bree soon came out holding a to-go bag along with a piece of paper that she handed to him. Charlie bristled at the sight of him giving her a hug.

Bree and the man continued talking briefly, the man occasionally looking back to Charlie. When she placed her hand on his shoulder, Charlie started to open his door but stopped upon seeing her lower her head and close her eyes. In turn the man lowered his. Charlie watched as his wife and a perfect stranger were lost in a moment that he knew not to interfere with. As her lips moved, the man's head slowly moved up and down. After a final hug, she was trotting back to the car, a huge smile on her face.

"What was that all about?" Charlie asked as soon as she opened the door.

She buckled her seat belt and turned to him. "Prayers."

"I got that but why?"

Bree's face was aglow. "Charlie, I've been praying for discernment, to know when and where to reach out to others, and God was answering that prayer."

"At McDonald's?"

"Why not? It could've been at the top of the Empire State Building, at the Piggly Wiggly, on a battlefield or even a golf course—it doesn't matter. The thing is, I've been asking him to help me know when to approach someone in need and in this case it was Peter."

"Peter who?"

"I-I don't remember—that's not the point though. The

point is that he's been on the street for the past couple years due to an injury that put him out of work and—"

"You know what you could've done? You could've bought him a burger then given him a *Following the Love* token."

"No!"

"No? Isn't that what he wanted, a handout?"

"He wasn't hungry. Not for food anyway."

Charlie angled his head. "I'm confused."

Her eyes begged for his understanding. "No, Charlie, what he wanted was prayers. That's all, just prayers."

He reared back. "A homeless guy stands outside a McDonald's and that's all he's looking for?"

"Yes. And that's what God was leading me to do."

"Just pray?"

"Yes!"

Charlie backed the car up beside where Bree and Peter had been standing. He glanced to the door and nodded. "Hmmm, prayers," he muttered.

Bree leaned in front of him and smiled. "Just prayers."

"Honey! We're home!" Bree shouted as they came through the kitchen door. The house was quiet. "She's probably still asleep. I'll just leave her lunch next to her bed." Bree made her way down the hall, making sure to be as quiet as possible. She cracked Ashley's door open and, as expected, found her with the covers over her head.

"How was church?" came a weary voice, thin and weak.

"I'm sorry, did I wake you?"

"No, I was just laying here," Ashley said.

Bree pulled the cover back and placed her hand on her forehead. "I think you've got a fever now, honey." She reached over to the nightstand and grabbed a thermometer. "Here," she said, placing it under her tongue. "If you're over ninety-nine, you're staying home tomorrow." The thermometer beeped.

"What's it say?"

Bree sighed. "Looks like you're staying home tomorrow."

Ashley groaned and pulled the cover back over her head. "Stupid fever."

"How's she feeling?" Charlie asked as Bree returned to the kitchen.

"Her temp's 101. If it gets any worse, I'm taking her to see Dr. Jenkins tomorrow."

"Do you want me to come?"

Bree's cell phone buzzed. "No, I think she'll be okay," she said as she stared at the message on the screen. "Hmmm…"

"What is it?"

"Peter just texted me."

"You gave him your phone number? Bree! Why?"

"He wants to have lunch tomorrow."

"No! There's no way you're going to have lunch with a man you just met, especially one who…" He waved a dismissive hand in front of her, his voice rising with each word. "You're not going. You hear me?"

Bree's eyebrows rose. "I hear you alright and so did the neighbors."

"Mom, Dad, what's wrong?" Ashley shouted from her room.

"It's nothing, dear," Bree replied. "I'll be back in just a minute."

Charlie closed his eyes for a moment, took a deep breath

then began in measured tones. "This man…this-this gentle-man you just met, as genuine as you might think he is, could possibly be deranged. For all we know he's a serial killer."

Bree rolled her eyes. "He's *not* a serial killer."

"You don't know that. Think about it. A homeless man who turns down food. There's something wrong with that. There's something sick about him."

"Which is exactly who Jesus came to save!"

"I get it, but this is different—"

"How's it different? Jesus didn't come to save the healthy. He came for all of us, especially the sick, not just the cutest, most handsome, nicest, richest or most influential or famous."

Charlie began to pace. "I still don't like it. I'm your husband and I'm going to protect you. This guy may be in need but it's about what you need more and that's protection."

"So, what're you saying?"

"That you're not going—I am."

Charlie was twisting the cap off an energy drink when Bree came walking into the kitchen, holding an icepack.

"How's she feeling?" he asked.

"She slept through the night but still has the same fever. It's another day at home, I'm afraid."

"Anything I can do?"

"Just take that bag with you to lunch today."

Charlie grabbed a brown paper bag at the end of the table with the name "Peter" written on it and began digging into its contents. "Hmmm, I spy one Hallmark card, one protein shake, an apple and an envelope." He pulled out the envelope. "Let me guess," he said as he plucked out the bills, counting them one at a time, "…ten, twenty, thirty, forty, fifty." He smiled as he reached into his breast pocket and pulled out a *Following the Love* token. "And if I find him to be a decent man with honorable intentions…" He dropped the token into the envelope. "A little something extra."

"Are you sure you want to do this?" Bree said. "I can still go and you stay home with Ashley."

"Oh no. I'm going. If your spidey-senses are right—"

"Would you please…It's not spidey-senses! It's God's way of helping me know someone needs to be touched." She pointed her index finger up to his face. "Don't even think about twisting that word either."

Charlie threw up his hands. "Sorry, I was just joking."

"Well, I wish you wouldn't."

Charlie took her into his arms. "I promise, no more joking."

She leaned her head on his shoulder. "I'm sorry too. I'm just worried about Ashley." She looked up at him. "You know, I think this is good that you're going instead of me. It'll give you a chance to connect on a different level."

"With Peter?"

"Of course, him, but more importantly with God. Charlie, when you reach out to help others, you're working to spread his word and that's a glorious thing." She touched his cheek, "God sees it and I see it." She laid her head back on his shoulder.

The coffee shop in the foyer of the Sinclair building buzzed with the hiss of steaming milk, muted conversation and the faint clatter of cups and saucers. The smell of pastries and roasted beans filled the air. Lydia sat in the farthest corner at a two-topper hunched over her laptop, her cell phone pressed to her ear.

"Hey, boss, what's going on?"

"I'm glad you called," Charlie said. "I wanted to see if we could do our daily online meeting either this morning or this afternoon. I've got something I need to do at lunch."

"How about this morning? And if possible, I'd like to do this one in person. I've got something to show you, and I think a face-to-face would work best."

"Sure, when and where?"

"Anytime you can get here. I'm at the coffee shop in the Sinclair building's foyer."

"See you in about forty-five minutes."

By the time Charlie arrived, Lydia was already on her second espresso and was maneuvering her cursor around her monitor, jumping from one line of code to the next at an alarming rate.

"Wow!" Charlie said, sneaking up from behind and causing her to jump. "I knew you were fast but never realized just how fast."

"Pop a squat, boss man. I've got something extra special for you today."

"Hot dog."

Lydia's lightning-fast coding came to a screeching halt. "Hot dog? Next you'll be using 'awesome sauce.'" She spun her laptop to him. "Check this out." On-screen was a pop-up video window. Frozen in motion was Dusty Harmon bending over to hand Ashley a token at the Bristol Motor Speedway. "Remember this?"

"Of course. It's the video that jump-started everything."

"And remember how engaging videos are, especially ones that are kindness related?"

"Yeah."

"And how powerful it'd be if we could add them to each token entry?"

"Right, for those that actually had a video taken during the kindness act."

"Well…" She held out her arms to the laptop. "Ta-da!"

"You were able to add that functionality?"

She grinned. "Yep! Awesome sauce, huh?"

Charlie stared at the screen, eyes crinkling around the edges. "How many videos have you loaded?"

"Only this one so far. I just ironed out the code. Besides, it's also the only one we have. We'll have to wait until our users get accustomed to being able to upload them."

"Of course. So have you debugged it enough to take it live?"

"Give me the rest of the day, but by this evening it should be good to go."

"Hey, since we're here, why don't we go up and show Sinclair! I'd love to show him firsthand what a great job you've been doing."

"No. I'm good."

"But you deserve recognition."

"I said no! I don't need it and don't want it!"

"Okay, okay, I'm sorry." He gave the moment time to simmer then looked her straight in the eye. "But just know how much I appreciate you…not only for your abilities but also for your friendship."

Lydia glanced away, unable to acknowledge the depth of his sincerity. All she knew to do was nod.

"Well then," he said, breaking the moment with a clap of the hands, "let's take a look at our numbers."

Lydia bounced in her seat, rubbing her hands together. "Prepare yourself because they're pretty good."

Charlie returned a wry smile. "Hot dog!"

Lydia snickered. "Give me just a second. I want to show you each section, one by one."

"Take your time. I'm gonna get a cup of coffee."

As Charlie approached the coffee counter, the young girl manning the station gave him a suspicious look before breaking into a grin. "Hey, you're that kindness guy, aren't you?"

"Excuse me?" Charlie said.

"You're the kindness king!" She turned to another young girl at the end of the counter who was applying foam to a steaming mocha. "Janey, it's the kindness king!"

The girl looked up and gasped.

Charlie blushed. "Do you guys happen to serve Mexican mochas?"

"No sir, but for the kindness king I'll make one special for you, Mr. …"

"Carraway," Charlie added politely.

"Mr. Carraway, we absolutely love what you're doing. Everybody I know looks at your site and uses your app."

The girl in the back held up her phone displaying the site. "I use it all the time!" she shouted as she continued applying her foam.

"I've even got a friend who got a token," the young girl continued. He was…"

As the girl prattled on, Charlie suddenly noticed several men in black suits carrying boxes coming out of the elevator. They were all fit and sterned faced, and they walked with a purpose, the type of men one might see guarding a dignitary. As they passed him, Charlie noticed they all had earbuds.

When he sat back down, Lydia was still setting up her demonstration.

"Does Sinclair use bodyguards?" he asked.

"Not to my knowledge," she said, not looking up from her computer. "I don't know…maybe." She stopped and took a breath. "Are you ready?"

Charlie remained fixated on the men who were now outside loading the boxes into a large black Suburban.

"Boss! Are you ready?"

"Oh, sorry. Yes, of course."

She flipped her screen to him and waited.

Charlie's jaw dropped. His eyes scanned the screen, a smile etching upward, growing larger and larger.

Lydia leaned toward him and clasped her hands. "Well?"

"You're getting a raise."

Chapter Eleven

Bree heard the crunch of tires on gravel and looked up from the dishes she was washing and peered out the window. A silver Cadillac Escalade rolled into the driveway. Behind the wheel was Charlie, all smiles. He put the car in park, reached over to the passenger seat and picked up the owner's manual. Next to it was the brown paper bag with Peter's name on it.

Before he could reach the back door, Bree was on the back steps, gaping at the vehicle taking up half their driveway.

He held out the owner's manual. "For you, m'lady."

"What on earth…"

"Honey, you're gonna love it. The salesman said it's the most popular luxury vehicle for wheelchair conversions, which I've already lined up for tomorrow afternoon." He led her to the back of the car and opened the doors. "Check out how wide they are and how much space there is inside. It's perfect for Ashley's wheelchair."

"It's nice alright but—"

"Nice? It's perfect! I even got a deal on it for being the kindness king."

Her eyes narrowed on him. "What's that mean?"

"It means they've seen our website and some of our TV exposure."

Bree rolled her eyes. "And that's what they're calling you?"

"Kinda catchy, don't you think? Xander said we can capitalize on it."

She closed her eyes and took a deep breath. "How much are the payments?"

Charlie took the owner's manual from her, replacing it with a sheet of paper.

She studied it for a long moment, shaking her head. When she looked up, her reaction cut to the chase without any tone. "We can't make these."

"Of course we can. And before long, I think we can even move out of this dump. Maybe to the Cliffs, maybe even on a golf course lot."

"But I like our house. And the neighbors, we love them. And you don't even like golf."

"I could probably get used to it. Honey, it's time we enjoyed ourselves."

She stared at the car, her contempt for it growing as she circled it. Opening the driver's door, she spotted the brown bag with Peter's name sitting in the passenger seat.

"Charlie! Did you forget to give Peter his gift?"

"I'm sorry. I forgot. Actually, I didn't forget. I just got busy with an update meeting this morning with Lydia. By the way, our numbers are through the roof. In fact—"

"The most important thing you had to do today, and you forgot!"

"I-I couldn't help it. I was in the meeting and the time just got away from me."

"Plain and simple—you forgot! And then you ran off and bought this tank! Something we can't even afford."

"But we can. Honey, your man has finally done good."

"My man forgot his mission. He left someone in need. My man chose the material world over helping others. How's that make someone the King of Kindness?" She turned and stormed back to the house, slamming the door behind her.

Charlie stood, dejected, staring at the ground. He looked into the car's passenger seat to the brown bag then pulled out his cell phone and began dialing.

"Hey, Lydia, I'm sorry but I'm going to have to cancel our lunch meeting tomorrow. I've got to return a purchase then run an errand for Bree. I'll call you in the afternoon."

The McDonald's smelled of burgers, fresh biscuits and coffee. The normal noonday rush was surprisingly light with only two people awaiting their orders. Charlie sat in a corner booth, drumming his fingers on the table, a half-empty coffee cup in front of him, his eyes flicking now and then to the door then out the large window to the parking lot. It was the perfect location to spot Peter as he came in. His plan was simple—exchange pleasantries, present him with Bree's gift bag, suffer through whatever sob story Peter wanted to share, then depart, his wife's wish paid in full. Nothing to worry about, yet as he waited, the more tense he became. He pushed his coffee aside and leaned toward the window, scanning the horizon for the tattered red poncho.

"Mr. Carraway," a man's voice came from over his shoulder. Charlie jerked around. There stood Peter wearing a warm grin and his red poncho.

"How'd you get in here without my…never mind," Charlie said. "Would you like a seat?"

"Thank you," Peter said. "Are you hungry? It's on me."

"You're offering to buy *my* lunch?"

Peter nodded with the sweet innocence of a child that had just shocked his parents. "Kind of, I've got a free coupon for a double cheeseburger." His smile widened. "Besides, you're the kindness king. You deserve some kindness just as much as anyone."

Charlie stared at him. "You know my website?"

"Of course."

"Soooo what do you think?"

Peter puckered his lips. "Very nice design."

"Um…thanks," he said. Realizing his gift bag was on full display in the middle of the table, he redirected the conversation to it. "I do have this for you." He pushed the bag to him unceremoniously. "Bree put it together."

Peter peeked inside, pulled out the card and read it silently. He held it to his chest, smiling. "Please tell her thank you."

A moment passed with Charlie's brow lines deepening as he worked to figure out Peter's angle for wanting to meet. Uncomfortable with the silence, he launched into his protective husband's speech. "Peter, Bree believes you're a nice guy and thought you were in need. She said you'd been out of work for a while due to an injury."

"That's right, but I'm getting better. I actually have a job offer beginning next week."

"Oh, that's good."

"You look a little confused," Peter said.

"I guess I am a little."

"Why?"

"I just thought you were in need of prayers. Bree mentioned the job and then—pardon me saying, but you look like you might be…"

"Homeless?"

Charlie's lips pressed tight.

Peter laughed. "That's partially true. I don't own a home, and I spend most of my time out on the streets but it's by choice. You might call it urban camping."

"Why?"

"That's where the mess is."

"What mess?"

"Under the bridges, in the alleys, on the sides of the road. Places where people have fallen and need help getting back up. Don't get me wrong, it doesn't mean this is where they all are—they're everywhere. But for what I'm doing, that's where I feel called to be."

"To do what exactly?"

"To pray for them."

"That's it? What about giving them something to eat or providing shelter or buying them clean clothes? That's what I'm doing with *Following the Love*."

Peter looked at him, his eyes softening. "Are you though?"

Charlie reared back. "Absolutely! My site has over 300,000 viewers in less than four months with close to a third of those doing acts of kindness for someone else."

"That's good, Charlie, but for what purpose?"

Charlie shifted in his seat. "I just told you!"

A lady in the booth behind them whipped her head around and gave Charlie the once-over for disturbing her meal.

Charlie leaned to Peter and in a restrained shout said, "That's—what's—important."

"But who are you doing it for?"

Charlie squeezed his eyes shut, unable to grasp Peter's questioning. His knee hammered the underside of the table, making it rattle with each jolt of pent-up frustration.

"I-I'm doing it for everyone!" he shouted. "I'm doing it to help mankind and to make this godforsaken world a better place. THAT'S WHAT I'M DOING." He stopped hard, his chest heaving.

"Excuse me, sir. I'm going to have to ask you to leave." Charlie looked up into the face of a stocky man with a neck the size of an ox. It was more about his balled-up fists than the manager's badge he wore that told him it was in his best interest to do as he said.

Charlie rolled his eyes back across the table to Peter only to find his seat vacant. "Where'd he go?" Charlie said.

"Sir. Go now."

Charlie gave the room a final glance. The only other person remaining was the lady in the booth behind him, her smirk indicating her pleasure in seeing his departure.

The moment Charlie entered the house, Bree approached him, hands out, bouncing in anticipation of details. "So, how'd it go?"

"I guess what I'd say is he's…he's a decent enough guy."

"Decent enough?"

"Well, yeah. Like if he was from England one would call him a nice enough chap. I got the feeling he's an okay guy."

"What did you talk about?"

"He wanted to give me a coupon for lunch."

"But what did you talk about?"

"He knew about *Following the Love*. He actually called me the kindness king."

"Did you find out more about him?"

"Um," he ran his hand through his hair, "let's see…"

"Did he ask for any prayers?"

"He's getting a new job. We can definitely pray about that."

"Of course. A prayer of thanks. What else?"

Charlie's patience with Bree's questioning began to wear at him as it had with Peter. "What else did you want me to do? I met him, gave him your gift and then it got awkward. By the way, he told me to tell you thank you."

"What was awkward about it?"

"I don't know, it just was."

"Charlie, could you not tell he was a good man?"

"I'll be honest, I did sense that—at first, at least—but then he started asking me about *Following the Love* and it got kind of strained. He started asking things like why I was doing it. It just became annoying and…"

"And what?"

"It was like he was judging me or maybe digging at me for something."

"Maybe he was." Her eyes widened. "So, what'd you say when he asked why you were doing it?"

"I told him I was doing it for mankind."

Bree held his gaze, as if wanting either more details or a better answer. "And then what?"

He shrugged. "That was the end of it. He just up and bolted."

Bree narrowed her eyes. "What did he say when he left?"

"Nothing. He just took off. No hug, handshake or anything."

"That's odd. That doesn't sound like him at all."

"Because you don't know him! That's what I've been trying to tell you. The guy's different. He's probably schizo-phrenic. But what I think is that he wanted you there and not me. He's a guy and you know he probably had thoughts that were more about—"

"Hush! Don't say that."

"You know it's true."

"No, I don't know that and neither do you."

"Mom! Can you bring the heating pad?" Ashley shouted from her bedroom.

"I'll can take it to her," Charlie said just as his cell phone buzzed. "Wait. This call's from Lydia; I might better take it."

Bree's eyes flashed white at his choosing a call over his daughter's needs. "Don't worry, I'll get it. You take your call."

"Hey, Lydia, what's up?"

"Charlie, it's Peter," came the voice on the other end of the line.

Charlie turned the phone over and double-checked the caller ID. The name "Lydia" still showed. "Peter, what're you doing calling me?"

"I wanted to say I'm sorry for the abrupt departure and that I enjoyed our brief chat."

"How'd you get my—"

"And I hope my questions weren't too much. I got the sense you may have wanted to continue our conversation."

"No, I was okay with ending it. I need to know how you got my number."

"I just wanted you to know we were going to be pray-ing for you."

"We? Who's we?"

There was a pause. Charlie felt his heart pumping faster. "Peter, who do you mean by we?"

"It's a rather large prayer group."

"Tell me! How did you get my number or else I'm—"

"Tell Bree thank you again for the gift. God loves you,

brother." The phone went silent for a second then began buzzing again.

Charlie pressed the phone to his ear. "I swear if you keep calling—"

"I don't understand. What'd I do?"

"Lydia?"

"Did I do something wrong?"

"Oh no. I'm sorry. I-I thought it was someone else."

"Boss…are you okay?"

"I'm fine. Sorry about that. I was just…never mind… So, what's up?"

"I've got some news. It's something you need to act on, like now! And then you need to call Xander."

Chapter Twelve

The muted thud of drawers opening and closing echoed through the house. Bree walked into their bedroom where she found Charlie feverishly folding and tucking clothes and toiletries into a backpack. Her fingers twisting at the hem of her sweater, "So that's it? You're leaving?"

He looked up, startled. For a moment he stood confused until he caught the welling of tears in her eyes.

"Oh, my dear. No. I'm not leaving you." He dropped the shirt in his hand and rushed to hug her. "I do have to leave but not because of us but because of the call I just got from Lydia." He took her by the shoulders and stared into her eyes, his excitement spilling out in a wave. "There's a university in Florida that wants to be known as the kindness college, and they want me to present to their board before they purchase 4,000 tokens for their incoming freshmen class. The board meets tomorrow morning, so I have to catch a plane this evening in order to make it!"

She wiped her eyes as she forced a smile that didn't quite hold.

"But here's the best news!" He clasped his hands. "On top of that, Xander's landed me a press junket. Not an ordinary junket either—a regional one, a major-market, ABC affiliates junket. Six cities including Dallas, Atlanta, Boston, Chicago, Philadelphia, LA and if all goes well, they want me back in New York!"

"What's that mean?"

"Probably one to two cities a day. Some might be a half day of interviews; others might include community activities or whatever the affiliate has in mind."

"How will you manage all this?"

"I'm not sure but Xander said not to worry because I'd have a handler to guide me through everything." He chuckled. "This must be how a movie star feels."

"How long will you be gone?"

"Probably ten to fifteen days." He turned to the clock on the nightstand. "And unfortunately, I better be going if I want to make my flight."

"Are you going to say goodbye to Ashley?"

"Of course." He threw his backpack over his shoulder and grabbed a small suitcase. "I'll call you when I land." He kissed her on the cheek and walked down the hall to Ashley's room. A sliver of muted light glowed from under the door. He gently pushed it open. On the other side a host of stuffed animals slid across the floor as he made his way in. "Honey, you awake?"

"Hey, Dad. Come on in."

He quietly maneuvered around the stuffed animals as he made his way to her wheelchair that sat waiting beside her bed. He plopped down.

She eyed his backpack. "Are you going somewhere?"

He nodded while sporting an over-the-top grin. "Hmmm… you might say that."

She scooted herself up to a sitting position, her eyes growing larger. "Where?"

On his fingers, he counted off all the locations of his junket, ending it with his half day at the Florida university. "You might call this the *Following the Love* tour." For the next ten minutes she sat listening as he explained, in exaggerated detail, how he would probably be wined and dined and meet some famous people along the way.

"Wow! After all this you'll be famous too. Is Mom going with you?"

"I'm afraid not. Somebody's gotta take care of our angel."

Her excitement turned sullen.

"What's wrong, honey?"

She hung her head. "I'm such a burden. If it wasn't for me, you and Mom could be taking a trip of a lifetime. I'm always pulling you guys down."

Charlie slid from the chair to her bed. "Listen to me. You are not now, nor have you ever been a burden. All you've been is a joy." He bent over, his forehead against hers. "You're the center of all things good in this nasty world. And don't forget you're the one who started this whole *Following the Love* shenanigans."

"Me?"

"Yeah, you! If it wasn't for the purple heart you drew on that poker chip and all those random acts of kindness reels you're addicted to on the internet, I would've never come up with the idea for the app." He smiled at her poster of Dusty Harmon sitting on the top of his #82 NASCAR. "Maybe your boyfriend helped a little too."

"Dad!" She threw her arms around his neck and kissed his cheek. "I love you."

That evening as Charlie waited to board his plane to Florida, he opened his laptop to check the *Following the Love* activity reports. Every other second Lydia's token notification system pinged, indicating one had been purchased. For several minutes, he sat in awe of his own success, gleaming down as the tally clicked higher and higher, the pinging growing steadier until morphing from individual notes to one solid beat. After muting the notification function he turned to the donations page. Across the screen appeared what had become a common and welcome alert—*Congratulations! You have received a donation.* Charlie's smile grew larger as he expanded the screen to display the last two months' activities. Peppered across the spreadsheet were dozens of donations that were more than $25,000 each.

His eyes darted from the laptop to his cell phone's calculator as he ran a quick summary of what had come in. The calculator popped up $323,000.

Another ding came from his computer, this one indicating an incoming email from Lydia. The subject line read, *Praying all goes well.* His smile slowly faded as he read. *Thinking about you and your trip. Be safe and may His glory shine brightly. Blessed be your journey. Peter.* Charlie whipped his finger across his contact list to Lydia's name. A distant recording played through from the other end of the line. "I can't pick up. You know the rest."

"Lydia, do me a favor. Check your text messaging and your email app. Both have been hacked!"

The steady drone of the plane's engine deepened, its lullaby hum reshaping into a distant thunder. From the darkness an arm reached out, fingers clawing toward him. Lightning flashed, and the ground shuddered before breaking into pieces. Charlie's head lurched forward, breath ragged, shirt clinging damp to his skin. Sweat traced his temple.

"Ladies and gentlemen, welcome to Orlando where the local time is 6:43 p.m. and the temperature is a pleasant seventy-seven degrees. Please remain seated with your seat belt fastened until the captain has parked the aircraft and turned off the fasten seat belt sign…"

As the attendant continued her welcoming monologue, Charlie dug into his backpack and pulled out his cell phone. A moment later the screen glowed with a text message from Lydia. *No hacks on phone or email.* He shook his head as he put the phone to his ear.

"Hey. Did you make it?" came Bree's voice.

"We just touched down. I'm just waiting for everyone to deboard or debark or whatever you call it."

She chuckled. "How about 'getting off the plane'? Was it a good flight?"

"Up until I dozed off."

"The courthouse?"

"Yeah. I don't know what it is about planes but…anyway, I need to ask you something. Did you happen to give Peter my cell number or my email address?"

"No. Why?"

"Are you sure?"

"I'm positive."

"Hmmm…"

"What's going on?" she asked.

"It's nothing. I just thought he might be trying to reach me and—"

"What? That's great! You made a connection, Charlie. I'm proud of you!"

"Well, I wouldn't say that…"

A man struggling with two duffel bags tapped him on the shoulder, motioning him to the empty section of the aisle in front of him.

"Oh shoot. I gotta run, hon. I'll call you later."

That evening, after checking into his hotel, Charlie called to wish Bree a good night and to find out how Ashley was doing.

"What're you doing tonight?" she asked.

"Just going over my presentation a few times then hitting the sack early. I want to nail this one. It'll be our first college."

"You know that's one of the colleges Ashley applied to, don't you?"

"No kidding! I didn't know."

A moment of silence followed, signaling that he had once again missed a milestone in his daughter's life.

"Ahhh!" He groaned. "I should've known. Dad blame it. Can you cover for me and tell her how excited I am to be presenting to one of her possible colleges…or something like that?"

"Charlie…just make your presentation. You can tell her what you want when you get back."

"Bree, you should have told me!"

The phone went silent again.

"I did." Her words dropped cold, sending shivers through him.

"But I don't remember—"

"Of course you don't! Ever since…" Her voice spiked with emotion but faltered before falling away. She began again, this time, without tone or any indication of frustration.

"Charlie, just make her proud. Practice your pitch and do your best. We'll both be praying for you."

Charlie breathed a sigh of relief knowing he had just received grace, a concept he had struggled with most of his life, the one thing Bree continuously provided.

"Thank you, honey. I promise, I'll do my best."

"And don't forget to pray."

An hour later Charlie sat on his bed, his computer on his lap. His head bobbed back against the headboard, preventing him from falling completely asleep. Unable to keep his eyes open any longer, he closed his computer and lay back on the stiff bedspread, shoes still on. Sleep came in fits as the vision of the dream he'd had while on the plane returned—the blurred edges of the arm outstretched, straining toward another just beyond reach. Lightning shattered the sky just as before, and the ground, again, crumbled and gave way to the abyss. He tried to shout but nothing came. His muted screams grew more intense, more real, more devastating.

He bolted upright, drenched in sweat. The air conditioner hummed, oblivious to the thunder within his dream. He rolled his head toward the nightstand, snarling at the digital clock as it flipped to 3:41 a.m. Beside it, his cell phone vibrated with the receipt of a text message. He picked it up and stared at the screen. *Xander*. He rubbed his eyes as he swiped his way to the message. He wiped them harder as he read. *Those who live in the shelter of the Most High will find rest in the shadow of the Almighty. Peter.*

Charlie jumped from his bed, holding the phone above his head, ready to slam it to the floor. Instead, he let it slip from his fingers and drop to the bed. He ran to the bathroom, frantically searching through his backpack. Seconds later he was clutching a prescription bottle in his hands.

He twisted the cap off and shook out two pills, swallowing them without water. He walked back to his bed, plopped down and buried his face in a pillow.

At seven thirty the next morning the hotel's bedside phone rang several times before kicking into a voicemail message. "Good morning. This is the front desk with your wake-up call, and a reminder that breakfast is being served and ends at nine thirty. Have a great day."

Charlie rolled over and stared blurry-eyed at it. "What, no morning prayer?" he muttered.

Charlie sat on one side of a long, polished oak table, a floor-to-ceiling wall of glass behind him. Outside, young men and women with backpacks flung over their shoulders and cell phones pressed against their ears walked along manicured sidewalks between carefully placed palm trees. Two middle-aged men, both in tweed jackets, sat on the other side looking very much like twins, except one wore an oversized tie and the other a skinny bow tie. Neither said anything.

A moment later, a tall elderly woman, her snow-white hair fastened into a bun at the nape of her neck, walked in carrying a leather binder. With the exactness of a military officer, she sat down at the opposite end of the table, placed a pair of horn-rimmed glasses on her nose, spread open the binder and laid a Montblanc pen parallel to it. Whereas the men smiled generously, her expression was sour and focused, a combination Charlie imagined was brought on by decades of dealing with rebellious youth and laborious school board meetings.

"It's a pleasure to meet you, Mr. Carraway. I'm Madeline

Bridgeton, dean of students. I trust your flight was a pleasant one."

"Yes ma'am. It was very pleasant."

She studied her binder for a moment. "So, you're from Asheville, North Carolina, I see."

"Canton to be exact, ma'am, it's just outside—"

"Asheville's a beautiful town. My second husband and I vacationed there several times in the fall and thoroughly loved it. A rather vibrant community, as I recall."

"Yes ma'am, it's…it's definitely vibrant."

"Why Asheville?"

"Ma'am?"

"You're a tech company. Why not Raleigh or Charlotte?"

"You mean why am I not located there instead of—"

"Exactly, why a tourist town instead of a tech hub? Your staffing and ability to scale have to be hampered, are they not?"

"No ma'am, not at all. Plus, me and my wife…I-I'm sorry, I meant to say my wife *and I* are from there. And our daughter…she absolutely loves it there We all do."

Ms. Bridgeton leaned down, scanning her binder's notes with more intensity. "Couldn't your daughter's condition be treated more effectively at somewhere like Duke? That's right in the heart of the Research Triangle Park."

Charlie straightened in his chair. "How do you know about my daughter's condition?"

"It was part of her application letter."

"Oh, yes…of course."

"So why not move your operation there and take advantage of Duke and all its advanced medical capabilities?"

"We have been. For the past seventeen years we've driven the eight-hour round trip every other month to Duke for surgeries and checkups. And every time I've begged her to let us move there but she won't let us. She loves our mountains, especially Canton and the people."

Ms. Bridgeton pursed her lips. "Yet she's picked a school near the ocean, in a city and state that's almost 600 miles away and listed a major that—pardon me for saying—doesn't make sense for a girl of her limited capabilities, not to mention her grades. Mr. Carraway, Ashley is a full grade level below our entrance standards. There's simply no way we could accept her."

Charlie looked outside, bewildered by her words. He turned back. "What major did she list?"

"Oceanography."

"Oceanography?"

"Were you not aware of your daughter's interests?"

He stared at the table. "Unfortunately, not as much as I thought."

"I'm sorry, Mr. Carraway. I now know you're not here because of her letter, but I had to broach it before moving on to discuss your website. To be frank, I thought her application might have been a tactic to gain an audience with me to sell me on your organization—especially considering the fact that you don't have any other colleges participating." She bent down, trying to catch his eye. "Would you like to proceed?"

"Yes. Most definitely."

She pushed her glasses up her nose. "Good, because if possible, we would like to purchase 4,000 tokens to be given out to our incoming freshmen the week they arrive for this next semester. Is that possible?"

"Absolutely. That gives us plenty of time to produce that quantity."

"Wonderful. Before we move forward, there are a couple things to discuss. The first is our school and what we're trying to achieve."

"To be considered the kindness college, right?" Charlie said.

"Correct! Your website and its app are perfect to help us do just that."

The two men in tweed finally made their presence known by nodding their heads and echoing her sentiments. "Perfect! Absolutely on point!"

"However,…" she continued, her tone becoming even more serious, "the first thing to discuss is the ability to white label the tokens with our school's name on it. We need to make sure that the pass-along feature of the tokens is associated with us."

"It's a must," said the man with the bow tie.

"Immensely important," said the one with the oversized tie.

Charlie scratched his chin. "I'm not so sure—"

"If you can," she said, tapping her Montblanc pen on the table, "we'll pay double the price for the tokens and also work out a deal next year with our sister college."

Charlie smiled. "Done! We'll make it work."

"Excellent," she said.

"What was the other item?"

She took a deep breath, tilting her head in preparation for the weightier issue of the two. "Your site," she began in a measured tone, "carries a certain gravity or rather a strong propensity for appealing to those wanting to do good, which in and of itself is extremely positive. These are the kind of people with whom we want to be associated."

"That's correct. It's those wanting to do good that we're after," Charlie replied.

"It is, however, a concern that the focus of your site remains intact."

"I don't understand. We're just wanting to promote good deeds."

"Yes! Exactly…but to just stay within that lane and not venture toward anything political."

"Oh no, of course not!"

"Or…religious."

Charlie's brow narrowed. "Religious? How do you mean?"

"You see, Mr. Carraway, our school is not affiliated with any one religion. We're open to all faiths and belief systems. We concentrate solely on academics and expanding the mind. That's our focus and what we seek out with any partnerships. From what I've seen, your site appears to align well with these same values." She pulled a checkbook from her binder and opened it, hovering her pen over a blank check. "If you agree and are able to stay aligned with us, then we're ready to proceed."

Charlie stared at the check. "Yes—we're aligned."

Chapter Thirteen

Charlie ducked into a corner of the airport terminal, dropped his backpack and wedged his phone between his shoulder and ear. "Hey, honey! Just checking in."

"Sooo, how'd it go?"

"Not so good."

"Oh no."

"It didn't go good—it went *great*! They signed for 4,000 tokens at twice the price."

"That's fantastic!"

"And the good news is that we'll probably get their sister college next year."

"I'm so proud of you."

"The numbers are good but it's not just that…it's the fact that it's a college so hopefully others will follow suit. They'll be our showpiece."

"No better one to have either."

"Well, I wouldn't say that. They're definitely not at the Ivy League level or anything like that."

"Charlie, I know they have a nice enough campus and all, but have you looked at some of the statistics…other than their academics?"

"No but—"

The PA crackled with a boarding call for Flight 276 to Dallas.

"Is that your flight?"

"Yeah, looks like my whirlwind press junket starts now. I'd better go."

"I love you."

"Love you too. Wish me luck."

Charlie trudged up the ramp and through the doors into arrivals at Dallas Fort Worth International. The place was alive with movement. Families jumped and shouted, balloons in hand as they greeted loved ones; businesspeople pushed through the crowds, intent on staying on schedule; and others swiveled their heads looking for their designated limo or taxi drivers.

He scanned the crowd for his own pickup signal. As he did, an odd sensation came over him. This was how a real businessperson must feel—one that was not just playing the role but the real deal, a truly successful one enjoying the trappings of their achievements. He raised his chin as he looked about, working to feel comfortable with this new identity. *Get used to it, Charlie*, he told himself. *You've earned this.* Just ahead he spotted a small figure in a black chauffeur's hat holding a chest-sized placard bearing his name.

He cut through the stream of travelers, closing in on the driver. As he drew to within ten yards, the driver lowered the sign and pushed the cap back.

Charlie froze. "Lydia!"

Her eyes sparkled with mischievous satisfaction. "Hey, boss! Wanna lift?"

"What're you doing here?" he said, caught between confusion and disbelief.

"Xander sent me. Just for this first stop on the tour anyway. He thought you might need a little support…you know…considering the first interview back home."

Charlie smirked. "Yeah, probably a good idea." He eyed her cap and laughed. "I know I've got you wearing a lot of hats but…"

She dangled a set of car keys in front of him. "Kinda nice to be in charge for a change. Now if you'll please follow me, sir, we'll proceed to your luxury vehicle awaiting you just outside."

Lydia led Charlie through the hallway to the TMTK studio, a makeup artist tagging along and lunging up to him, swiping his face with a brush. "You got this, boss," Lydia said, straightening his collar from behind. "Remember. Don't sit down until she asks you."

The set's lights burned bright, bathing the room in a warm glow that accented a rich mahogany desk. Behind it sat the host, a striking blonde woman with her own makeup artist primping her just as Charlie's had done. Behind her, a set of floor-to-ceiling monitors affixed together displayed Ashley's heart-inspired *Following the Love* logo.

"Ten seconds, everyone," a deep baritone came from behind the lights.

Charlie squinted out into the darkness. Just beyond the stage, the cameras' red lights blinked to life one by one. The makeup artist rushed in for one last dab on his forehead before retreating into the shadows. A second later it was just him, the lights, and the hush of the set.

"Good evening, ladies and gentlemen," the host said, her Texas drawl pouring out like honey. "In tonight's special-interest segment, we'll be meeting a man who some people are calling 'the Johnny Appleseed of Kindness,' or as some have referred to him 'the King of Kindness.' Please welcome Charlie Carraway!"

A hand from behind Charlie nudged him forward as a canned applause track kicked in from off camera.

"Your throne, good sir," the host said, motioning him to a plush leather chair next to her desk.

Charlie sat stiffly, his eyes darting out into the darkness searching for Lydia.

"I couldn't help the throne reference, Mr. Carraway," she chuckled. "After all, the nickname 'King of Kindness' seemed to beg for the pun."

For the next five minutes, the conversation between them was a pleasant one. Charlie's nervousness from the first interview was gone as the host guided him from topic to topic, including how the site began and the excitement over the site's one millionth token being passed. But it was the playing of the video of Dusty Harmon handing Ashley a token that brought a tear to her eye and sniffles from behind the cameras.

She wiped her eyes. "And all this love and kindness… it's all from you?"

"Oh, no ma'am. There's also my associate Lydia Phelps, Xander Whitman and the main supporter, Thomas Sinclair of TS Enterprises. Without his—"

The crash of metal clanged against the marbled flooring, breaking Charlie's response mid-sentence as a six-foot tripod toppled onto the edge of the stage causing him and the host to jump. Next to it stood Lydia, shoulders pulled in tight with a petrified look on her face.

"I-I'm sorry," she squeaked.

"Dan?" the host said, looking out into the darkness. "Are we good?"

"Yeah. I think we got what we need."

She turned to Charlie, her hand outstretched, and smiled. "Nothing like going out with a bang." She shook his hand. "I'd like you to know I truly think what you're doing is awesome."

Lydia walked up beside Charlie. "I'm sorry about the tripod. I hope I didn't ruin the spot."

"No worries," the host said, "they'll just edit those last couple lines. It'll be perfect."

Lydia sighed. "Thank goodness."

Charlie held the door as Lydia brushed past him, eager to put the building behind her. The sun made her squint, but she didn't slow down, her shoes stomping all the way to the rental car.

"I can drive," he said.

"Nope. I got it. It's in my name plus I need to get you to the airport ASAP. You're flight boards in an hour."

Charlie jumped into the passenger seat and sat quietly as Lydia pulled out of the parking lot. A moment passed. His cheeks puffed, his lips quivered. Unable to hold it in any longer, he burst out laughing. "Lucky thing there was no camera on that tripod, or we'd have to sell another couple thousand tokens."

Lydia remained silent, eyes glued to the road.

"Too soon?" he snickered.

"Charlie, you absolutely nailed this!"

"Thanks. I actually felt pretty comfortable this time. In fact, I'm kinda looking forward to the rest of these."

"That's great. I'm sure you're gonna be awesome."

The conversation dropped off into an uncomfortable silence.

Charlie leaned forward, trying to catch her eye. "Are you okay? Don't let that camera stand get you down. They said they could edit it out."

She took a deep breath. "Charlie, you've got to do me a favor."

"Of course."

"You can't mention Sinclair again. We've talked about this. He doesn't want to be included in any conversation or public acknowledgment about his involvement."

"It just doesn't make sense. We're doing good."

"You need to listen to your wife. She's got some great insight into the whole do-gooder thing."

"You've been talking to Bree?"

"A little. I really like her."

"What's she been telling you?"

"She's just been helping me with some things…but that's beside the point. You just can't—"

"You tripped over that tripod on purpose, didn't you?"

"Charlie, listen to me. Just don't bring up Sinclair anymore, please. For me and Xander—okay?"

"Xander! Why him? What's going on, Lydia?"

She pulled up to the drop-off curb at the gate. A moment passed. "Sinclair referred me to work with you, right?"

"Yeah."

"And Xander's been working for him for years, right?"

"So?"

She looked around as if searching for prying eyes. "So, we have to deal with his wishes. Whatever he says goes. If he doesn't want to be associated with what we're doing, then that's all we need to know. Besides, we're free and clear of him and his initial financing, so for all intents and purpose we're on our own anyway."

"That's true."

"So next time Sinclair's name pops into your noggin maybe you could think about…oh, I don't know…maybe Xander's cute little…I-I mean goofy sideways grin."

"Wait a minute—that's the second time you've tripped today. You like Xander!"

Lydia slapped on her fake chauffeur hat and smiled. "Time for you to go, sir. This limo driver has her own plane to catch."

For the next several weeks Charlie jetted around the country, playing not so much the Johnny Apple Seed of Kindness but rather the King of Kindness. In Atlanta he was met at the studio by a throng of fans waving signs with the title next to his name. In Boston and Chicago, the station affiliates took him out to see their respective sports teams in action. In Philadelphia they presented him with a three-foot Philly cheesesteak sub and in LA they wined and dined him at Spago. And since the junket was a resounding success, they flew him back to New York for a wrap-up segment, took him on a cruise around Manhattan, and followed it with dinner at Peter Luger Steak House.

Along with the pounds his celebrity status was adding, his confidence was growing as well. Every interview became more engaging. He cracked jokes, poked fun at himself and managed to develop a lovable self-deprecating persona that charmed every staff member and fan he met. He grew to love signing autographs while the stations loved the guaranteed ratings boost he gave them. The more he spoke, the more the affiliates and the communities he visited became enamored by him, and as he promised Lydia, he never mentioned Thomas Sinclair's name again.

Charlie stood at the edge of his hotel bed, stuffing his suitcase and backpack in preparation for his trip home. He bounced an awkward jig while singing with the playlist coming from his cell phone. Along with the hum of the air conditioner and the street noise pouring in from his open balcony door, he almost missed the buzzing of his incoming text message from Bree. Happiness surged through him as he swiped it open, ready to savor the moment of reading how much he had been missed.

His chest tightened as he read the simple message across the screen. *The "pride of life" is vanity, a worldly distraction from Him. Peter.*

Charlie squeezed the device, ready to fling it across the room, then stopped and dialed.

A moment later Bree picked up. "I was just about to call you."

"Honey, tell me the truth—did you give Peter any kind of access to your phone?"

"Of course not. Why would I?"

"Somehow he's gained access to your phone or cloned your number because I keep getting messages from him."

"What kind of messages?"

"I'm not sure. They're rather cryptic. For instance, this

one read, 'The pride of life is vanity, a worldly distraction from Him.'"

"Hmmm, I can't place that as actual scripture but there's something there. I'll have to think about it. But, honey, I promise I haven't given him your number."

Charlie shifted the phone to his other ear, pacing the length of the room. "I know. It's just kind of strange though because I've gotten similar messages through Xander's and Lydia's emails and texts. Honestly, I'd file for a restraining order but there's no way for the cops to serve him since he lives on the streets. What do you think I should do?"

Silence.

"Bree?" He checked the screen to see if the call had dropped. "Bree, are you there?"

A second later her voice returned, softer and breathless. "I'm sorry, I had to check on Ashley. She's been throwing up and I needed to help her. What were you saying?"

"Nothing." He stopped pacing. "Is she alright?"

"That's why I was about to call you. I don't know. I think it might have been some bad sushi we had last night but she's got a fever again. I wanted to find out when your flight arrived this evening so I can run some errands when you get back. I just don't want to leave her by herself."

"Oh honey, I'm sorry but…"

"But what, Charlie?"

"I, um…I've got a couple more days in front of me."

"What's that mean?"

"Remember the grocery chain that turned down my shopping app? They want to purchase 500 tokens for the opening of one of their stores in Newark the day after tomorrow. Lydia is overnighting them, so they'll have them on time."

"So, what's that have to do with you coming home this evening?"

Charlie hesitated with an audible gulp. "Well…they've seen my interviews and since I'm right across the river, they think having me at the opening—like a meet and greet—will be a great way to introduce the program." His voice brightened. "And, like the college, if it goes well, they'll purchase 500 for all their other stores!"

Silence.

"Bree…honey. Did you hear? Every store will buy 500! Just think about it. That's 500 times—"

"I get that it's a lot! And I know that you'll be home two days later than you said you would. Hand out your tokens, spread the kindness and get your butt back here. Your family needs you!" The phone went silent once again.

Thomas Sinclair sat staring out the massive windows of his office into the glare of the afternoon sun, a cigar in one hand, a manila folder in the other. His chief accounting officer stood patiently on the other side of the desk, await-ing his superior's next exhale. The cigar met Sinclair's lips then left with a flume of smoke that encircled his head, the sun's rays casting a halo about it. He spun his chair around, simultaneously sliding the folder across the marbled table. "Your thoughts, Mr. Drummond?"

The old man smiled. "Very nice figures, sir. Better than we could have imagined."

Sinclair pulled another sheet of paper from another folder and added it to the one in front of Drummond. "Not only has he managed a successful press junket, he's got former business prospects wanting to participate."

"A diamond in the rough."

"Indeed," Sinclair said. He took another draw from his cigar, arched his head back and released its cloud into the air. "And not a peep."

"No sir. Not a peep."

Sinclair smiled up at him. "Feel free to quickstep it, Mr. Drummond."

Chapter Fourteen

Charlie swung the front door open and stepped inside his house, suitcase trailing behind him.

From the kitchen came the shuffling of slippers. Bree appeared, her face lighting up when she saw him. "You're home!" she said, crossing the room to wrap her arms around his neck. The warmth in her voice was genuine, though lines of doubt crossed her brow, as if she were struggling with his sudden presence a day ahead of schedule.

He kissed her cheek, the faintest smile tugging at his lips. "I would have been home yesterday like I originally planned but I had already changed my flight."

"But what about the store opening?"

"I told them they didn't give me enough notice, and I needed to get home."

Her embrace tightened, then loosened almost too quickly, when he told her they were going to reschedule for another opening in a couple days in Charlotte.

For a moment Charlie felt his early return had delighted her, but not the way she might have hoped for, and not in the way he was expecting.

He dropped his backpack to the floor. The sound of

it thudded against the hardwood, marking the end of his journey and the beginning of something more fragile.

"How's Ashley?"

"Better. Her fever went away, and she's not been throwing up. In fact, she's over at Sally's house right now."

"So, I came home for…"

Bree stood waiting for him to complete a statement he knew better than to finish.

"You came home for what?" she demanded.

"I think that was about to come out wrong. What I meant to say was I came home early because I was concerned about her."

"Well, it sounded like it was going someplace else."

He grabbed her around the waist, hugging her tight. "I'm sorry, honey. It's just that my mind has been all over the place. This junket's been such a whirlwind. I-I don't know how to even explain it, but it's got my head spinning. Things have been moving so fast and going so well. The site's got over a million users now, revenue is beyond projections, and the donations are through the roof. And the people… oh my gosh! You know how there were a few who were referring to me as the 'King of Kindness'? Now *everyone* is! Everywhere I go, that's what they're chanting. For the first time since the courthouse, I feel…"

"What?"

His eyes glistened. "Worthy."

"Worthy of what?"

"That I've done something right in my life…something good."

She placed her hand to his cheek, looking into his eyes. "You do that every day, as a good father, a good neighbor and a friend."

"I guess," he said his voice softening. "It's just that this makes me feel something else too. Like I'm special."

"Hold that thought." She rushed into their bedroom and returned a moment later, her Bible in hand. She began flipping pages. "I think our friend Peter was trying to tell you something when he said, 'the pride of life is vanity, a worldly distraction from Him.'"

Charlie's lips skewed.

"Here," she said, dropping her finger to a page. "1 John 2:16 says, 'For all that is in the world, the lust of the flesh, and the lust of the eyes, and the pride of life, is not of the Father, but is of the world.'"

"I'm sorry, but I don't get the connection, especially the lust part…like it's sexual."

"No, lust can also reference all kinds of different desires. In this verse I think it's saying when we look for things in this world to make us happy or feel satisfied or even worthy rather than seeking God, then we're focused on the wrong thing." She looked at him, her eyes begging. "Does that make sense?"

"Maybe." He ran his hand through his hair. "All I know right now is that I'm bone tired. Philosophical questions like that are too much for my fuzzy little brain to comprehend. Can we talk about this later?"

She smiled with a promising look that the conversation had the chance to continue. "Sure. Why don't you go take a nap? I'll have supper ready in about an hour."

Bree woke to the blare of her 7:30 a.m. weekday alarm. She reached across the bed, her hand finding only the taut covers of a freshly half-made bed. A note from Charlie lay on the pillow.

I didn't want to wake you, but Xander texted me late yesterday evening after you'd fallen asleep to let me know he's driving to Charlotte today to help the store where I'm handing out tokens. Since Ashley is feeling okay and since he has something major to discuss with me, I thought it would be okay to go with him. I hope that was okay. I'll call you later today.

Bree stared at the note, read it again then tossed it in the waste bin. It had made sense but not enough to make her feel any better about not being able to see him off. In all the years they had been married this was the first time there hadn't been a goodbye kiss. All she had was the unsettling light of the morning sun as it glared in her face.

Miles down the road, Charlie raised a hand to shield his eyes from the same sun as his other hand shook his breakfast biscuit wildly about, crumbs scattering over his lap. "Geez, Xander, drive much?"

"Sorry, buddy. I had to swerve to keep from hitting a box turtle jogging across the road."

"Sorry, I didn't see the little guy."

Xander laughed. "Nah, there wasn't one. I just couldn't bear watching you enjoy that fluffy biscuit while I'm stuck driving."

Charlie shoved the remaining morsel into his mouth. Through stuffed cheeks he grinned. "You've got what's called a case of bitter biscuit envy."

Xander smirked. "Give me one of those hash browns and I'll tell you the big news."

Charlie looked into his bag. "I don't know. Is it worth it?"

"Hmmm, let me think on it. One hash brown for details

on a podcast for the website called *Following the Love*. I guess it could be."

"A podcast? Who—what—why?"

"It'll be your podcast. It'll be all about spreading kindness. And why? That's easy, because you're the King of Kindness, that's why!"

"Are you kidding?"

"Nope. You did such a great job on the junket, the network wants to create one just for you!"

"You're serious?"

Xander bobbed his head as a smile stretched across his face. "I'm telling you, Charlie—the world loves you. I even commissioned a popularity study to gauge what people thought of you. Actually, the network required it."

Charlie remained staring out the window, muttering, "A podcast. I'm gonna have a podcast."

"Want to know what the study showed?"

"Sure."

Xander cleared his throat. "For all these categories one is considered poor and ten is best. So, Mr. Carraway…your category standings as of today are as follows. Sincerity 7.2, intelligence 8.2, articulate 7, appearance 7.2, humor 8.0, and finally…overall likeability…9.2! Booyah! Not bad, young buck! The masses have spoken—Charlie Carraway is a bona fide star!"

"Would you stop it!" Charlie laughed. "How many people even took your silly test?"

Xander averted his eyes refusing to respond.

"Mister marketing man…how many?"

"It doesn't matter."

"Seriously, how many?"

"Oh…okay. Forty-two."

Charlie snorted. Probably all family and friends.

Xander's eyes fell back to the road. "Mark my words, my friend. Charlie Carraway, the King of Kindness, is soon to become a household name."

Lydia's yellow bug eased into Bree's driveway. The moment she opened the door, Bree was out on the front porch, waving her in.

"Quick—inside," she said.

Out the corner of her eye, Lydia caught a guy on an electric bike holding up his cell phone at her while another man sat in his car pointing a camera with a telescopic lens at Bree. "Hurry," she said, pulling Lydia through the door.

For a moment they just looked at each other, breathless.

"Wow," Lydia said. "Who'da thunk Charlie would be getting this type of attention?"

"See? I wasn't kidding about these camera crazies. It's not every day but they're popping up more and more."

Lydia looked at her with a moment of regret. "I'm afraid the reason I'm here is to let you know there might be more of them showing up soon."

"I know."

"You do?"

"Charlie called an hour ago to tell me the news about the podcast."

"Phew! I thought I was going to have to break it to you. How's it made you feel?"

"Honestly, furious at first. I thought it was going to be just another reason for him to be pulled away from home, but when he told me he could do it from here, I was better."

"Better, but not great?" she said.

"Here," Bree said nodding to the kitchen table, "let's sit and chat a bit. I'll get us some coffee. Between the paparazzi, the podcast and helping Ashley weigh the pros and cons of which college to go to, I need the caffeine."

A moment later steam curled gently from their mugs, the scent of cinnamon rising up. Barely a beat passed before Bree started. "I'm so glad you're here. I've been aching to talk to someone about all this."

As the refrigerator hummed steadily in the background, Bree, holding her mug with both hands, leaned forward. "You're in the thick of this crazy thing too. I was curious, first of all, how you also feel about it?"

Lydia blinked, appearing shocked that it was her opinion Bree immediately sought.

"It's been great. I mean from a strictly programming standpoint it's been incredible. And the user figures and donations and all the revenue generated have been almost miraculous."

"What about the personal side of it?"

"I'm not sure what you mean."

"Like…how's it affected you personally. Are you happy?"

"Yeah, sure," said Lydia. "It's a job and I do like that it's all for a good cause. So yeah, I'm happy."

"And what about Charlie as a boss. Has he been good to you?"

"Um…yeah. Actually, he's the best boss I've ever had. You know I call him 'boss,' but it feels more like we're partners. Right now, while he's doing all the promo stuff, he's basically got me running everything. He trusts me, which I kinda dig." She angled her head. "Bree, I don't mean to pry, but is there something going on?"

Bree took a deep breath as she put her coffee down. "Kinda."

"Anything bad?"

"It's just that all this success has me concerned. You see…Charlie's always been extremely driven."

"And wicked smart," Lydia added.

"He is. But through the years he's had idea after idea and they've all fallen through. But now there's all this hoopla over the website. I'm not sure he knows how to handle it."

"You think it's going to his head?"

"Lydia, you've never been married, have you?"

"No," her lips skewed. "I've thought about it though."

Bree placed her hand on Lydia's arm. "If you ever do, just make sure you're equally yoked."

"Oh my gosh, that sounds like a torture of some kind."

Bree laughed. "No, no…it's quite the opposite. Being equally yoked means that a man and woman share the same faith, values, and spiritual direction so they can walk together in unity."

"Is it a biblical thing?"

"Very much so."

"Are you and Charlie equally yoked? I know you're a Christian but is he…are you guys yoked?" She shook her head. "I-I'm sorry. I don't mean to screw up the phrasing. It's just not in my vocabulary."

Bree patted her arm. "That's quite all right. To answer your question, it's been a journey. I came to Christ when I was a little girl. I had a solid foundation where both parents were believers as well as my brother and sister. Through the years it's grown stronger."

"And Charlie?"

Bree turned to the window, her eyes growing misty

as she revisited a memory from many years past. "When I met Charlie, he was—as he puts it—damaged goods." She leaned her head back. "Oh, I hate that tired cliche, but unfortunately it applies all too well."

"I won't repeat it, but what made him…that way?"

She swallowed. "Something happened within his family, something horrific that tore them apart."

"Can you say what?" Lydia.

Bree turned away, her voice growing distant. "All I can say is he's battling something powerful, something that comes from a dark place that's had a hold on him most of his life. And unfortunately, Ashley's being born with a frail immune system and without the use of her legs has only made it worse. He feels like—"

"He's being punished," Lydia said.

"Exactly," Bree said, turning to find Lydia staring into the table, her hands cupped together as a tear dropped between them. The edge of one sleeve was turned up, exposing the underside of her wrist and the faint image of a jagged scar.

Bree wrapped her hands around Lydia's. "Enough about Charlie. We can talk about the boss man later." Her eyes softened. "Right now, I'm here for you."

Lydia sat frozen, her lips quivering. A moment later she laid her head on Bree's shoulder, and the sobs came.

Chapter Fifteen

The Charlotte trip had gone better than hoped. The satisfaction from handing out tokens lingered as Charlie and Xander sat in Charlie's office, revisiting the excitement over how much joy they had generated with the grocery store's clientele.

"Remember the look on that one little lady's face when I handed her a token and forgot to explain it?" said Charlie.

Xander chuckled. "What I remember is how she gave you the stink eye like you'd given her a coupon for free laundry detergent. Remember how sly she was slipping it in her pocket, like we were running some kind of scam?"

"Pretty sure she thought it would start beeping at checkout." Charlie turned and surveyed his office, taking inventory of the challenge of prepping the room for his podcast series. Boxes of sound equipment and a rat's nest of wires cluttered his desk along with a shiny microphone still smelling of new plastic and waiting to be tested. He lowered himself into his chair with the slow satisfaction of someone settling into their element, while Xander leaned against the wall, his arms crossed and wearing an easy grin.

"That's right, old boy. Strap yourself in 'cause this pod-ship's about to take off!"

From the kitchen came the sound of the back door opening, then the warm notes of laughter. Bree's voice rose, followed by Lydia's—light and happy, then talking over each other in a way that spoke of mutual trust and genuine joy in one another's company.

A moment later, Bree was leading Lydia into Charlie's office.

"Good timing," Charlie said, rising a little straighter in his chair. "We're ready to get started."

Xander's reaction was hard to miss. His grin sharpened into something brighter, less guarded, and for a beat too long his eyes lingered on Lydia as she crossed the room. If she noticed, she gave no sign. She glanced back at him and smiled.

"I thought you fellas would be finished setting up by now."

Xander held up a common power cord plug, turning it back and forth with a quizzical look. "Still trying to figure out where this thing goes."

Bree laughed. "I've got to run some errands. Lydia, try and keep our boys from electrocuting themselves."

The door had barely closed before Lydia began bouncing—a sparkle in her eyes. "Can we hold off on the podcast setup for a bit?"

"Why? What's up?" Charlie asked.

She leaned in, her expression full of purpose. "There's something I've been working on while you've been out shaking hands and kissing babies. It's a game changer that we've been hoping for but never had the answer to."

"What're you talking about?" Xander asked.

She pulled out two tokens and handed one to each of them.

Xander glanced at Charlie then back at her. "Are you okay…because we already have a few of these floating around."

"Not like these, we don't. Boss, would you fire up the website and log in under your user account."

Charlie placed the token down, navigated to the site then leaned back. "Now what?"

"Click on the token location tab."

Charlie made the click. He stared at the screen then turned to her, pressing the tip of his finger to the heart icon hovering over the outline of his house on the Google street map. "Is this the token you just gave me?"

She nodded.

"Did you scan the QR code or enter it already?"

She reached down and flipped the token over. The backside was barren, no text, no image, just a plain white circle.

"What's going on?" Xander said.

Charlie tapped his finger on the heart icon. "This is the token!"

Xander scratched his head. "I'm sorry but I don't get it."

"Our programming genius here has figured out how to allow our tokens to be located without having to scan the QR code or enter the alphanumeric code on the back, which means a token's journey will never be lost."

"These are prototypes," Lydia added. "The real ones will still have the codes on the back."

"Why?" Xander asked. "If they don't have to enter the codes and can still be tracked, doesn't that eliminate the entry need?"

Charlie shook his head. "The codes are still needed for the first person to start the token's journey. They'll also be needed in case someone wants to add a comment or post a video—"

"But," Lydia interjected, growing more excited, "if someone wants to just do an act of kindness and pass it along without a comment or video, they simply pass it on."

Xander's eyes widened. "This way a token will never die off?"

"That's right!" said Lydia.

"Wherever it's at…that token will appear on the map?"

"Yep! Only one downside," she said. "They're expensive. The nano-chip tracking technology is cutting edge, so it comes with a hefty price, not to mention the actual embedding of the chip into the token."

"So, what're we looking at?" Charlie asked.

Lydia's face contorted into a painful frown. "At least 80 percent."

"Our profit margin per token is a whopping 87 percent. A 7 percent decrease is well worth this added functionality."

"No. The cost to produce the chips will increase 80 percent."

Charlie's expression went blank.

Lydia sat in the corner of the Sinclair building's marble foyer, rubbing her palms back and forth on the chair's stiff leather strap armrests. The droning of conversations, the receptionist checking in visitors, the echo of shoes on stone, the distant chime of elevators—all louder than usual, as though everything was testing her composure. For the past five years, she'd only had a handful of meetings with him, each one filling her with more anxiety than the previous.

And for the first time, she prepared herself in a different way—she prayed.

The elevator pinged. She looked up to find Xander stepping out, his smile growing bigger as he strode across the foyer. She exhaled with a breath she hadn't realized she'd been holding.

"Hi there," he said, voice full of cheer. "Are you ready?"

She hesitated, shifting her weight. "As ready as I can be. Do you mind sitting with me a bit? I think I need a minute."

"Sure, your presentation's not for another ten minutes." He smiled. "Just remember, you're a superstar. Without you, none of his tech initiatives would have ever gotten off the ground. He needs you."

The knot in her stomach loosened a fraction. There was something in his tone—a confidence in her she wished she had for herself. For a moment, she almost forgot why she was there. The warmth in his eyes held more weight than his speech. It was genuine, carrying with it something she liked, something that put him in a light that had gradually brightened. The butterflies in her stomach suddenly fluttered happily about.

"Do you want to go over how you're going to propose the new chip technology?" he asked.

"I think I have it down. It's not complicated. It's just that I'm afraid of the cost. It's so expensive."

"Yeah, he probably won't like that, but hey, he has to know sometime." His eyes darted upwards as if finding a solution that was hovering above. "I'll be there with you, so why don't I chime in when you bring up the cost? That way he'll turn to me with all his questions and if he gets bent out of shape, he'll vent on me, not you."

"You'd do that for me?"

"Of course." His voice softened while at the same time resonating a reassuring tone, displaying the type of character she had never experienced with men in her life—at least not one who cared enough to be there for her in a time of need.

As the elevator doors opened again, he looked down at his watch. "What do you say? Ready to hit one outta the park?"

"Yeah, I think I'm ready." As they walked to the elevator, she caught the briefest spark in his gaze—something unspoken but undeniable. Nerves still fluttered inside her, but now they were threaded with something else entirely.

Xander entered Sinclair's office first—his gate steady, unflinching. Lydia lingered a timid half step behind.

Sinclair motioned them in yet didn't rise to greet them. "Lydia." His voice rolled off his tongue sounding as if attached to something he owned. With a mere hand wave, he motioned them to two empty seats in front of his desk.

She kept her eyes down as she took her seat, fingers folding in her lap. She pressed her wrists against the fabric of her sleeves, just enough to keep the cuffs in place, concealing what lay beneath. *Don't draw his eyes there*, she pleaded to herself.

Sinclair placed his elbows on his desk, gently tapped his fingers together twice then smiled. "What have we today?" His tone was matter-of-fact. Like a simple entry in a ledger.

Lydia shifted to the edge of her chair. "Good morning, sir." The words stumbled out in slow motion. She glanced at Xander and found a reassuring nod. "As I'm sure you know, the website has been performing well."

"Very well indeed," Sinclair added.

"Yes sir, very well. And with Charlie being on the road and handling all the promotional aspects of the business—"

"Which we want him to continue with."

"Yes sir, I believe that's the plan." She turned to Xander.

"That's correct, sir. Charlie's on board with that." Xander gave her a discreet wink followed by a welcoming, yet over-the-top complementary segue into her pitch. "I think you'll find our brilliant technical mastermind has been working on what could possibly be the most unique selling proposition of any website within the random acts of kindness segment."

Sinclair glared at him with an understood message to cut the pretense.

"Sorry, sir. Lydia's got a great idea for making it easier to track the tokens." He handed him one. "This is an example."

"Looks the same as all the others."

For the next ten minutes, she ran through the details of the new feature, explaining how much easier it would be on the users and how a token would always be able to be tracked. Her points were clear, concise and logically presented. Xander nodded through it all and offered statements affirming her brilliance.

"And with this new capability, we're sure to increase our volume," Xander added. "Our revenue—"

Sinclair ground his sales pitch to a halt with a cut straight to the jugular. "How much?"

Understanding the man's patience limitations had been reached, Xander came right out with it. "Unfortunately, the technology's rather expensive. It will eat into close to 80 percent of our profit margin." He waited.

A smile crept up Sinclair's face.

Xander continued undeterred, stating again that the dramatic cut in revenue could ultimately be made up in the increase in users, and that they could potentially raise the price of the tokens slightly.

Sinclair looked down at his watch, his smile continuing to grow. "If you'll excuse me, I have a meeting." He walked to the door. Just as he was about to exit, he turned, all traces of a smile gone. His brows pinched tight. "There will be no new tracking feature." He looked at Xander and began to laugh. "Eighty percent! Are you serious?" He turned, his eyes locked on Lydia, his voice void of emotion yet packed with intent. "And you'll make sure our Mr. Carraway continues to live and breathe kindness." His heavy, unyielding gaze held hers uncomfortably long. "Understood?"

"Yes sir." The words slipped out, quiet, automatic.

Sinclair held up the token. He turned it over and tilted his head as if trying to understand its new power. He chuckled, stuffed it in his pocket and disappeared into the hall.

The heavy glass door swung shut behind them, muting the muffled tones of the Sinclair building's foyer. Outside the rays of a harsh noonday sun combined with the roar of car engines, blaring horns and people scurrying up and down the street, all adding to Lydia's stress. She stood stiff, her shoulders tight, hands trembling slightly as she clutched her laptop.

Xander paused next to her, studying her. There was something there, something they didn't speak of during the elevator ride down. She stared at the pavement.

"You okay?" he asked. "I know it didn't go the way we wanted but it's not the end of the world. We'll just keep moving on as we have been. Things are going great anyway. And who knows? He may change his mind, and the cost of the technology may even come down in the next year or two." He placed his hand on her shoulder. "By the way, I think you did great in presenting everything."

She offered up a halfhearted nod that convinced neither of them. It was just a rehearsed gesture designed to end the pain of obligatory conversations such as this.

Xander wanted to press on, but something lurked beneath the surface, something that warned him off. Whatever had occurred inside that office, it wasn't his to unpack.

He stood with her in the lingering silence, letting the city noise fill the gap. After a moment, he reached for her hand and took it gently in his.

She turned her gaze up to him, warm but distant. In that moment, Xander was certain the girl he had started to care for was being haunted by something left unspoken, something that reached into a past that held her in its grip.

Chapter Sixteen

Charlie pulled a handful of envelopes from his mailbox and stood sorting through them. In the distance Ashley practiced her basketball skills in the driveway, spinning her wheelchair in circles while dribbling. "Anything from the colleges?" she shouted.

He flicked through the stack. "Doesn't look like it." His eyes stopped on the last item, a plain white index card. On it, written in red ink, was a single sentence: *Words that you may pass so that she may be strengthened.* It was signed, *Peter.*

His eyes jumped straight to Peter's name then back to the strange message when a car horn blared, snapping his focus up to a van pulling to the curb. The side door flung open. Three Pisgah High School cheerleaders, one brunette and two blonds, jumped out, waving pom-poms as if running onto the court for a pep rally. They all waved to Ashley as they bounced about and giggled. A second later Ashley was sitting beside them, shaking her own pom-poms.

"Okay girls…" the brunette said. With military precision the blonds fell in line next to her and began a choreographed routine of leg kicks and pom-pom maneuvers. Ashley followed along in her chair with her own brand of pom-pom moves. In perfect unison, Ashley led them off in a high-pitched chant. "Charlie, Charlie, he's our king, spreading kindness, that's his thing! Goooo Charlie!" A series of fan kicks, scissor jumps and more pom-pom shaking accented the ending.

"Thank you, girls," Charlie said with a modest bow and nod of the head.

"You're welcome, Mr. Carraway," the brunette said.

One of the blonds blushed like the shy little girl she was back in middle school. In a timid voice she said, "All of Pisgah High thinks you're great." The other blond nudged up to him, batted her eyes and smiled. "All of Canton does."

"Um…thanks," Charlie replied, glancing over at Ashley who looked a bit confused yet entertained.

"Alright, girls, game starts in thirty minutes," said the brunette. She spun around to Ashley. "Ready, girlfriend?"

"See ya, Dad!" she said, waving over her shoulder as the brunette rolled her onto the chair lift that had magically appeared out the van's back door during the makeshift kindness rally. The brunette pressed a button inside the van and the door eased closed. Inside Ashley beamed. "Love you, Dad," she yelled as she faded away.

"Don't worry, Mr. Carraway," the brunette said. "We'll have her home by midnight." She smiled. "I mean ten."

A car door slammed shut from the other side of the driveway. Charlie turned to find Xander walking to him, his hands over his heart, lips puckered in mock adoration.

"Now that's what I call love!"

"How long have you been there?"

"Just pulled up in time to witness the show." He smacked his lips. "From eighteen to eighty, you got 'em all eating out of your hand."

Charlie waved away the compliment with a smirk. "Where's Lydia?"

"She's not going to be able to make it."

"But we're launching the podcast in forty-five minutes, and I was going to introduce her. She was going to be our first guest. I was even going to let her announce the new token technology."

"I'm afraid that's the reason she's not going to be here."

"What?"

Xander put his hand on his shoulder. "Come on inside. I'll tell you all about it."

The kitchen was warm with the hum of the dishwasher and the aroma of freshly brewed coffee. Bree pressed the last slice of bread into place and smoothed her palm gently over the sandwich, etching the letter X into it with a butter knife. She carefully arranged two plates in her hands and turned toward the hallway leading to Charlie's office.

From down the hall came his and Xander's muffled laughter.

Bree smiled.

Over the past months, since the launch of the *Following the Love* website, Xander had drifted into their lives in that easy, unrushed manner as some people do, unforced and natural as if they had always belonged, very much the same way Lydia had snuck into their hearts. Neither was blood, but they might as well have been. Charlie trusted Xander with things he didn't often share, and Bree had grown to think of Lydia as a little sister, often sitting with her for hours discussing heartfelt subjects meant only for them. With Charlie being gone so much, the amount of time they had together provided a level of intimacy that some friends never saw in a lifetime.

She nudged the office door open just as Xander stepped out. His cheeks were flushed from laughter—or more likely the excitement of successfully pulling off their first podcast.

"Hey, Bree," he said, stopping short upon seeing the sandwiches. "For us?"

"Can you guess which one's yours?"

"Hmmm." He pointed to the one with the engraved letter. "X marks the spot?" He chuckled. "Would you mind if I take mine to go? If I don't leave now, Charlie will talk me into one more final tweak on the episode."

She laughed softly. "So, it's finished, then? The great podcast launched?"

"Up, up and away!" Xander said, his eyes lit with the type of pride that came from a successful communal effort with friends. "Your hubby will tell you all about it. He's still in there floating around on cloud nine." He skewed his lips. "Wonder what's up with clouds one through eight?"

Bree, accustomed to Xander's sometimes lame humor, shook her head and glanced through the half-open door. Charlie sat at his desk, leaning forward as though there was still work to be done. She looked back at Xander, lowering her voice. "Thank you for all you do. It warms my heart that you guys are working together again."

"Funny how life circles back sometime," he replied. For a moment, he stood there, content with not so much what he had helped achieve but how it had been received. "Well then, you'd better get in there before he forgets to eat." With a small wave, he slipped away.

Bree lingered a moment in the hallway then strode in,

sandwich plate stretched out as if making an offering for the intrusion. "Still at it, huh?"

The only response was the clatter of his keyboard tapping.

She stepped closer and leaned in front of him, making him jump.

"Oh shoot. I didn't hear you come in."

"I made you a sandwich."

He pushed himself away from the computer.

"Xander told me you guys had a successful launch."

Charlie took two big bites of his sandwich then tried to speak, the words coming out muffled and uneven. "I'm telling you—" he swallowed, "everything just keeps working out for us. Well…everything except the new tracking technology."

"It doesn't work?"

"It works great. Lydia nailed the programming, but Sinclair shot it down."

"I didn't think he was involved anymore."

"I'm a little confused by that myself. On paper he's not but because he brought Lydia to us, he kinda is, and in hindsight I don't believe we'd ever have gotten off the ground without her. The girl's an absolute genius."

"So, you feel beholden to Sinclair because of it—and you're willing to let him still make decisions?"

"I-I guess so. I still feel obligated to him. It's like he's a silent partner." He chuckled. "Actually, an invisible partner. And to be honest I kind of like it this way. Everything is working out better than I could ever imagined, so why rock the boat?" He started to say something else, but his words trailed off as his gaze fell onto his desk, his sandwich forgotten in his hand. "I'm just curious as to what it is that he has over her."

Bree's head slowly moved up and down. "I think I may know some of it."

Bree settled into the chair opposite Charlie. He leaned back slightly, watching her with quiet patience.

She inhaled, her fingers curling together in her lap. "You know Lydia and I have grown pretty close, right?"

"Yeah, I think so."

"Since you've been gone so often, she's been over quite a bit."

He looked down, averting his eyes to avoid the condemnation of his time away from his family. Yet she didn't go there, not this time. This was about Lydia, not his lack of presence as a father or husband.

"It's not easy to explain." Her eyes flicked to the door then back to him. "And to tell you the truth, I don't have the full story so what I tell you could be out of context. Just promise me you won't say anything—not a word to her."

"I promise."

"Good. So…it seems that Lydia's father worked for Sinclair for many years as his IT guy. In fact, he was with him since the beginning when he launched his first business. According to her he was even smarter than she is."

"Wow, that's hard to believe."

"She also said that he was much more involved in Sinclair's businesses than just IT. The picture I got was that he may have been his partner or at a minimum his right-hand man."

"You're saying all this in past tense. Did something happen to him?"

She nodded. "Somewhere around her senior year he up and left—just vanished!"

"Any idea why?"

"No. To this day she has no clue."

"What about her mom?"

Bree shook her head. "Evidently the marriage was toxic and so was her relationship with Lydia. Things only got worse after he left, and her mom turned to drugs and alcohol."

The room fell silent. Charlie stared out the window. A sudden chill came over him as the vision of him reaching out his own hand into the darkness appeared followed by a clap of thunder snapping him back to Bree's story.

"Are you okay?" she asked.

"Ye-yeah, I'm fine." He ran his hand down the side of his face. "So, how's this all related to Sinclair?"

"It appears that when her father took off, he left them with nothing. Bank accounts were emptied, credit cards gone and the bank even foreclosed on the house…that's when her mom overdosed…"

"You mean…"

"She had no one." A tear rolled down Bree's cheek. "The scars on her wrist are a result of how she tried dealing with it."

Charlie's expression dropped. "What?" His voice came out quieter than he intended. "Oh no… I never noticed." He ran a hand over the back of his neck. "How did I miss that?" He paused, still trying to process it. "I still don't see how that involves Sinclair."

"That's when he came to her rescue. Sinclair came in and took care of all her bills, including all her college tuition."

"So that's it—she's indebted to him financially. She has to pay him back."

"I thought that too, but she said he doesn't want payback. All he's ever done is to ask her to occasionally help him out with IT issues and—in our case—to help you launch a website."

"That's… that's just amazing. I'm feeling rather guilty now."

"Why?"

"I had started questioning his motives but now this! The man's a saint."

The words still hung in the air when Bree's attention drifted to the pile of mail he'd brought in. The top piece caught her eye—Peter's index card, its edges slightly bent, as if it had been handled too many times. Almost without thinking, she reached for it.

"Did this come today?" she asked.

"Yes. And to tell you the truth, I'm sick of it. First thing tomorrow I'm contacting the police—"

But she was already reading. "Put on the full armor of God, so that you can take your stand against the devil's schemes. For our struggle is not against flesh and blood, but against the rulers, against the authorities, against the powers of this dark world and against the spiritual forces of evil in the heavenly realms."

Charlie leaned over and flipped the card in her hands. "And this…"

Bree lowered her gaze, pausing for a beat before reading more quietly, "Words that you may pass so that she may be strengthened. Peter."

She went still; eyes fixed on the card as the meaning settled in. Then her eyes widened.

"Oh my gosh… this isn't meant for you," she said,

looking up at him. "It's for Lydia. Peter wants you to give this to her."

Charlie reared back. "How do I pass something along when it doesn't make sense?"

"It's Ephesians 6:11-12. It's scripture that means life is like a battle, but the fight isn't against other people. The fight is against evil influences we can't see. In Lydia's case we don't know what she's up against but whatever she's dealing with is definitely evil. And whatever that might be, she needs God's protection." She took a deep breath, letting the moment sink in for them both. "Charlie, I don't know who he is but I'm telling you, these aren't just random messages."

"I don't care. I say he's a psycho and I'm calling the cops. Somehow, he's gone and dug into the business. Not only is my family in jeopardy but my employees are now as well. Soothsayer or whatever he is, I—DON'T—CARE."

Chapter Seventeen

Charlie paced in circles in his office, one hand pressing his phone to his ear, the other flying about in animated frustration. "I told you—he's stalking me," he said, voice rising. "He's hacked into me and my coworkers' emails and now he's mailing cryptic messages to my house." He gripped the edge of his desk. "I don't know exactly how he's doing it—he just is!"

On the other end of the line, the police officer's tone was flat but politely asking for information Charlie couldn't provide.

Charlie groaned. He was getting nowhere.

Just then a text message from Lydia popped up. *Call me ASAP.*

"I'm sorry, officer, I have to go." Without any goodbyes Charlie switched straight to speed dial.

"Hey, what's up?"

Lydia's voice filled the line with a hesitant tone. "I think we've been hacked."

"What?" he shouted. "How? By whom? What've they got into? Has the server been—"

"Calm down. It's not bad. They didn't corrupt anything,

and nothing's been stolen. It appears to just be passive reconnaissance."

"What about data from our users? Was any of that scraped?"

"No," said Lydia. "Our firewalls appear to have prevented anything like that."

"What about emails?"

"No. I just told you our firewall kept them secure."

"What about the donations and all the transactional data?" Charlie asked.

"All secure."

"Are you sure? A hundred percent sure?"

"Yes."

"This will ruin us, Lydia. If we're hacked, we're toast!"

"Charlie! Listen to me. We're okay. Nothing's been jeopardized."

"I bet it's Peter. He's trying to take us down."

"Charlie, would you stop a minute and listen to me?" said Lydia. "The site is still completely secure."

"Are you sure?"

"Yes. Completely. I just felt I should keep you posted."

The line went silent. Charlie filled the void with an extended sigh.

"You okay now?" Lydia asked calmly.

"Yeah…I'm sorry. It's just…well, it's been one of those mornings, you know?"

"Well, don't worry, I've added another layer of security to the site. Not even the CIA could get at us."

"Okay…thank you."

"So, who's Peter?"

"Nobody. I-I was just thinking about something else."

"Something else? It wouldn't be the dip in visitors to the

site would it, because that's probably just a cyclical thing. I spoke to Xander, and he agreed it's nothing to worry about."

"I'm glad you guys think that, but I can't help but be concerned."

"Every site has its ebbs and flows. It's normal."

Charlie's grunt did nothing to assure her that he agreed.

"When was the last time you had a vacation, boss?"

A moment passed. "I don't know, maybe a year or two ago. To be honest I can't remember."

"Maybe it's time you and Bree had one. You know you've earned it."

"Thanks, but right now I just want to make sure we're tight."

"Boss, you're plenty tight for all of us. Please take some time off. It'll do you a world of good. And I know Bree would love it."

"I'll think about it."

"Oh, for Pete's sake. You're impossible."

Bree stepped out the back door, a towel draped over her shoulder, her hair still wet from her morning shower. She flung the towel to the ground as she headed to the end of the driveway where Charlie stood struggling to position a large black box into the trunk of his car.

"Don't you want to take the van?" Her tone was more of a command than a suggestion. "Charlie, what on earth are you doing?"

"Hey," he said, a little too casually as he angled a microphone stand in beside the black box.

Bree glanced inside the trunk at the neatly stacked boxes

and cases—mixers, microphones, headphones and loops of cable and power cords. "Did the podcast not work out?"

"No. It's actually been a big hit."

"Then why are you returning all the equipment?"

He slammed the trunk shut. "I'm sorry. I wanted to get everything packed before you woke up and then I was going to tell you—I have to take advantage of my grocery store relationships and take the podcast on the road."

She drew back a step. "An actual road show?"

"Yeah, you might say that."

"And you're going with it, I presume."

He choked back a laugh. "Of course, it's my show."

Her eyes froze over, and she stood speechless.

Charlie summoned a slender smile, his voice soft but deliberate, carrying the measured cadence of a speech he had rehearsed in the sleepless hours of the night before. "Bree, honey, I know this is rather sudden but it's something I have to do. The website's been hacked into and our effectiveness and overall usage has dropped. Lydia has put out the fire from the security breach, but in order to revive the downward visitor trend I need to get out in front of our fans—I-I mean users—and give them a level of confidence that all's well."

Bree shook her head. "Do you hear yourself? You sound like this is some kind of battle or natural disaster."

"I'm sorry if it comes off that way but in my world that's what it is. And if you don't react fast enough, you're dead." He wiped his forehead with a trembling hand.

"Are you okay? You're shaking."

"Just too much coffee this morning." His voice was faulty, each word coming out uneven.

"Are you sure? You're acting like you've just had one of your nightmares."

"I'm fine. It's just that I know I have to do this, and I know there's never going to be a great time for it but…" He swung his head back and forth, as if trying to shake unwanted thoughts away. "I just have to go. I have to keep the success going. I have to, I have to, I—"

"Slowwww down," Bree said, placing a hand to his cheek. "Just breathe. Everything's going to be okay."

Charlie stood looking into her eyes, his breathing coming in short anxiety-filled bursts. "I…I'm sorry. I just have to do this—for me, for us."

Bree moved her hands down to his right hand, her fingers curling gently around it. She pulled it up to her lips and kissed it. "Listen to me…"

Charlie jerked his head down the street then back in the other direction. "Paparazzi. I know they're out there."

She tugged at his shirt. "Charlie! Are you listening?"

"Yes. What?"

Bree leaned her forehead against his and stayed there, drawing in a slow, deliberate breath. For the next minute, she breathed with him, helping him steady whatever had taken hold of him. A moment later. "Feeling better now."

He nodded.

"Good, because if you keep this up, you're gonna have a heart attack."

"I know, I know."

"So, if you feel you have to do this, just remember it's your daughter's birthday this Saturday."

"I won't miss it. I promise. I swear I'll—"

"No need to swear. Just promise me you won't miss it, okay?"

"I promise." Charlie drew an X over his chest with his finger. "Cross my heart, hope to die."

"That reminds me—is Xander going with you?"

"No." He cocked his head. "What made you think of Xander?"

"You just made an X. He's been on a kick lately with this whole 'X marks the spot' thing, like he's got the phrase trademarked. Guess now I can't un-hear it." She tilted her head, her eyes glistening. "So, are you leaving right now or can you come back in for a breakfast?"

"I'm afraid I have to go. The first gig's on the other side of Raleigh just after lunch so I have just enough time to get there and set up."

"Then you'll be back by tomorrow afternoon for Ashley's birthday party?"

"I've got another store early in the morning on the way back in Charlotte, but yeah, I should be back by lunch."

Bree raised an eyebrow. "Are you sure?"

Charlie took her into his arms and kissed her on the cheek. "I'll see you tomorrow."

A minute later he was pulling out of the driveway and waving goodbye. The moment the house was out of sight, he reached into the center console and pulled out a small orange bottle. At a stoplight, he unscrewed the top, shook out two tiny pink pills, and popped them into his mouth.

Lydia walked up to Bree's front door. It was already cracked open as though Bree had been listening for her.

"Come on in," Bree called softly from inside.

Lydia stepped in, her footsteps hesitant, a quiet unease settling over her. Something was wrong. She'd heard it in

Bree's voice. She set her purse down on the foyer table and found Bree in the living room, perched on the edge of the sofa like she might spring up at any moment. A half-empty mug sat forgotten on the coffee table.

"Thank you for coming," Bree said, her voice tight, almost breaking.

Lydia took the chair across from her. "Of course. Is it something about Charlie?"

Bree nodded, twisting her wedding ring around her finger. "He's left."

"He's what?" Lydia said, jumping to her feet.

"No. No! It's not like that. He's gone on the road with his podcast."

Lydia fell back into her chair as she blew out a sharp breath. "Oh Bree…don't do that to me."

"I'm sorry. It's just that he up and left so abruptly."

"I'm sorry too. When you said he left, I should've known what you were talking about. He called me a while ago to let me know how the Raleigh podcast went."

"I should've figured he would."

"He said he'd call you when he checked into his hotel." Lydia tilted her head to her. "Soooo…is there more?"

"I don't know. I just needed to talk to someone. I-I'm just worried about him, you know?"

Lydia nodded, though her eyes lingered on the floor. "I'll be honest, I am too…a little that is. I mean not crazy concerned, but I have noticed some things."

"Like what?"

"He's been rather keyed up lately. He's normally pretty chill but of late not so much."

Bree returned a knowing nod.

"I told him you guys needed a vacation."

"One hundred percent," Bree said. "He's so worried about the website being hacked into and how it's started to decline and—"

"Oh my gosh! Bree, I told him he didn't have anything to worry about, that those things are normal. For one, the site is super secure. That hack was something that many platforms like ours experience and two, the decline was temporary. It's already trending back up."

"So do you think he's okay, that this is typical nerves?"

"At first I didn't but the more I sit here thinking about it, I kinda do. Having as many users as we do definitely carries a burden. And I'm sure he feels a certain obligation to them, especially considering that it's based on doing good."

"I guess you're right."

"By the way, during his rant about the site being hacked, he mentioned somebody named Peter. Is he a friend or something because it didn't sound like it."

Bree stood up. "Hang tight a minute? There's something I want to show you."

A minute later she returned with her Bible. Sliding a chair next to Lydia, she flipped it open to the page where Peter's note to Charlie was tucked. "This message was sent to Charlie...but I believe it's meant for you."

For the next twenty minutes, Lydia listened to Bree interpret Ephesians 6:11-12 and how important applying the armor of God was to battling one's demons. When she had finished, Lydia sat silently fighting back the tears. "Does Charlie go with you to church?"

"Sometimes."

"Would you mind," Lydia hesitated, her voice soft as a child, "if I came with you—sometimes, that is? I think I need to know more."

The words lingered for a long moment, leaving Bree unable to speak. All she could do was let their warmth settle in. "Yes! Yes…of course you can." The house fell silent again as Bree sat there stunned that she had done something she'd always prayed about and even professed to Pastor Dan that she felt lacking. It was the one thing she had failed to do with Charlie but had just done for Lydia. She had planted a seed that was finally beginning to break through the surface into the light.

Bree threw her arms around Lydia, and for a few heart-beats the rest of the world faded away. When they finally pulled back, it was with a shared exhale followed by a silence that said no words were needed. Bree straightened, brushing a strand of hair from her face. She cleared her throat, her tone shifting just enough to tether them back to the everyday. "Hey," she said lightly, "you're still coming to Ashley's birthday party tomorrow, right?"

"Absolutely!"

"Awesome, and don't worry about a gift. You being here is enough."

"Too late—done got it!"

Bree clapped her hands. "She's going to be so surprised."

"Is Xander coming?"

"Of course…is that okay?"

"Oh yes!"

Bree gave her a sideways look. "I know you like him. Uh huh…you like that boy, don't you?"

Lydia grinned and walked to the front door. As she was about to leave, she turned back and smiled. "I'm looking forward to church."

Charlie sat on the edge of the hotel bed watching an ant wrestle its way across the carpet's deep fibers, somehow feeling sympathy for the insect's silent persistence along the uneasy path he had chosen.

The room was too quiet, the hum of the air unit too steady. His shirt still clung to him from the long day, and his crumpled tie hung loose like a flag of defeat. Restless, he rose, pacing a few steps before his choice became clear.

By the time the elevator doors opened onto the lobby, he had already decided which bourbon to order. The low amber glow of the hotel bar called to him, an oasis of relief from a hard day of faking smiles while handing out tokens and struggling for something witty to add to his podcast. He slid onto a stool, nodding to the bartender without a word. The first glass went down quickly, burning the back of his throat. The second lingered, heavy in his trembling hand. By the third, the edges of his restlessness began to soften, and a quiet settled over him. Finally, he could relax.

"What're you drinkin' there, handsome man?" came a silky voice from behind him. A tall blonde with high cheekbones, an ample amount of mascara and a come-hither smile nestled up to him. "Did I see you someplace today?"

Charlie shrugged.

"You look familiar." She scooted a little closer to him. "Are you familiar?" she smiled wryly.

Charlie narrowed his eyebrows. "I'm not sure what that—"

"I got it! You're that kindness guy!"

A flash lit the room as two college students snapped a selfie while downing shots at the far end of the bar.

The blonde tapped Charlie on the shoulder, drawing his attention back to her. "I saw you at the grocery store this afternoon. You were at a table doing some sort of show about those kindness chips. That was you, wasn't it?"

"Yeah, that was me."

She batted her fake eyelashes as she gushed, "You're a celebrity!"

"Not really."

"Are you staying here?" she asked.

"Yep."

She gazed into his eyes then glanced toward the exit. "What do you say we go spread some kindness up in your room?"

Charlie raised his left hand and tapped on his wedding ring.

"So? I had one of those one time. Didn't stop me."

"Sorry, ma'am," he replied.

"Ma'am?" Her tone went sour. "You're calling me a 'ma'am'? I'm no ma'am. My grandmother's a ma'am." She stormed off, shouting over her shoulder, "Ain't nothing kind about you, mister." As she turned into the hall, the frustrated clicking of high heels on marble was the only thing left, along with her muttering, "I reckon *calling me* a ma'am!"

Charlie turned back to the bar to find the bartender leaning toward him with a big grin. "Would you care for another round, sir?"

"No thank you." He threw out two twenty-dollar bills. "Keep the change."

Back in his room and still unable to sleep, Charlie opened his laptop. Instead of going straight to the *Following the Love* analytics page as he always did, he clicked into the *Dealer's Choice Gaming* website. The screen glowed with a bright neon-green message: *Welcome back, Charlie!* Below it, in small text, was the time stamp of his last visit, the day before he launched the *Following the Love* website.

He rubbed his hands together, clicked the pulsating *Place Your Bet* button and smiled.

At six thirty the next morning, Charlie jolted awake. His eyes locked on his laptop. The *Dealer's Choice Gaming* website glared back. *Account Empty. Better luck next time!* He slammed the screen shut.

Chapter Eighteen

Through her window Bree watched as Xander's car rolled to a stop outside her house. He was already grinning before he cut the engine. A moment later Lydia pulled up behind him.

Bree stuck her head out the door. "You guys are kinda early for the party but come on in. I could use some help decorating."

"Is Ashley ready?" Xander said, sliding through the door with Lydia following.

"I think she's been ready since the sun came up."

"How about you?" he asked.

Bree turned to Lydia with a questioning look, one that Lydia could only respond to with a shrug.

"I'll be ready as soon as I get the decorations up. Then all we have to do is wait until Charlie gets home."

Xander's eyes darted from Lydia back to Bree.

"What's that look about?" Bree said.

"I'm afraid Charlie's not going to make it."

Bree's eyes flashed red. "What do you mean he's not going to make it? He said he would. He told me, point-blank, he was going…" She looked at Lydia. "He promised me."

"I'm sorry, Bree. He also made me promise not to tell."

"Not to tell? What's going on, you two?"

"It's okay," Xander said with a healing tone. "It's a surprise that we've been working on for a while now. One for both you and Ashley." He turned and smiled at Lydia. "A special apology to you for having to drag you into such deceit."

"Would someone tell me what deceit you're talking about?"

Xander placed his hand on her shoulder. "Bree, you wonderful, caring, special lady…would you please trust me on this and allow us to take you on a little trip? If you do, I guarantee your birthday angel will have the best time of her life. All we need are the keys to that broken-down vehicle you call a van." He turned and smiled warmly at Lydia. "Then leave the rest up to us."

Just then, Ashley rolled into the room in her wheelchair. "What's going on?"

Bree sighed. "Looks like we're going on a trip."

Bree's van rolled off the highway just outside Charlotte and down a small service road that opened into a sea of asphalt scattered with shiny trailers, huge chrome tool chests, and the glow of a dozen race cars lined up ready to be worked on. In an adjacent field sat a sleek black helicopter with the number 82 across its side.

Ashley pressed her nose to the back window, her eyes widening as a monstrous garage came into view. Across the front, in bold lettering, were the words: *Dusty Harmon Racing.*

"Ohhhh my gosh," she murmured.

Xander eased the van up to the open bay doors where several mechanics were inspecting an engine block. Inside the garage, the air was thick with the tang of oil and rubber, the kind of smell that clung to concrete floors and well-worn overalls.

Xander jumped out of the van and ran to the back, standing at military attention, waiting for Ashley's chair lift to lower her. "Ready to party?" he said, doing a less than impressive overbite jig. Lydia laughed out loud.

"Yes! Yes! Yes!" Ashley squealed.

"That's what we wanted to hear!" The voice was familiar but not immediately recognized.

Ashley's mouth dropped. She spun her chair around. "Dusty! You're—you're here!"

Everyone laughed. "Yep, this is pretty much where I live."

Suddenly the chaos of the garage was at a standstill as everyone in the shop, from mechanics to the cleanup crew, gathered around the van. Dusty bent down and gave her a hug. "This is your day, Ashley Carraway! Happy birthday!"

"How'd you know?" she replied, still wide eyed with surprise.

"Why don't you ask the King of Kindness himself?" he said, tipping his chin toward Charlie as the crowd opened around him. In his hand, he held the strings to a dozen black and gold balloons along with one oversized mylar unicorn.

Charlie walked up, handed her the balloons and dropped down for a hug. "Happy birthday, angel." He looked up to Bree. "Hey, babe," he said, smiling. "I hope Xander and Lydia's road trip didn't throw you for too much of a loop."

Bree shook her head while wiping away tears. "Couldn't have been any better."

"It actually does get better." He stretched his hand toward Dusty with a nod.

"On behalf of myself, my crew, and our sponsors, we'd like to present to you…the Dashley!"

And just like that, a brand-new black luxury BMW van rolled into view, gleaming in the sun, the *Following the Love* logo emblazoned across its side.

Dusty cleared his throat. "By the way, the name came compliments of your marketing guru."

To the delight of the crowd, Xander provided a comical half curtsy followed with his urgent need to explain his naming strategy. "See what I did there…mashed up the D from Dusty with Ashley to come up with—"

Lydia patted his shoulder. "We all get it," she said with a gentle laugh. Her smile and gaze lingered on him, warm and unhurried.

Charlie shook Dusty's hand. "From the bottom of all our hearts, we thank you for such an incredible gift."

Dusty smiled. "What makes the Dashley so amazing isn't just that it'll hit the road for the podcast tour. It'll also serve its namesake! Packed with every gadget and convenience you could imagine, it even has the latest, state-of-the-art chair lift in the industry."

Ashley beamed. "What's her top speed, Mr. Harmon?"

Charlie skewed his lips. "That would be whatever the speed limit is, young lady."

The new Dashley van cruised down the highway, its engine purring like it had just been tuned by a professional pit crew.

Ashley sat in her special chair, raised effortlessly by the van's state-of-the-art lift, a grin spreading across her face. She spun around in awe at the rich burl wood dashboard, hidden compartments, and every dazzling feature built just for her.

Up front, Charlie and Bree exchanged thankful glances for a van that was more than a vehicle, it was a gift that made life easier, brighter, and full of possibilities. As the newness wore off, their appreciation turned to reflecting on the overall fun of the surprise party.

"Thank you again for setting it all up, Dad," Ashley said.

Bree patted Charlie on the knee, acknowledging her own appreciation.

"So now that you're another year older and preparing to go off to college, the question remains…have you narrowed it down to where you're going?"

"I have."

Bree turned and winked at her.

"And I've done more than narrowed it down. I'm choosing UNC Asheville."

"Hallelujah! Hallelujah!" Charlie shouted. "When did you decide?"

"About five months ago."

"Five months! You little minx…all this time I thought you were heading to Florida to learn oceanography."

"Nah, that was kind of a joke."

"Kind of? I'd say a full-fledged gut buster."

"Not all of it, Dad. Just the oceanography part."

"Bree, can you decipher what the alien in the back is talking about?"

Ashley laughed. "Dad, let me ask you some questions. What's the crime rate in the county where that school is?"

"I don't know."

"It's almost 52 percent per 100,000 people, which is in the top ten in the United Sates. What's the poverty rate in that county?"

"Uh, I don't know."

"It's 53 percent, which is within the top 10 percent in the country. And what's the unemployment rate there?"

"I'm guessing it's pretty bad?"

"You're right. It's 7.4, putting it in the top twenty."

"Okay, I get it, but what's that gotta do with why you pretended to want to go there?"

"Mom…did Dad forget what *Following the Love* is all about?"

Bree lowered her chin, letting her eyes meet Charlie's in a moment of parental pride. "While our dear girl was doing her research on colleges, she found out just how bad off that area is…"

"And when I found out they wanted to be known as 'the college of kindness,' I figured including being the daughter of the kindness king might just plant the seed to contact you about *Following the Love.*"

Charlie rubbed his forehead. "Ohhhh, of course!"

"Do you see now?" Bree asked.

"Yes! Because that school is surrounded by so many in need, it's a target-rich environment for doing good."

"Honey!" Bree said. "Can you phrase it just a little softer?"

"Oh—sorry. Yes, it's a place that's in need of kindness. A lot of it."

"And?"

"And love."

"Of course, love," Bree added. "But what else?"

Charlie looked into the rearview mirror to Ashley for help. "Honey?"

"God. They need God, Dad."

Charlie swung his head in amazement. "Wow! I can't believe how well you thought that through, honey. You know who'd be impressed by that? Xander. All that research and to come up with a tactic like that to get us in there. That's just genius."

"Or maybe it's the Holy Spirit," Bree added.

"All I know is that when you graduate, you can come work with Xander to help market us. What do you say?"

No answer.

"Honey, what do you think about that?"

"Oh, I'm sorry. What'd you say?" came a groggy reply.

"You okay back there?"

"Just tired is all."

Bree turned to check on her. "You looked bushed, hon. When we get home, it's a bath and off to bed."

A moment passed. "Dad, you never asked me what I wanted to major in."

"I'm sorry, honey. What do you want to major in?"

"Social work," she murmured, already half-asleep.

"That's great. Do you know what field?"

"No," she whispered, her voice fading. "God will decide for me…"

The words slipped away, blending with the steady hum of the road beneath them.

Chapter Nineteen

Bree knocked on Ashley's bedroom door before pushing it open and sticking her head inside. The soft glow of a bedside lamp glistened off her wheelchair's metal handles. Her mylar unicorn balloon, wrinkled from loss of helium, hovered just above its seat as if recovering from the prior day's birthday party.

"Hey, honey," Bree said softly. "Are you coming to church this morning? Dad's coming?"

"Did you tell him?"

"That it was your birthday wish? I didn't have to say another word. As soon as he heard that, he was in."

There was a pause, then a quiet, almost hollow reply. "I'm sorry, Mom. I'm just too tired."

Bree studied how she hadn't lifted her head or even turned it to her. She sighed, forcing a smile. "Okay, dear. Do you want me to pick up anything for you on the way back?"

"No, I'm fine. I just think yesterday wore me out."

Bree paused at the door, watching the gentle rise and fall of Ashley's chest. "I love you."

"Love you too…"

Charlie pulled on his tweed jacket and headed for the door with Bree trailing him, her heart lifting at the simple sight of him joining her for church. The neighborhood was quiet, save for the rustle of leaves and the distant hum of someone mowing their lawn. Charlie led the way to the driveway where their new van sat, sunlight glinting off its windshield. Charlie smiled. "Can't wait to see the faces of the congregation when we roll up in the Dashley."

"No, dear, please not the van. Can't we just take the car?"

"But I'd like to show it to Pastor Dan."

"It's—it's so showy, with the logo and everything. It just looks…it's just too much."

"Are you serious?" His voice rose an octave.

Her expression took on a calm, borderline sternness. "Yes, we're going to church, not a trade show."

With the church bell's final chime hanging in the air, Charlie and Bree jumped out of their car and scurried up to the front door, Pastor Dan waving them in, a broad smile stretched across his face. "Well, I'll be hornswoggled," he crowed, arms stretched out for welcoming hugs. "Welcome back, brother Charles!"

"Sorry we're late, Pastor," Charlie said, still huffing from their little run.

"No worries, but you two might want to duck on in. We have a new lead singer on the worship team, and you don't want to miss her first song." He slapped Charlie on the shoulder. "It's one I think you'll like. It's called, 'Come Back to Me.'"

Bree gave the pastor a covert nod for his perfect song reference, although it was lost on Charlie as he was already halfway inside. "I'm sorry, honey, but I've gotta run to the little boy's room."

Inside a stall he reached into his jacket pocket and pulled out the small orange bottle he had begun to carry with him wherever he went. He dropped a single pill into his hand. A quick swallow with no water and he was back with Bree in the rear of the church, scanning for seats.

Hand in hand they stepped down the aisle as the worship team began to sing, the warm, layered harmonies of "Come Back to Me" resonating over the congregation. Sunlight spilled through the stained glass, blanketing the crowded pews in a rainbow of soft colors.

The congregation was on its feet, clapping to the rhythm, voices joining in praise. One by one, heads began to turn, eyes brightening, as looks of surprise and excitement spread across the sanctuary as they realized the King of Kindness was among them.

Bree's cheeks flushed under the growing attention. She smiled politely, nodding to the familiar faces beaming their welcome, all the while her fingers fidgeted with the strap of her purse. "See what you've done?" she murmured out the side of her mouth. "If you'd come more often, we wouldn't have to be in the spotlight like this."

Charlie only smiled. "But that's the whole point," he teased lightly, guiding her forward with an easy confidence. He greeted people along the aisle, nodding and mouthing "good morning" here and there.

Bree hung tight to him, scanning for a place to sit. "It's so packed, we'll be lucky to find a spot."

"There's two seats down at the…" Charlie hesitated, his eyes landing on a pew halfway down the right side. He squinted, not sure who he thought he was seeing. "Is-is that…?" he began.

Bree followed his gaze. "Oh my gosh, it's Lydia. And…Xander!"

Charlie blinked, still a little unsure. "Xander?"

Bree's grin widened as she gave a small, delighted wave that caught Lydia's attention. Lydia smiled back and nudged Xander, who gave an awkward half wave in return.

Suddenly Bree was in front of Charlie, pulling him down the aisle and squeezing into the pew next to them. Bree snuggled gleefully beside Lydia as Charlie leaned across her, trying to catch Xander's attention, only to find him with tight lips and puffed cheeks, looking as if he'd been caught petting a kitten at a bullfight.

For the first half of the sermon, Charlie tuned out Pastor Dan's message, content with torturing Xander with his adolescent eye rolls and lopsided smirks. To his frustration, Xander only acknowledged his antics once, choosing instead to lean more and more into the pastor's words. It was Bree's pinch to Charlie's underarm that brought him back to his own focus. For the remainder of the sermon, Lydia, Xander and Bree were locked onto the pulpit while Charlie remained detached, visualizing himself being interviewed by a famous reporter and sitting at his podcast table surrounded by adoring fans.

As soon as the service ended, a well-meaning elderly man, clearly a fan of *Following the Love*, approached Charlie from behind, leaving him to politely accept the man's compliments while Bree, Xander, and Lydia headed outside. By the time

Charlie had broken free and made his way out to the front steps, he found them deep in conversation with Pastor Dan.

Seeing him approaching, the pastor said aloud, "Let's see what this young man has to say on the matter."

"Sorry, I got ambushed back there," said Charlie.

"No problem. We were just discussing the verse and what it means."

"I'm sorry, what verse was that?"

"The last one I spoke about in the sermon—Ecclesiastes 3:1–8. It's the one I mentioned was hard for many to interpret."

Charlie stared blankly at them, prompting the pastor to enlighten him.

"To everything there is a season, and a time to every purpose under heaven: a time to be born, and a time to die; a time to plant, and a time to pluck up that which is planted…"

Xander poked Charlie. "Come on, you've heard it before."

Bree looked away, knowing her husband was completely out of his element.

"Well, I'm inclined," Xander began with a playful, professorial tone, "to agree with the musical theologians, Kansas."

"Kansas?" The pastor tilted his head.

Lydia giggled. "He's talking about the band Kansas."

Pastor Dan clasped his hands together like a toddler awaiting a treat. "Do tell…"

"In 1977 the band known as Kansas," a nod to Lydia, "thank you, my dear…penned 'Dust in the Wind,' which included the prophetic lyrics 'All we are is dust in the wind,' which, if I correctly understood your message, reflects life's fleeting nature, the inevitability of change, and the reminder that everything is temporary."

Lydia looked up at him with a gleam in her eye.

Xander raised his index finger. "Further to the point, I do believe Pete Seeger penned a similar message in his song titled 'Turn, Turn, Turn,' which The Byrds released in 1965, with the line 'a time to be born, and a time to die…a time to keep, and a time to throw away.'"

Pastor Dan stood speechless, a tiny smile creeping up.

"Oh! Oh! What about 'Circle of Life'?" Charlie chimed in.

"'Circle of Life'?" Pastor Dan said.

"From *The Lion King*, nineteen something or another. You know… 'It's the circle of life and everything moves… yadda, yadda.'" Determined not to be out done, he broke into an off-pitch, staccato repetition of the same line ending with the same yadda, yadda.

"Oh brother," Bree said grabbing him by the sleeve, "it's time to take this one home for a nap."

The Dashley glided along the highway, sunlight streaming through the windshield. Bree adjusted her sunglasses and glanced at Charlie, his eyes locked on the road.

"So, Mr. Bible scholar," she teased, gently nudging his arm, "did you get anything out of today's sermon other than learning that Lydia and Xander are an item now?"

Charlie's lips twitched, caught between a smile and a frown. "Evidently not," he said, with a lingering hint of embarrassment from his post-sermon performance on Pastor Dan's scripture quiz.

Bree leaned a little closer for another playful poke at him—but then noticed something that held her back from any more teasing. His right hand, resting on the steering wheel, trembled slightly, a barely perceptible shake that didn't match the rhythm of the road.

"Honey…" she said softly. "Your hand…are you okay?"

He forced a smile, tightening his grip as if the motion could hide the truth. "Yeah, just…a little chilly."

In that moment, the warmth of the Sunday morning's sun felt distant, replaced by an icy tension that grew colder when he told her he'd be leaving for another road show podcast right after lunch.

"How come you're just now telling me this?"

"I'm sorry, I just forgot. With planning Ashley's birthday party and then being dragged to church—I just forgot."

"Dragged to church! You thought you were dragged?"

"Maybe 'dragged' isn't the correct word," he said, back-pedaling. "More like coerced."

Bree slapped her palms down on the dash, her chest heaving, and stared straight ahead for the duration of the ride home. Nothing Charlie could say or do could pry her gaze away. The moment they pulled into the driveway she was out the door and into the house, the front door slamming behind her.

An hour later Bree was still in her bedroom with the door closed. Inside she sat on the bed with her Bible open, scanning the pages for the answers in scriptures, searching for enlightenment on patience and forgiveness. She turned her face toward the window, the verse from Ephesians echoing in her mind: "Be kind and compassionate…forgiving each other." She wasn't sure which part was harder—the kindness or the forgiveness. She rushed to the door and down to his office only to find it empty. All his equipment was gone, everything with him on the way to another one of his events—the events that were slowly driving a wedge between them.

Lydia's phone buzzed on her nightstand. She glanced down, her heart skipping a beat. *Thomas Sinclair.* She paused before unlocking it. *I need you in my office tomorrow, 11:00 a.m.*

Her fingers lingered over the screen as a wave of anxiety rolled over her. She dialed Xander without thinking. He picked up after only one ring.

"Hey, are you in your office tomorrow? I've got a meeting with Sinclair and…I could use backup." Her voice peaked higher than intended.

"Ah shoot, I'm out of town with Charlie at that event down in Charleston."

Lydia let out a soft exhale, trying to steady her thoughts. "Oh, that's right. I forgot about that."

"I'm sorry. Are you going to be okay?"

"Yeah, it just that…"

"Lydia," he said tenderly, "if you want me there, I'll skip the event and come back for you."

"Thank you. But that's okay. I'm sure he wants you with Charlie. And I don't want to get you in trouble."

"Don't worry about me. You just say the word, and I'll be there."

"No, no…it's fine…I-I'm just happy to know you would."

She ended the call and stared at the ceiling. A moment passed. She turned to her computer, opened a blank Word document, and began typing.

*Dear Mr. Sinclair, this letter is to inform you
that I regretfully…*

Chapter Twenty

At precisely eleven the next morning, Lydia sat rigid in Sinclair's office, a worn leather satchel clenched against her knees. She shifted in her chair, her fingers fumbling with the brass clasp. Sinclair's seat, behind the massive marble desk, sat empty. Only the hum of the air conditioner and the muffled sounds of the streets below filled the void. Five minutes passed. She wiped her forehead. Ten minutes passed. She wiped her brow again. The calm of the office continued as her inner peace eroded. A minute later, she heard a door slam far away and then stomping feet as one man shouted and others replied in apologetic tones. The footsteps grew louder as did the shouting—clearly Sinclair. "I want it done without the mess is what I want!"

A moment later he was storming through the door. Two men followed, one large and burly with a tattoo of Thor's hammer on his neck, the other sharp in both physique and dress with a tight blond ponytail. The latter was apologizing in a distinctly Scottish accent. "We're sorry, Mr. Sinclair."

"Good morning," Sinclair said evenly as he passed Lydia on his way around the other side of his desk. He sat down, waving the two men off with a dismissive hand, then yanking them back with a curt directive to the one with the ponytail. "Murdock, you make sure Thor—and his hammer—don't lose their composure next time. You understand?"

Murdock nodded reverently as he backed out of the office. "Aye, Mr. Sinclair. It'll nae happen again. I promise."

Sinclair picked up a remote and pointed it at the door drawing it shut. "Now, Miss Lydia," he said, pressing his fingertips together, "let's discuss our little project, shall we?"

Lydia pulled an envelope from her satchel, holding it in her hand, the edges shaking. "Sir, before we begin—"

"I'm concerned," Sinclair said, not waiting for her to complete her thought. "I'm concerned that the young Mr. Carraway might be having a little difficulty with—how should we say—maintaining the pace."

"Sir, I assure you Charlie's working as hard as he can."

"It appears so, but it's not the current pace I'm worried about. My concern is his ability to keep it up."

"Trust me. He's honestly doing whatever it takes. He's on the road constantly with the podcast and doing whatever he has to… so much so that it's starting to affect his marriage." She stopped and stared at him. "How'd you know he might be having troubles?"

One of Sinclair's lips curled up like a snake. "I didn't. But I do appreciate your willingness to enlighten me just now."

Lydia's shoulders dropped.

"What I need from you, my dear, is a little encouragement. Cheerleading, if you will."

"Yes sir, of course…that wouldn't be hard because I like Charlie, but sir…" She hesitated, her eyes dropping to the envelope in her lap. "Here," she said, thrusting it out to him, "this will say it better than I can."

Sinclair eyed the envelope as he took it from her. He

silently read the letter inside, his eyes moving deliberately over each line. A flicker of understanding crossed his face. He paused, tilting the paper, letting its message sink in. He leaned back, fingers tapping the corners, as he formed his response. "I understand."

"You do?"

"Yes, and I agree. You simply can't do this anymore."

"That's right, sir. I'm just not able to. Things have changed for me."

"That's why you'll be getting some help."

"Excuse me?"

"I'm going to provide some support for you. And quite frankly, it's a perfect solution."

"I'm sorry, sir. Can I ask what you're referring to?"

"Your letter requesting help…" He popped his lips, turning the page toward her. "Right here where it reads, 'Two are better than one.'"

She took the letter and silently read. "Dear Mr. Sinclair, this letter is to inform you that I regretfully must admit that 'two are better than one, because they have a good return for their labor: If either of them falls down, one can help the other up.' Ecclesiastes 4:9–10. Peter."

"I'm sorry, sir, but I'm not sure where that came from…"

"Don't be ashamed, dear girl. To be honest I thought you would have come to me before now. And even though I believe your use of scripture is a bit over the top, I do enjoy some good theatrics."

Lydia sat gripping the letter, unable to take her eyes off it, baffled as to how it had replaced her original.

He gently placed both palms on his desk. "So, here's what I want you to do…"

Lydia turned her head to him, her lips parting but nothing coming out.

"I want you to take the rest of the day for yourself." He pulled out his wallet and slid a credit card across his desk to her. "Go on a little shopping spree. Buy a nice outfit. Go to the spa and this evening have a nice dinner with your boyfriend."

"Sir, I don't have a boyfriend."

"Of course you do." He smiled. "His name's Xander." In an instant his smile went flat.

Lydia sat frozen, staring at him, her mind spinning, trying to piece together everything he had said and how he knew about her and Xander. After a long, painful pause, she broke the quiet. "Who are you going to send to help me?"

"In time, my dear, you'll know, but for now here are the specifics on what to do in order to maintain young Carraway's productivity level, which, thanks to you, are exactly what is needed."

For the next ten minutes Lydia sat and listened to Sinclair present a strategy that she had helped craft, a strategy that from all angles made sense—only with a risk.

As if in a trance she walked to the door. Before she could leave, he stopped her.

"About your letter…it was Solomon."

"Sir?"

"It was that know-it-all King Solomon, not Peter as you have credited."

The grocery store smelled of coffee from the Starbucks located next to the produce section just yards away from the *Following the Love* podcast table. Charlie sipped on a latte while leaning over a table, spreading pamphlets and tokens, humming under his breath. Xander adjusted the pop filter on the mic until it clicked into place.

"X, X, X marks the spot," Xander said into the mic. "Testing X, X, X…X marks the spot. The sound levels are *excellent*," he said, emphasizing the X.

Charlie groaned. "Oh brother. You know you don't own that letter, don't you?"

"I know," Xander chirped. "Just allowing you to use it rent free in your head." His phone buzzed. He tapped the screen. "Hey, Lydia."

Her voice came quickly, a little uneasy. "Have you got a minute?"

His voice mirrored the smile on his face. "Of course."

"Has Sinclair contacted you?"

"No."

"Good, I wanted to catch you before he did. We had a rather strange conversation this morning and—well…" The phone beeped then went silent.

"Lydia, you there?"

"Sorry about that," she said, coming back online, "that was Bree. She's been trying to call Charlie, but his phone keeps sending her straight to voicemail. She wants him to call as soon as possible. You might want to go tell him now. We can talk later."

"Are you alright? You sound a little out of sorts."

"I'm fine. Just make sure to tell Charlie."

"He just sat down to begin the podcast, but I'll let him know. I'll call you when it's over and I'm on my way home."

Xander grabbed a pamphlet and magic marker from the table and jotted down "Call Bree ASAP." He slid it next to the mic, not wanting to disrupt the call-in conversation

Charlie had just launched into about the impact *Following the Love* was having on the Charleston community and how the grocery store was playing a major part. Without looking at it, Charlie stuffed the pamphlet into his pocket.

Xander pointed to the pocket. "You need to read it," he mouthed.

Charlie shook his head, annoyed at having to deal with the caller while being pestered by his friend.

Charlie slammed the van door shut.

Xander looked down, grinning at a cable dangling out of it.

Charlie opened the door and snatched up the frayed wiring that now hung limp, almost cut in two. He looked back to the grocery store's neon sign buzzing faintly in the background then back to the cable, his cheeks red as if about to explode. He squeezed it tight as if trying to choke it back into a solid piece. "Next major expenditure's gonna be a road crew," Charlie said, climbing into the van.

"Don't forget to call Bree," Xander called over his shoulder, heading to his car. "See you back at the ranch." He paused, smiling. "Proud of you, buddy. Don't know how you keep it going."

Charlie watched him pull out of the lot. The moment he was out of range the answer to Xander's observation came in the form of the orange pill bottle in his hand. A single tablet slipped into his palm—the little dose of magic he could no longer live without.

A mile down the road Xander's prodding him to call Bree came back to him. He picked up his phone. A moment later she was on the other end, her voice ice-cold with a hint of sadness.

"Why haven't you called?" she said.

"I've been doing the podcast. You knew that."

"I probably left two dozen messages. Did Xander not tell you to call?"

"No." The word landed after an uncomfortable hesitation.

"I told Lydia to tell him to tell you that…"

To Charlie's relief a dead zone dropped the call. He stared at his phone, ready to call her back, but the pill's effects had just kicked in telling him no. All was good with the world. Whatever Bree was on about was nothing more than a request to stop on his way home to pick up something for dinner.

A moment later his phone buzzed again. His hand hovered over it for a few seconds then found the knob to the van's radio volume. He turned over his phone, muffling the next five minutes of Bree's attempts to reach him while adult contemporary rock blared from the custom speakers Dusty had installed in the Dashley.

After an impromptu stop at a roadside bar for a couple beers to calm the tremors brought on by his pill popping and an extended layover at a Kentucky Fried Chicken, he finally rolled into his driveway. The clock on his dashboard read 11:05 p.m. All the lights in the house appeared to be off.

As he tiptoed past the kitchen and down the hallway toward his bedroom, a sliver of light spilling out from beneath it caught his eye. Bracing himself for the consequences of not calling, he forced himself forward. As he passed the living room, Bree's voice penetrated the stillness.

"What took you so long?"

He turned to find her on the edge of the sofa, hands clasped in her lap, just a dark silhouette in the dim light.

"I thought you'd be in bed."

"No." The single syllable was the tip of the iceberg Charlie knew lurked within her.

"Honey," he began, slow and deliberate, "I know you're probably upset but it's just been a long day, and I honestly didn't mean—"

"Ashley got sick today." Her voice was firm but weak from a long day on an emotional roller coaster.

"What do you mean sick?"

"I'm not sure."

"Like a cold, flu…what?"

"During graduation rehearsals this afternoon she fainted. For about half a minute, she was unconscious." Her voice began to quiver. "A paramedic even got called in to help."

Charlie rushed to her side, wrapping his arms around her. "Oh dear. I-I'm sorry. I would've come home immediately had I known."

"But you didn't!" Bree said wrenching free from him. She bolted up. "And you lied to me, Charlie. You lied! Lydia spoke with Xander this evening. He told you to call me. And he even told you it was important, but you didn't do anything. You went back to your stupid podcast and… and…you forgot about your family." She spun away from him, arms crossed tight. From behind, Charlie could see her shoulders rise and fall, full of rage at him, full of fear for their daughter, the weight of the day bearing down on her.

"How is she now?"

In the dark room Charlie could hear only his own heartbeat in his ears.

"Bree…how is she now?"

"She's in her room, asleep."

"But is she okay?" he said more gently.

"She's alright but the paramedics are recommending we take her in for a checkup."

"When?"

"Soon."

"Like how soon?"

"I'm not sure!"

"Why not?"

"It depends on the schedule."

"Whose schedule?"

"The doctor's, Charlie! Whose else would it be?"

He threw up his hands. "I'm just asking!"

"If you were ever here, you might not have so many questions."

Through the darkness he could see her eyes burning red with a feeling he'd never felt from her before—disgust.

The house had gone still. Bree had long since retreated to their bedroom, the soft click of the door closing behind her echoing louder in Charlie's mind than any slam could have. He stood alone in the hallway, the taste of their argument still bitter on his tongue.

He drew an uneasy breath and turned toward Ashley's room. The ticking of the grandfather clock punctuated the silence as he rested a hand on the door frame. He eased the door open an inch. The soft glow of her night-light spilled past her wheelchair and onto a dozen stuffed animals all snuggled up to her.

Charlie lingered there, watching her chest rise and fall,

letting the rhythm quiet the panic in his own chest. After a moment, he turned and made his way down the hall to the bathroom. The mirror greeted him with unflattering honesty—eyes bloodshot, skin drawn tight around a jaw still locked from tension. He reached a shaking hand into his pocket and brought out the orange pill bottle from earlier, stuffing it quickly back before retrieving another one filled with white tablets. Following the same routine, he tapped one into his palm, then another for good measure, before swallowing them dry. The chalky bitterness clung to his tongue, but it didn't matter. He needed the calm—the stillness—to wash away the remains of the rush from the orange bottle's stimulant and the anxiety brought on by Bree's rebuke.

For the next ten minutes he stood over the sink, gripping the edges as if to keep from falling apart. As the pill began to settle his nerves, he crossed the hall to his office. He sank into his chair and turned to his computer, seeking refuge, looking for anything that didn't feel broken. But the screen soon blurred. His head bobbed, his shoulders slumped. A moment later his cheek rested on the keyboard.

The next morning, he awoke to find the house as still as when he had passed out at his desk. A note was stuck to his computer screen. The message was simple. "Love you! Ash." Beside it was a heart drawn in pink magic marker.

He wiped his face, rubbing the sleep from his eyes, the aroma of coffee luring him to the kitchen where half a pot still sat warm. He poured a cup and walked to the back door window reaffirming what he expected—the Dashley was gone; in its place a silver Porche 911 was using his driveway for a quick U-turn. Only the backside of the driver's blond ponytail was visible. A second later it was gone. "Paparazzi dogs," he muttered.

Just then his phone vibrated in his pocket, rattling against his pill bottles and causing him to flinch.

It was a text from Lydia. *Great news! New token tracking green-lit!*

Chapter Twenty-One

Charlie's fingers fumbled over the phone screen as he pulled up Lydia's number, his heart thudding with excitement. With every ring of the phone, his grin spread. This was it. This was the answer to making social media history. Visions of him alongside the likes of Steve Jobs and other technology visionaries played out in his mind. "Come on, Lydia, pick up, pick up…"

"Hey, boss."

"Talk to me!"

"He's given us the go-ahead to move forward with the new tracking technology," she said matter-of-factly.

"That's awesome! So, what happened?"

"He just called and said move forward with it."

"What about funding? Is he going to pay for it? I thought he said it was too expensive. What about—"

"Slow down, boss. Geez. What kinda speed are you on?"

"I-I'm not on any speed, I'm not on anything," he said, fidgeting between the two bottles in his pocket. I'm just excited."

"Okay, but there's a catch. He wants to make sure you're all-in and that you're committed to its continuing success."

"But I've done that already. I'm living and breathing this thing."

"I know and so does everybody else but that's just how he operates."

"So, what's he want?"

"He needs you to share in the cost of producing the first six months of tokens."

"What do you mean 'share'?"

"He wants you to front the money for them. After that he'll reimburse you for the cost. From that point on the uplift in their usage should pay for them just like we think it will."

Charlie mulled over the request. "How many tokens are we talking about and how much?"

"I figure every token with the new tracking chip will be $3.75 and you'll need at least 125 a day, based on the current usage. That brings the total to $84,375."

"That's a lot of money—nothing I just have lying around. I'd have to…"

"Charlie. Are you still there?"

"Yeah…I'm just trying to figure this out."

"I forgot to tell you, but he also said he was expecting a large donation to come in a couple days which will probably pay off half that."

"Are you sure?"

"That's what he said."

"Okay, then yeah! I think I can do this!"

"You sure you don't want to think about it? Like you said, it's a lot of money."

"No, I'm good with it. Absolutely—all-in!"

"There's one more thing. He wants you to announce it on a podcast live in a major metro area, like the Research Triangle Park in Raleigh-Durham. Xander's already setting things up. All you have to do is show up in the Dashley van and do what you do."

"When?"

"Tomorrow, right after lunch."

"Can do!"

"Great, that way you'll be back by Sunday and can go to church with Bree."

"Church? Did Bree have you say that?"

"I haven't talked to her. I just think it's something you should do, don't you?"

"Why? What do you know? Why should I go? Is the devil gonna take me out? God gonna smite me or send plagues down on me?" The words came fast but sporadic, a mishmash of thoughts brought on by one of his little pills.

"Nothing's going to happen to you, Charlie, but whatever you've got going on you might want to throttle it back. You're sounding a little too amped up."

"I'm not amped. I just want to get all this done. How come you're not more excited? This is your baby, Lydia. You should be freaking out right now. You're about to become a tech superstar."

"I'm just a little tired is all. Aren't you?"

"No, I'm good to go."

"Great, because there's one last thing. Sinclair wants you to make the purchase before the podcast."

"Excuse me?"

"He doesn't expect them to be in hand by then, of course…" Her voice started to waver.

"What is it, Lydia? You're spooking me."

"It's nothing. Like I told you I-I'm just tired."

"So, what happens if I can't make the purchase before the podcast?"

"I don't know. The only thing I *can* tell you is that he's always testing people."

"You think he could pull the plug on the new technology? Because I know—in my heart—I know it's going to skyrocket us."

"He could."

"And you're sure that big donation is going to happen?"

"Charlie, please don't hold me to that. I'm just relaying what he told me."

The phone fell silent. "Okay, wish me luck."

Charlie heard the front door open, followed by the shuffling of footsteps and light moments of laughter. The murmur of voices reached him—Bree's low and measured, Ashley's weary but content.

A moment later, Ashly wheeled into his office, an ornate dress box in her lap.

"Hey, pumpkin," Charlie said, "Whatcha been up to?"

"Shopping!"

"Shopping for what?"

"A graduation party dress," Bree said, standing in the doorway with her arms crossed. She didn't look at him at first, just set her purse on the table beside his office door. Her movements were calm and deliberate—the kind of calm that showed she was still carrying the weight from the previous night's argument.

"That's good," he said.

"I'm gonna go try it on. Will you come help me, Mom?"

"I think you need your rest, honey. Let's have the fashion show tomorrow, okay?"

Ashley nodded. "Yeah, I guess I should." She pushed

herself up next to Charlie and gave him a quick peck on the cheek. "Night, Daddy."

"Night, sweetie."

As Ashley headed down the hall, silence settled between Charlie and Bree. He wanted to say something to bridge it but wasn't sure how. Bree finally looked up, her gaze level, tired, yet sharp. "Dinner's in the fridge," she said quietly, then walked out.

"Wait," Charlie blurted.

She stopped.

"Don't you want to hear how the podcast went?"

She shrugged.

"It went great!"

"Okay, that's great that it went great." She turned and started out again.

"But! But it gets better."

She turned back to him, slower than before, her lips pinched and brow furrowed. "Better how?"

Unable to temper his excitement, he let loose in rapid-fire succession all the details of launching the new token tracking systems—everything except how it would be funded.

"And when will this launch take place?"

"This Saturday." He quickly held up his hand. "But not to worry, I'll be back on Sunday, and we can go to church. What do you say?"

"Fine, I guess. But you'll have to go alone."

"Don't you want to go?"

"I won't be here and neither will Ashley. I'm taking her on a women's Bible retreat this weekend. And Lydia's coming with us."

Charlie shifted in his seat, his stomach tight as the banker in his charcoal gray suit sat opposite him, expressionless, dissecting the paperwork before him.

"Charlie, your current account has just over $6,000 in it and you're asking for $84,000," the banker said void of emotion. "Unfortunately, that leaves you well short at $78,000. And with the second mortgage on your house, you don't have anything to borrow against either." He pulled two other sheets of paper from a folder and began tapping his index finger on them as if sending a telegram. "And these other loans that were defaulted on several years ago don't help matters." The banker leaned forward. "Charlie, your kindness site seems to have taken off. By chance, would there be any other assets you could rely on?"

"Things are going great, it's just that there are a lot of technical expenses that go along with it as well as advertising and other stuff," Charlie said. "But as I said, it's doing well. The thing is—it's this new technology that we're going to use the money for that's going to make it explode!"

"New technology?"

"Yes sir. It already exists but it's new to using it in this application. What we have planned for it is basically revolutionary!"

"That does sound great and I'm sure it'll be a huge success, but given your current financial situation, my hands are tied. There's nothing more I'd love to do than help out the King of Kindness, but I'm afraid I just can't."

Charlie's throat tightened. "I do have something."

The banker raised an eyebrow.

Charlie slid a folder across the desk. "A van that was recently donated to my company. Clean title. Very high-end. And best of all it's completely paid for."

The banker scrolled to the bottom-line value. "Oh wow…$93,000 is certainly high-end alright." He leaned forward; fingers steepled. "And you say your company owns it?"

"Yes, and of course I own the company," Charlie said.

A calculating smile crept across the banker's face. "That changes everything. We can secure the loan against the vehicle, and you'll sign over temporary control of the title. If the loan isn't repaid, though, we take possession. Simple—but risky."

"How fast can it happen?" he asked.

The banker tapped away at his keyboard. "If you sign within the hour, we can release funds by the end of the day."

Charlie grabbed a pen. "Where do I sign?"

A minute later he flipped over the last page that granted title of the Dashley to the bank if he defaulted.

"Now," the banker said, "Where would you like the funds to go?"

"Directly to the manufacturer," Charlie said. "They're producing the items, so I need it transferred immediately."

The banker pressed a few keys, then swiveled his monitor toward Charlie. "Done. Wire's set. They'll have it within the hour."

Charlie stepped out of the bank into the midday sun. Around him the city buzzed with car horns, snippets of conversations, the rhythmic clack of heels on concrete. He closed his eyes and inhaled, filling his lungs then releasing his breath in a victorious exhale. Despite his debt, his loan history, and countless unmentioned gambling losses, he had secured the next level of success for his company, all thanks to one talented NASCAR driver. For a moment, the world felt bearable without the help of pills.

His stomach grumbled. It had been hours since he woke, and he hadn't had breakfast. A hot dog cart sat at the corner, under a bridge calling out to him. Above them, cars rushed past, the sound rumbling through the space below.

Litter, abandoned shopping carts, stray dogs and lost souls lay curled up in thin woolen blankets or bent over and shaking from whatever withdrawals they were enduring.

Charlie hastened his walk to the cart, pulling a crumpled ten-dollar bill from his pocket.

"What'll it be?" the vendor said, plunging his tongs down into the pile of dogs.

"Just one," said Charlie, "no, make that two."

"Plain or all the way?"

"Plain will be fine."

A young girl, not much older than Ashley, rolled past him in a battered wheelchair—its wheels wobbling, one armrest missing, the frame squeaking with every turn. It was nothing like Ashley's clean, well-kept chair. This one was barely holding together, a reflection of the life she'd most likely endured beneath the bridge. Her true age was buried under layers of dirt and years of surviving in that dim sanctuary, where the darkness offered shelter but stole everything else. Her smile had vanished long ago, lost alongside the other walking dead.

As she passed, Charlie caught her out the corner of his eye. He turned, anticipating her hand to be stretched out to him, begging for a crumb of what he might offer. Yet she passed with only a nod. Charlie scanned the length of the underpass, counting, mumbling a string of numbers.

"Hang on a minute," he said, holding up his hand to

the vendor. "How many hot dogs do you have in your steamer there?"

"Around fifteen."

"And the tub," Charlie said, pointing to a cooler. "Any in it?"

"Probably thirty or so. That's my reserve."

"Great. I'll take 'em all."

"Awesome! You got a picnic or something?"

Charlie tilted his head. "Sure…a little one right here. Can you help me round up our guests?"

"Sorry, sir, but I don't get what you're saying."

"Just follow my lead. Oh, and I'll take all the drinks you have too."

With the vendor following him, they canvassed the entire stretch underneath the bridge, inviting everyone to join them at the hot dog cart for his impromptu picnic. Within minutes a line of more than thirty had formed.

"Can you make some more?" Charlie asked.

"Sure. How many?"

"Enough so that everyone gets two."

The first up to the cart was the young girl in the wheel-chair who had passed by earlier. A fragile smile crossed her lips as she took the hot dog from Charlie's hand.

"Thank you," she said in a thin, frail voice. She turned and began to wheel away.

"Hang on a minute," he said, digging into his pocket in search of a *Following the Love* token. He smiled and held it out to her, but before she could take it, he pulled it back and tucked it away. "I-I'm sorry." He reached back into this pocket, pulled out a handful of crumpled bills and placed them in her palm. "Here, take this," he said wrapping both hands around hers.

She smiled at him, her eyes turning from sorrow to gratitude. "God bless you."

"Hey! You're that kindness guy," the vendor blurted. "I thought I recognized you. You were going to give out one of your—"

Charlie put his finger to his lips, shaking his head.

"Oh," the vendor said. "I understand."

Charlie smiled back at the young girl then looked up to survey the crowd. Across the street a man stood alone, watching. He wore a red parka with a tattered backpack over his shoulder, the same as Peter had. His dark skin and wiry frame were identical to his as well; only a cell phone held up in front of his face hid his true identity.

Charlie stepped to the side for a better look. "Hey, you!" he shouted.

The man took a step back.

"You there," Charlie called out again.

The man turned and stuffed the phone underneath the poncho—enough proof for Charlie.

"Peter! Is that you? What're you doing?" In a split-second Charlie was running across the street, out from underneath the bridge into oncoming traffic and a horde of pedestrians. He dodged cars, weaving his way onto the sidewalk in pursuit of the man in the red poncho until suddenly he was gone. No alley, no doorway, no side street, no sign of where he'd gone.

Chapter Twenty-Two

I-40 stretched wide and empty beneath the fading pink sky over the approaching Appalachian Mountains, the hum of the Dashley's tires blending with Xander and Charlie's laughter into a low, steady harmony.

Xander leaned back in the passenger seat, his voice animated as he replayed every reaction they'd gotten at the Research Triangle Park podcast. "Man, did you see the call lines light up when you announced the new token tracking?"

"I was having a hard time concentrating on the callers because I kept looking at the spikes in the website traffic," Charlie said.

Xander grinned. "You'd think we'd just pulled a rabbit outta a hat!"

Charlie laughed, the sound genuine but tempered by the weight of the risk he had taken to secure their new technology. "Yeah, it was a good show." He gripped the steering wheel harder. The new technology had dazzled but would it be worth it? As the city lights of home flickered into view, it felt as if it would.

Xander was still talking as they rolled into Asheville,

his words full of plans and possibilities. Charlie remained engaged, laughing at the right moments, playing the part.

When they finally pulled into Charlie's driveway, it was already dark and quiet outside. Xander stepped out and stretched his legs. "Alright, partner," he said, slapping the side of the van. "You rest up now. Oh, I just about forgot. When do you wanna meet to discuss the ad campaign for the new technology?"

"How about tomorrow morning? All our girls are out of town."

"Sorry old chum…church."

"You're going without Lydia?"

"I reckon so if she's not here. You wanna come with me?"

"Nah, I'll pass."

"Alright, suit yourself ya heathen," Xander chuckled.

"What about Monday lunch? You call it."

"Mills River Diner. And it's on me."

Charlie watched his taillights fade down the street. He turned to his house. For a moment, everything was exactly as it should be. The road behind them full of accomplishment, the night ahead calm and still. He could hear the faint buzz of the city in the distance, and for once, it felt like all of it—the risks, the long hours, the tension—was all going to pay off.

Charlie walked into his house, surprised to find several lights on. He eased down the hallway, expecting the place to be empty and everyone already asleep. Just as he was about to reach Ashley's room, her door slowly opened. Bree was backing out of it but stopped halfway. "Good night, my love."

"G'night," came Ashley's voice, sounding miles away.

Bree closed the door. She turned and jumped when she saw him. "You scared me," she said, clutching her blouse.

"I'm sorry," Charlie said. "What're you doing back. I thought the retreat was all weekend."

She took his hand and led him into the kitchen.

"It was," she said, her voice thinning. She took a breath, her eyes shifting, searching for the right words. "But… something happened to Ashley."

"What?"

"This afternoon we were breaking up into small groups to share testimonials…halfway down a hallway she suddenly couldn't push herself anymore and she started wheezing."

"How bad?"

"Uncontrollable for at least five minutes. Maggie Johnson, who's a nurse, took her pulse and said it was around 100."

"It's not that now, is it?"

"No, it came down within the hour." She ran her hand through her hair. "Charlie, she was so pale. I didn't want to chance anything, so we packed up and came home. Lydia monitored her the entire way, keeping her hydrated and comfortable and checking her pulse."

"But you think she's okay now?" he asked, already moving before she could answer. "I'm gonna go check on her."

"No, you don't want to wake her. Maggie said to let her rest as much as she can until we get her checked."

"Checked?"

"She's got a regular physical in two weeks, but I called and got it pushed to Monday. They're going to squeeze us in at lunch. But don't worry, it's just with her primary care doctor. Lydia wants to come so you do whatever it is you need to do."

"I have a lunch meeting with Xander, but I can cancel. I just—"

"No, seriously, you do the business. Maggie said they'll probably say it was just all the excitement going on at the retreat."

"Alright then. If Maggie said it's okay…then I guess it's okay."

Just before noon on Monday, Charlie sat in the Mills River Diner parking lot surrounded by huge eighteen-wheelers. In his lap was his computer, opened to the donations page of *Following the Love*'s admin dashboard. He clicked the refresh button, biting his lip, hoping for the contribution figure to spike to the amount Lydia said Sinclair had promised—no spike. He clicked again, still nothing. He grumbled and clicked refresh again. Nothing. A minute passed and another click. The old saying *a watched pot never boils* sprung to his mind, yet he clicked once more, willing it to do produce results. Again, no spike. Again and again, he refreshed the page until finally resorting to his bottle of pills for relief.

"You coming?" Xander's voice rang out, causing him to bobble the bottle and spill pills across his lap and into the cracks between the seats.

Charlie jerked his head up to find Xander standing at the diner's shiny chrome door waving him in.

Two minutes later the bell above the door jingled as Charlie entered the diner, its air thick with coffee, grease, and the hum of tired conversation, compliments of a half dozen road-weary truckers.

"Over here!" Xander shouted from a corner booth.

Charlie walked up and slid into the seat across from

him, his jawline still tense from his fruitless attempts at summoning the donation to his website.

"What were you so into out there?" Xander said.

"Just reviewing the website's traffic."

"Everything okay? You look a little tense."

"I'm just a little out of sorts this morning. Feeling a little—"

"Edgy?" Xander said, staring down.

Charlie followed Xander's gaze to his trembling hand and quickly moved it under the table.

"Oh no, you don't," Xander said. "Something's going on."

"Nothing's going on."

"Charlie, you're as nervous as a long-tail cat in a room full of rocking chairs. Something's up."

"I'm telling you, it's nothing."

"Buddy…you were fine the other evening and now this morning you're Mr. Shaky Paw."

"It's nothing I'm telling you."

"Charlie, come on now. Is it Ashley?"

"No, it's…well, it partly is. Say, how'd you know about her?"

"Lydia called and told me about what happened at the retreat."

"She's at the doctor's right now for a checkup."

"Lydia and I are praying everything's okay."

Charlie nodded.

"So, what's the other thing?"

"What do you mean?"

"You said 'partly'…I asked what had you so edgy and you said partly Ashley. What else is there?" He leaned forward looking into Charlie's eyes. "Remember, this is your best boy here. Nothing goes beyond this greasy spoon."

Charlie looked around the room as if scouting for prying eyes, then back to him. "Lydia didn't tell you about her meeting with Sinclair?"

"Just that he's all about the new tracking technology and all those stipulations on how to announce it."

"And nothing about funding it?"

Xander reared back. "No. Why?"

Charlie lowered his head, took a deep breath, then slowly began his story about Sinclair giving him the ultimatum of funding the technology through his initial tokens purchase and how he had to put up the Dashley as collateral.

All the while Xander sat with his fingers to his temples as if trying to soothe a headache that had just set in.

"I'm sorry for dumping all this on you," Charlie said.

Xander shook his head quickly. "It's fine." But it wasn't. The color had drained from his face. His eyes darted to the door before forcing their way back to Charlie. His lips parted but nothing came.

"What is it?" Charlie said.

"I-I have to tell you something…something I should have long ago." He hesitated. "Before I say anything else, just… know this. I've made mistakes. Plenty of them. Stupid ones." His voice wavered. "But this—this is the worst."

He paused, eyes distant now.

"I thought it was behind me. I tried to bury it." A breath caught in his throat. "I never thought it would come back."

"Why am I suddenly wanting to run?" Charlie said.

Xander took another deep breath. "Remember, this is in the past."

"Sure. It's in the past," Charlie said.

"During my time working with Sinclair, he's usually kept me at arm's length. All I've done is handle his advertising and that's it, I promise. Straight up, nothing else. But there's been a couple times I've had to look the other way."

"Something illegal?"

"Kinda."

"Kinda? Was it illegal or not?"

"A little. It-it's a little gray."

"What did he do?"

"He shorted vendors on payments."

"How much?"

"There were two small companies and between them it came to around $350,000."

"How do you know he didn't pay?"

"Because I was the one who placed the media buy."

"Did you go to the police?"

"I couldn't."

"Why not."

"You remember after I left the company you and I worked for I started my own ad agency?"

"Yeah."

Well, things went well for a while, but when COVID hit, clients started slashing their budgets and the business folded. One of my clients during that time was Sinclair." He began wringing his hands. "Right before I shut down, he asked me to place a media buy for him that was about half a million dollars."

"Was the $350,000 part of that deal?"

Xander nodded.

"And you couldn't go to the police because…?"

"Because I was the one responsible for it."

"How? He's the one who placed the order."

Xander shook his head. "It was me. It was my company,

and I purchased it in my name and then marked it up 12 percent. It's a typical agency up-charge."

Charlie shook his head, trying to follow.

"Don't you see?" Xander said. "I placed the media buy under my agency's name because Sinclair wanted it done before I officially closed my doors. So, I took out loans to cover it, and he promised—guaranteed, actually—to pay me back if I agreed to come work for him afterward. And he did pay everything back *except* the $350,000 to those two companies."

"Did they try to sue you? I mean, they could have since it was you who was on the hook for it—right?"

"They could have, but they didn't do anything. I don't know why, but they didn't."

Charlie leaned back in his chair, running his hands through his hair. "Holy smokes, you dodged a bullet."

A dark cloud came over Xander, his gaze lost back in the details of his confession. "Not really because not long after this all happened, the companies that were shorted went out of business…probably because of me."

"You don't know that," Charlie said.

"No, but it doesn't make it right." He swung his head away. "A sin is a sin and that's what I did."

Charlie sat staring out the window. His mind parsing through the underpinnings of Thomas Sinclair's operating methods. A moment passed as Xander watched him, waiting for the realization to hit.

Charlie gasped. He looked Xander in the eyes, his gaze acknowledging that Sinclair had capitalized on his situation using basically the same tactic he had used on him. Just as he was about to hit rock bottom, Sinclair had pulled him up by getting *Following the Love* off the ground and to cap it off he was now in jeopardy of Sinclair disappearing on his promise to pay him back. All he had was a dangling hope that the would-be donor would come through in the next few days.

Xander looked at him, his eyes remorseful in reliving his past indiscretion. "He owns us Charlie. Thomas Sinclair owns us."

Charlie closed his eyes.

"And Lydia too."

Charlie's eyes flashed open. "Lydia?"

"I don't know how," Xander muttered, "but he does."

Charlie white-knuckled the steering wheel, his chest still aching from Xander's words. Over and over they played in his head—questions he didn't have answers for, accusations he couldn't get his mind around. The more he thought about things, the more he convinced himself that there were only two paths before him. One, Xander was simply delusional and his newfound religion was causing him to project his own past sins onto Sinclair; or two, he would simply have to make sure the new technology paid for itself quickly enough to pay off his new debt while clinging to the hope that the donation Sinclair had mentioned would come through. Either way, he was determined to work through this.

By the time he turned onto his street, his thoughts had refocused on Ashley and her doctor's appointment, which summoned a new wave of anxiety. As he eased into the driveway, his spirits rose at the sight of Bree sharing a laugh with her as she helped her from the van. From a distance it appeared as if Ashley was her old self, full of energy and vigor.

"Hey, Ash, how about a spin around the neighborhood?"

"Can't right now dad. Gotta start my fast and do some relaxing. Got a big test coming up."

"Uh…okay," he said, passing Bree a questioning look.

Bree stayed behind, waiting as Charlie walked up. Together they stood smiling as Ashley wheeled herself into the house.

"Looks like things went pretty well."

Bree's smile faded. Her head fell onto his shoulder. "Let's go inside."

Chapter Twenty-Three

"What did the doctor say?" Charlie prodded as they stepped inside.

Bree hung her purse on the hook by the door, her movements slow and deliberate, giving herself a few more seconds to compose herself.

"You want some coffee or tea?" he asked, knowing her well enough to see her need for more time.

Bree forced a tiny smile. "Coffee would be nice," she said, her voice absent of its usual sparkle. She went back to her purse and began digging through it.

By the time she made her way to the kitchen, Charlie had two mugs on the counter.

"Is that her diagnosis?" he asked, staring at a piece of paper in her hand.

"No, it's a list of the tests she has to have."

"Couldn't they have done them there? The lab's in the same building. And didn't she just have blood work done six months ago?"

"It's not routine blood work. And it's other tests too. Ones that cardiologists have to do."

"A cardiologist!" Charlie put down his coffee, took the

paper from her and began reading. "Electrocardiogram, chest X-ray…and not just one, but two, three, four, five—five blood tests!"

Bree bit her nails. "And they all need to be done immediately."

"Why immediately?"

"He said it's just part of their procedure." She sighed. "And there might be other tests."

"What're they looking for?"

"They don't know. He just kept saying it's part of the protocol in how they go about ruling things out."

"But it's a cardiologist so it has to be something with her heart."

She nodded. "He said based on her recent fainting spell and the issue at the retreat, along with her suppressed immune system, that's a possibility. He suggested having them done soon."

"How soon?"

"Tomorrow."

"How serious is this?"

"I told you. I don't know. All I know is that she needs to be there by eight in the morning."

For a moment, the image of the girl in the wheelchair Charlie had met at the hot dog stand wavered in his mind, Ashley's face overlapping the girl's then fading away. "I'll take her," he said. "You've done so much already. You should sleep in."

She hugged him. "That's okay, we'll both go." She pulled back, looking at him.

His face was pale, sweat running down his temples.

"You look like you're not feeling so good. Are you okay?

And you're shaking again. Maybe we should get you in to see the doctor too."

"I'm alright. I just have a lot on my mind and now this."

She took him by the hand. "Charlie…the devil is real and he's attacking us. We need to pray. Will you please pray with me?"

He closed his eyes turning his head from her. "Bree…" his voice trailed off, his silence answering for him.

"Okay then…" She turned and walked away. Halfway down the hall she stopped and turned back. "Then I'll pray. I'll pray alone for our daughter." Her voice faded to a deeper sadness. "And I'll pray for you…and for us."

Charlie watched her vanish into their room. A moment later his hand was in his pocket searching for the bottle of white pills that would provide the relief he believed her talks with God never could.

Charlie sat with his elbows on his knees, hands clasped tight, staring down at the tiled floor of the cardiac diagnostic laboratory. Bree sat beside him, both closed off in silence, lost in their own thoughts, wrapped in the same worries.

The hallway door creaked open. A doctor in a white coat stepped out, clipboard in hand, his expression calm but unreadable. For a second Charlie forgot how to breathe. Bree reached for his hand, her fingers trembling as she laced them through his.

"Mr. and Mrs. Callaway?" the doctor asked softly. "I'm Dr. Keegan." He glanced down at the clipboard, then back at them. "Why don't we step into my office?"

Charlie pushed to his feet, a tightness gathering beneath his ribs. Bree stood with him, her fingers still wrapped around his hand, afraid to let go. Together, they followed the doctor to a small office.

The doctor gestured for them to sit. He took the chair opposite, folding his hands over the clipboard as if steadying himself before speaking. "First," he began, his tone gentle, "Ashley did very well today. She's such a bright young lady too, and a fellow NASCAR enthusiast as well." He chuckled. "She almost had me switching my loyalty over to Dusty Harmon."

Bree managed a tiny smile. "That sounds like her."

"So," the doctor said, nodding as he eased into the conversation, "most of the tests gave us useful information—but they also raised a few questions. To get a better idea of what's going on, I'd like to run a few more."

Charlie leaned forward. "What kind of tests?" His voice came out rough, like he'd been holding it back for hours.

"Mainly core diagnostic imaging."

"Which means…?"

"It would basically be an echocardiogram and a cardiac MRI, both of which are to evaluate how well the heart is pumping and where the problem lies."

"So, there *is* a problem?" Charlie said.

"I'm sorry. I meant to say where there *may be* a problem. Also, the blood work that was done should be back when we do these tests as well."

Bree swallowed hard. "So, you don't know what's wrong yet?"

"Not yet," the doctor said softly. "But we're getting closer. Right now, we're just playing it safe and checking all the boxes. I've gone ahead and ordered the tests for day after tomorrow."

Charlie glanced at Bree then at the doctor. "The urgency of all these tests has me kind of concerned."

"I totally understand." He took a measured breath. "At this stage all I can say is that when it comes to the heart we always rely on caution, especially when it comes to someone as young as Ashley." He smiled. "Most of the time it's a temporary issue but we want to make sure." He stood. "If you'll follow me, I'll take you back to the waiting room. Your young race fan should be out any minute now."

Neither Charlie nor Bree spoke on the way back to the waiting room. The silence between them was heavier than it had ever been.

The drive home was quiet with Bree staring out the window and Charlie's hands locked on the wheel. In the back seat, Ashley sat buckled in, her head resting against the window. A small hospital band was still wrapped around her wrist. "Did I ever tell you how much I love the Dashley?" she said softly.

Charlie tilted his head toward the rearview mirror and chuckled. "Yes, dear…about a million and one times."

Bree turned to her. "How're you feeling, honey?"

"Fine. Still just tired."

Bree's phone buzzed, vibrating it across the dashboard and down into her lap. She glanced down at the screen. "It's Lydia," she said softly. "She'll want to know how things went." Bree glanced back to find Ashley asleep. She swiped the screen to answer. "Hey," she said, her voice low, not wanting to wake her. "We just left. She's asleep in the back now."

She paused, Lydia's muffled concerns coming over the line, barely audible.

"They don't know anything right now." Bree replied. "We have to bring her back in for more testing."

A pause.

"We probably need to cancel but I'll ask." She turned to Charlie. "Lydia was asking about dinner tonight. I said we probably need to cancel."

"No! You can't cancel," Ashley shouted, rising from her cat nap. "You need to go."

"But honey, I don't—"

Ashley leaned forward. "I know it would be because of me and I'm saying you need to go. Sally can come over if you're worried about me. Dad, please tell her you're going!"

Charlie shrugged. "I didn't even know we had plans."

"I'm sorry," Bree said, "I forgot to tell you. Last week Lydia and Xander asked us out for dinner tonight."

"Please, Dad! Don't make *me* the reason for not going. Pretty please."

"Here," Bree said, handing him the phone. "You can make the decision."

Charlie took the phone while sharing a smile in the rearview mirror with Ashley. "Hey Lydia, it looks like the pretty please did me in, so sure, we're in for dinner. Only one request. Can we do it at our house?"

"Yay!" Ashley shouted.

Charlie switched the phone to his other ear. "Okay great. Chinese will be perfect."

Another long moment passed as he listened to her passing along information that suddenly caused him to swerve, his voice taking on an edge. "No, absolutely not. If it's that important to him then he can do it himself." Another moment.

"I don't care!" His voice rose to a fevered pitch. "And let him know I'm still waiting on that donation!"

A horn blared as the van barely missed sideswiping an oncoming truck.

"Charlie, please," Bree said, poking his shoulder. "Watch the road."

His voice fell back to a calm hush. "Just tell him what's going on and that I just can't…not now." He nodded. "I know you understand. Thanks. Okay, we'll see you tonight."

He tossed the phone onto the dashboard, his grip on the wheel tightening.

"Let me guess… Sinclair?" Bree said.

"Yes." The word came flat and final.

Lydia rang the doorbell, shifting the paper bags marked "Chang's Garden" in her arms. Beside her, Xander tugged at his collar. She smiled at him. "You're not nervous, are you?"

"No, of course not."

She nudged his arm. "Yeah, you are. But it's okay. I think it's cute."

"We're not late, are we?" he said.

"No, you're right on time!" Bree said, opening the door. She smiled at Xander as she ushered them in. "Our doors are paper thin, you know."

"No kidding," he replied while holding out a bottle of champagne to her. "For you, m'lady."

Bree took his offering with a mock curtsy. "Thank you, good sir. The lord of the castle is with the princess at the moment but should be out shortly."

Lydia handed the bags to Xander and turned to her. "How is she?"

"Why don't we go into the kitchen," Charlie said, walking in. "We can give you all the details while we lay out this most excellent meal."

"Is Ashley going to be able to join us?" Lydia asked.

"She's pretty wiped out right now, but she asked me to come get her before you leave. I'm not sure what's going on—just that she made me promise I would."

For the next thirty minutes, Bree led the conversation on how things went that morning at the cardiology lab. While the heaviness of the situation loomed over them, Xander kept things light by occasionally ribbing Charlie about something from one of his podcasts or back to the days when they had first worked together.

"You know what Charlie really likes?" Xander said, glancing from Bree to Lydia.

The two shrugged. "Token sales?" Lydia said.

"Stringing zeroes and ones together?" Bree said.

Charlie shook his head at Xander and smiled. "Inside joke."

"I get it!" Lydia howled. "That's a good one B."

"B, is it now?" Xander said. "Bree not short enough for you?"

Everyone laughed.

"I'll tell you what my boy likes and that's a good toast. Lydia, would you please pour a glass of champagne for everyone?"

"What's going on?" Charlie asked.

"Yeah," said Bree, "what're you guys up to?"

As Lydia handed out the drinks, Bree's eyes suddenly lit up, a hushed gasp escaping her lips.

Xander raised his glass. "In the presence of our friends—correction, our best friends—we'd like to announce that I am officially handing in my resignation of bachelorhood in exchange for matrimonial bliss with this beautiful lady next to me."

Charlie and Bree sat, mouths hung open.

Xander turned to Lydia, his eyes glistening. "I fell in love with her the moment we met and with all my shortcomings she has still chosen to love me back. Today, tomorrow and aways I will love you."

Lydia wiped her eyes as Bree jumped up to hug her while Charlie sat shaking his head, a huge smile appearing. "It's about time!" He jumped up and wrapped Xander in a bear hug, then turned to Lydia for the same, while Bree bounced over to Xander for a kiss on his cheek.

For the next several minutes the house was full of clinking champagne glasses, more hugs and laughter.

"I guess the cat's outta the bag?" Ashley's voice came from the edge of the room. Everyone turned to find her sitting in her wheelchair, a small box with a bow on it in her lap.

"Cat's out alright!" Xander chuckled.

"Wait," Bree said, looking confused. "Did—did you know?"

"Sure did!" she smiled.

Lydia beamed. "Had to make sure the most important Carraway was going to be here."

"And…" Ashley said, wheeling herself to them, "I come bearing congratulatory gifts." She held up the box to Xander. "For you and the missus," she giggled.

"Aww, thank you." He took it, pulled off the bow and handed it to Lydia. "We'll want to put that someplace special." He gently pushed up the lid. A tilt of the head accompanied by a curious grin followed. With two fingers he pulled up a gold ribbon. On the end dangled a *Following the Love* token customized with glitter, the edge circled in minuscule fake diamonds.

"You like my bedazzling?" she said, eyes bright with anticipation. "By the way, those are zirconia around the edge."

"They're beautiful is what they are," Lydia gushed.

"Turn it over."

Xander's smile grew wider as he flipped it. "Now that's awesome!"

Lydia clapped her hands. "Let me see, let me see!"

Xander held it up for her to examine. On the back where the QR code had been was now a decorative letter X.

"X marks the spot," Ashley chuckled. "Now you can track your man wherever he goes."

"Uh oh," Charlie laughed. "Can't hide now."

"There's one to keep an eye on you too, Lydia," Ashley said.

"Looky, looky," Xander said, pulling out another customized token necklace which he immediately turned over to reveal a large L.

"Looks like nobody gets to hide out anymore," Bree said, laughing.

Inside the kitchen, Bree stood at the sink, looking through the window as Xander walked Lydia to his car while Charlie struggled to cork the half-empty bottle of champagne behind her.

"Aww, he just kissed her and is now opening the car door for her. They're so good together," she said softly. "I love seeing that kind of happiness."

Charlie nodded, looking out the window as the taillights disappeared down the drive. "It does feel right, doesn't it?"

"They're my favorite of all your friends," Ashley said, rolling into the kitchen with a stack of plates in her lap.

"Thanks, honey," Bree said, setting the plates in the sink before turning to Charlie. "Lydia mentioned something tonight about Mr. Sinclair wanting you to do another podcast in Charlotte, the same day Ashley has her cardio tests. Ashley and I talked it over, and we both think you should go."

Charlie froze, his hand still on the cork. "Well, I'm not."

"Honey, I realize now how important this one is, especially with the new tracking thing and all. And they're just tests. Plus, I'm sure they won't even be able to get the results back for a couple days, so it's not like you can do anything."

"I can support my daughter is what I can do."

"Dad, I know you want to be there, and I love you for it, but seriously, it's just more tests. None of them are painful and Mom's right, it's not like you can change the outcome of them anyway."

Charlie set the bottle down, his eyes darkening just a little. "I said no."

Ashley pushed up next to him. "Dad, please go. I'm going to be alright. Besides, it's all in God's hands anyway."

Charlie turned back to Bree; her lips were pressed into a thin smile.

"Hard to argue with a child of God."

Chapter Twenty-Four

Charlie was up before sunrise, determined to get to Charlotte early. He hoped to persuade the grocery store hosting his road show to let him start ahead of schedule so he could make it back to Asheville sooner. If he wasn't going to be there for Ashley's tests, he would do everything he could to be there soon after. Skipping his usual coffee, he popped one of the pink pills and headed outside.

With the sun yet to peek over the mountains, the yard was still a dark landscape, the dim light from a nearby streetlight making everything look strange and unfamiliar. Something was different. Long white ribbons hung from the trees fluttering in the breeze, and the bushes looked oddly heavy, tangled in thin strips of tissue. Across the lawn, in and out of the flowerbed and around the mailbox were pieces of the same white material. He scanned the length of the yard, squinting, trying to make sense of it, when it hit—the Carraways had been the victims of the age-old schoolyard practice of being toilet-papered.

"Kids," he muttered, yanking off at a strand of tissue draped over the holly bush by the front door. A minute later he stopped, realizing it was a lost cause. Why ruin the moment anyway? Letting Ashley see that her friends cared enough to pull off the harmless prank wasn't such a bad thing. She would get a kick out of it for sure. After all, only the coolest kids usually earned that kind of attention.

A moment later he was in the Dashley, pulling out of the driveway. He smiled as he looked up in his rearview mirror to see the mischievous perpetrators had even left their calling card in the way of a yard sign with their initials—EKAF. He chuckled, thinking how much fun Ashley would have with the decoding process.

By late afternoon, Charlie pulled back into the driveway, feeling proud after wrapping up his most successful road show yet. His spirits lifted higher when he saw the yard was completely free of toilet paper. It had to be a good sign. Clearly, Bree and Ashley had found both the time and energy to clean up, which could only mean the tests had gone well.

As he walked to the front door, he could hear someone stuffing the big green trash can out in the garage. He walked over to find the door pulled up. In the back corner Bree was feverishly cramming piles of toilet paper into the receptacle, punching it down, grunting as if taking out some hidden aggression.

"Honey, I'm back!"

Bree jerked around. Her eyes were bloodshot and swollen with tracks of dried tears down her cheeks. She stopped without a word then turned back to hammering away at the mounds of paper, trying unsuccessfully to move it down then ripping it back out and throwing it behind her and out across the garage.

"Bree…" Charlie said tenderly, inching to her, "dear… what's the matter?" He stood motionless behind her. "It was just a joke."

Ever so slowly she turned back to him, her lip quivering. She stared at him, looking as if she wanted to speak but was unable.

"Honey, it was only a harmless prank. As popular as Ashley is I'm surprised it didn't happen sooner."

Bree fought unsuccessfully to hold back the tears. A moment came and went then she spoke the words that shook Charlie to his core. "Ashley's heart…is dying."

"What did you say?"

"The tests…they came back."

"I-I don't understand. The tests? How could they've come back so soon? There were others to be done too." He held out his hands to her. "Bree?"

Her head swung back and forth in an agonizing sweep.

"Bree! What happened? Talk to me!"

She squeezed her eyes hard and long, her fingers curling into fists that she raked across them, unable to stop the sobs that came.

Charlie took her into his arms, pressing his head against her, waiting. A moment passed. "Tell me exactly what the doctor said."

She cleared her throat softly then began, her breath catching on the verge of more sobs. "The-the doctor said th-the bl-blood work came back showing that her heart was in severe distress, something about the enzymes showing muscle damage—a lot of it. And the other tests that they took today all pointed to it no longer being able to supply her body like it should. The rest of her body's starting to feel the effect of not getting the oxygen or nutrients it needs."

"But all these tests take time to get results! The doctor said—"

"I thought so too, but he moved everything along quicker

than normal because he had his suspicions from the first tests. He said he just didn't want to alarm us with the first ones in case they were negative."

Charlie grabbed the edge of the trash can, his legs weakening. Each second stretched out, pressing down, every breath a reminder of the news that would not leave him.

"You said her heart was dying. Is that what the doctor said…those were his *exact* words?"

She nodded then buried her head into his chest, holding him tight, weeping uncontrollably while he stared off into the corner of the garage.

A minute passed, then another, his mind numb as wave upon wave of anxiety crashed over him. He pulled back then jerked toward the door. "I have to go see her!"

"No, wait!"

"But I have to—"

"She doesn't know!"

"The doctor didn't tell her?"

"No, he said it'd be better to tell you first then we decide. Plus, they still have to do a few more tests. Ones that will tell us…" Her head dropped, unable to speak the words.

Charlie's voice fell to a whisper, finishing what she could not. "Ones that will tell us how much time she has?"

She nodded. "Besides, she's still upset about the toilet-paper prank and that sign calling her a fake."

"A fake? No—that sign was just their initials. It—" He froze as the image of the letters EKAF read backward in his rearview mirror snapped into place. "Why would they call her fake? Ashley's one of the most popular kids in town. I swear I'll track down everyone who had anything to do with this and I'll—"

"Do nothing!" Bree cut him off, holding a finger to his chest. "You'll not do a thing, you hear me?"

Charlie stood for a moment, his hand clenched. He slammed it against the trash can, gnashing his teeth.

Bree placed her hand on his arm. "Listen to me. We're going to go back inside and for the rest of the day and into the night we're not going to say or do anything to upset her. Tonight, we fight against all the anxiety—tonight, by prayer and petition AND with thanksgiving we're going to ask the Lord for a miracle."

Charlie reared back, his face contorted into a twisted look of confusion. "What on earth are you talking about? You're asking me to be thankful for this? She's been stuck in a wheelchair her entire life, suffering, and now…I'll be—"

"Stop!" Bree shouted, throwing her hand over his mouth. "Don't say it! Please, Charlie, don't say anything else. Just pray with me."

"You can pray for both of us if you want. Right now, I'm going to see my daughter." He turned and headed into the house.

Bree's eyes turned upward, her lips moving as she silently called out to God.

The sound of children playing outside the doctor's office was lost on Charlie and Bree as they sat waiting for Dr. Keegan to come in. Charlie sat hunched forward, his elbows on his knees, staring at the floor, while Bree's hands were clasped so tightly in her lap her knuckles were white. Several minutes passed.

"I can't stand this," Charlie said, jumping to his feet. "I'm going to go see what's taking so long."

Just then the doctor came in. "I'm sorry, I wanted to make sure I had the last of the test results before we discussed Ashley's condition."

Charlie sat back down, teetering on the edge of his seat while the doctor pulled up a chair rather than taking the one behind his desk. He sighed—a single breath that sent Charlie's heart pounding—then sat with the stillness of someone who had delivered the words more times than he had ever wanted.

"I wish I had better news," he began quietly, his voice carefully measured. "The tests confirm what we feared. Her heart muscles are indeed failing. At this point..." He glanced down at the folder on his lap as if to avoid making eye contact.

"How long?" Bree asked.

"I'm afraid not that long."

"How long?" Charlie asked.

"A year at most." He shook his head. "Or it could be months. There's just no way to tell."

"There has to be something that can be done!" Bree pleaded.

"There has to be," Charlie added, his tone sharp and demanding. "A special drug or surgery—something."

The doctor exhaled, his shoulders dropping. "The only possibility would be a transplant. That's the only way. She'd have to have a new heart." He shook his head. "But even if we could get her on the list today..." He hesitated, the silence finishing the sentence for him.

Bree covered her mouth with her hands, her voice trembling. "There might not be enough time?"

"Not if her condition accelerates."

The room fell silent, time fading away, leaving

only despair. Bree's breath came in starts and stops. When she finally spoke, her voice was barely there. "How… how do we tell her?"

"Together," the doctor said softly. "When you're ready."

The soft, steady rhythm of the van's tires on the road offered a small comfort after the oppressive silence of the cardiologist's office. Bree pressed her forehead lightly against the cool window, watching the trees blur past, willing her thoughts to slow or vanish all together. Beside her, Charlie kept one hand loosely on the wheel, eyes forward but tense, the other hand curled into a fist that couldn't relax.

In the back seat, Ashley slept, her head leaning against the window, her #82 Dusty Harmon NASCAR blanket tucked under her chin. Each gentle rise and fall of her chest was a quiet promise that, at least for now, she was safe.

Bree turned to her, glad to see her at peace yet imagining the horror of it lingering beyond. "She looks so peaceful."

Charlie's gaze softened in the rearview mirror. "Good," he said quietly. "She needs her rest more than ever right now."

Ashley stirred, blinking up at them with groggy eyes. "Why's that?" she murmured.

Charlie smiled back at her. "We'll explain everything when we get home, dear. For now, just rest a little longer."

Several minutes later Charlie was lifting her out of the back seat into her wheelchair.

"Dad, why don't people like me?" she said, brushing the sleep from her eyes.

"What do you mean, honey? Everybody loves you."

"Then why did they put that sign in the front yard?

They called me a fake. Do they think I'm faking being in this wheelchair?"

"No! That's not it at all. They…um…that was…" He glanced at Bree for help.

"That was Xander playing a trick on your dad," she said, jumping in. "He was just ribbing him about being a fake celebrity."

"That doesn't sound like Xander at all. He's too nice. He'd do anything for us."

"Of course he would," said Charlie. "Come on, let's get you inside. Mom and I need to talk to you."

"Hey look," Ashley said, pointing to the front door. "Someone left us a letter."

"Probably Xander apologizing," Bree said.

Charlie dropped the keys onto the foyer table as they stepped into the living room. Ashley tossed the envelope next to them.

"Who's it to?" he asked.

"To you. If it's from Xander, can I read it?"

"Not now, dear," Bree said.

Inside, the quiet hum of the house was comforting but somehow almost too soft. Charlie guided Ashley toward the living room couch, each step full of unspoken love. Bree lingered at the doorway, her eyes meeting Charlie's in a silent exchange of courage and fear. "Would you like to lay down?" she asked Ashley.

"No, I'm fine." Her eyes darted between them. "What's going on? Why're you guys acting so strange?"

Charlie knelt beside her, taking her hand in his, squeezing it gently. Bree moved to her other side, her hand brushing Ashley's hair back from her face. "There's something about your health we need to talk about," Charlie said, his voice a trembling mix of steadiness and heartbreak.

Ashley's eyes widened, fear and trust mingling in a silent plea. Bree's hand found Charlie's shoulder, squeezing it as if to share the weight of the moment. The room went quiet, the familiar comfort of home still around them as they braced for words that would change everything.

The lamp beside the couch cast a warm light over the framed family photo next to it. Ashley sat between Charlie and Bree, her hands resting on her lap as she stared at the picture of the three of them smiling against a backdrop of the Great Smoky Mountains.

"The doctors are going to do everything they can," Charlie said, forcing optimism into his tone. "They're some of the best in the country. And they think—well, they think there's a chance you could even get a new heart." He looked to Bree with a hidden request to back him up.

Bree leaned forward. "That's right. They've already put you on the list for one. In the meantime, you're still you, sweetheart. You can still do your homework, hang out with your friends, and play your video games."

"Just maybe no basketball for a while," Charlie said.

"Heart failure," Ashley said softly. "I just thought I had some kind of virus or something. She looked between them, her voice small but steady. "So…my heart's just tired?"

Charlie nodded. "That's right. It's tired because it's been working extra hard and needs rest. That's why you haven't had any energy. But we're going to do everything possible to give it that rest."

"So does this mean I won't be able to go to college?"

Bree squeezed Ashley's hand. "We'll have to wait and see."

"Maybe we can take that beach trip next month," Charlie said. "After all, if you're going to be a marine biologist like your application letter said, we'd better get you acquainted with the Atlantic."

Ashley smiled, putting her head on his shoulder. "You think they have floaties for wheelchairs?"

For a few moments, they sat together in silence. Outside, a light rain began, the pitter-patter of drops filling the spaces between their breaths. Charlie wrapped his arm around her shoulders as Bree pulled Ashley's hands up to her lips for a gentle kiss.

"I'm okay," Ashley said softly after a while. "I just… need a little time to think."

In the stillness, with hope and uncertainty binding them closer than they had ever been, they sat, Bree praying quietly as the rain came down harder.

Chapter Twenty-Five

Charlie pressed the phone to his ear as he paced his cluttered office, the air stale with neglect, a hospital bill trembling in his hand—the numbers showing how far his financial situation had fallen.

"Rough morning?" Lydia's voice came through the line, warm and steady, cutting through his cluttered thoughts.

"The worst six months of my life is more like it. Between all the doctor visits, the endless bills and the website drop-off, I feel like I'm juggling chainsaws."

"How's Ashley this week?"

Charlie's voice caught. "They're still running them. But the bottom line is the doctor said her heart's continuing to weaken. They're now worried about the rest of her body and the effects on it, which is pretty much what I imagine Sinclair's thinking about the effect my absence has had on the business. And before you ask, I'm still not doing those road shows anymore. I can't. I won't leave Ashley right now—or ever."

"Good," she said firmly. "You shouldn't. Anyone with any decency would understand that."

"You think he's done with us?"

"Could be. Has he still not contacted you?"

"Not a word."

"It doesn't surprise me, given how he's continued to distance himself from us."

"If you ever do talk to him, let him know that the donation he promised coming through never did…so it looks like the Dashley will be the bank's pretty soon."

"But how're you going to transfer Ashley back and forth to her doctor appointments?"

"A neighbor's got one that's been sitting in his backyard that he's going to let us use."

"Charlie…if you need Xander or me to help out, let us know."

Charlie smiled. "Thank you. We appreciate how you and he have stuck by us during all this."

"Well…we love you guys, boss. And speaking of Xander, he and I do have something we want to run by you regarding our wedding."

"Whatever it is—yes."

"Great because we want you all to be a part of it. You as best man, Bree as maid of honor, and Ashley to deliver the invocation. Would you consider it?"

"Of course! Bree will be thrilled." His voice dropped in a moment of gentle reflection. "But you know we're planning a year out from now." He hesitated. "The way things are progressing we're not sure Ashley will—"

"Charlie," she interrupted him so he wouldn't have to finish, "we've changed the date to the week after Easter."

"That's in less than two months."

"I know! Are you still in?"

"Absolutely!"

He hung up and set the phone down beside a haphazard

stack of bills. He sunk down into his chair, stared at them for a moment then buried his face into his hands. He finally raised up and with a groan started to sort them into separate piles—each with a different index card above them. The first was labeled two months past, another three months past, and a third simply had a huge red X on it. Just as he was about to place another bill on top of the X pile, something caught his eye.

Sticking out from underneath a foreclosure notice was the letter Ashley had pulled from the door the day they first talked to her about her heart. He stared at his name on it—no address or even his last name—just Charlie. In a second it was opened. As he read, his pulse pounded, and his eyes burned with a mix of anger and disbelief. Without thinking, he crumpled the paper in his fist and stormed out of his office. "Bree! Where are you? We need to talk!" He stomped down the hallway. "Bree?" His voice carried through the empty house, but there was no answer—only the distant ticking of the grandfather clock.

The living room looked like it hadn't been touched in months. Dust gathered on picture frames, and a blanket still lay crumpled on the couch where he and Bree used to curl up to watch TV.

He stepped over a forgotten pile of laundry, the letter crumpling slightly in his hand as he turned into the kitchen. She stood at the sink over a stack of unwashed dishes, staring out the window, unaware he was there.

"Bree," he said again, lower this time.

She didn't turn.

He set the letter on the counter next to her, smoothing out its wrinkled edges. "You want to tell me what this is?"

His voice cracked with the fury of an anger that had festered too long.

She glanced at it, then back to the window, her eyes hollow.

Charlie took a step closer. "What's this mean? This-this note sounds like something you'd say. It even sounds like what you said the night we talked to Ashley about her condition." He snatched it up and read, his voice rising. "Do not be anxious about anything, but in every situation, by prayer and petition, with thanksgiving, present your requests to God. And the peace of God, which transcends all understanding, will guard your hearts and your minds in Christ Jesus." He thrust it out in front of her, pressing his finger into the last line. "And look who it's from! Your friend…Peter!" He held the paper in front of her face, shaking it. "I don't understand what your connection is with this man, Bree? Are you and he trying to make me go insane or something?"

Bree's blank stare suddenly vanished as a smile etched across her face. She gently took the paper from his hand, looked down on it then turned back to him and said, "He's reminding us of what we should do." She lifted the page to her lips and kissed it. "It's Philippians 4:6–7." She smiled at him. "Don't you see? He's doing it again."

"Doing what again?"

"Providing us with hope."

Charlie's eyes flashed wide. "I don't buy that. What I think is that this is just your way of sending me stuff that'll get me praying alongside you. This message isn't from anybody, is it?" He held the paper up again, pointing to the name Peter. "This is you. Admit it, Bree. This is…" His trailed off.

"What is it?" she asked.

"I-I don't know."

She gently pulled the paper from his fingers. On the other side of the paper, at the bottom, was the single line that had brought his tirade to a screeching halt. *When you're ready, I'll be waiting on the steps of the courthouse.*

"What's it mean?" she asked.

"The courthouse," he muttered.

"Charlie?"

He didn't answer, lost in thought, miles away and years long past. "He knows. Somehow he knows."

"Knows what?"

Charlie slowly turned to her, his eyes narrowing into slits. Through them his gaze turned from confusion to one of revelation. "You've talked to him, haven't you?"

"No. Not since the very first time at the McDonald's."

"Yes, you have, or else how would he know about the courthouse?"

She gasped, throwing her hand to her mouth. "Oh, my gosh! You-you think he's talking about the Devil's Courthouse?"

"Of course. And you told him!"

"No! I promise, I didn't. Honestly, I've only spoken to him that one time. That's it!"

"How dare you tell anyone about it! How dare you invite someone into my life like that!" He reached over and picked Bree's phone up off the table. Grabbing her hand, he pushed it onto her palm then jerked around and headed to the door, stopping halfway out. "Call your friend. Tell him I'll meet him there now—right now. Do it, Bree! Call him, because I'm getting to the bottom of this!" The door slammed behind him, leaving her staring at the phone.

Charlie stormed onto the front lawn, refusing to look back, his words and accusations still ringing behind him—hurled too fast, too loud, and too late to take back. He ground his teeth as he looked to the curb where the Dashley was already halfway up the ramp of a flatbed tow truck. The tow driver, a guy in a soiled denim vest chomping gum like it was payback for something, pretended not to notice him coming up on him.

"Great, just great," Charlie muttered, rubbing a hand over the back of his neck.

"Morning," the tow driver said, still not looking at him.

"That's my van."

"Was your van," the guy said, tapping something into a tablet, "now it's the bank's."

Charlie pressed his tongue against his teeth. He'd known this day was coming. He could still argue. He could still demand answers. He could let everything boiling inside him spill out right there, but he didn't. Instead, he reached into his pocket for his pill bottle. "Fine," he said, popping one straight into his mouth. "Just…fine. Take it!"

A moment later he was standing on the front doorstep of a neighbor's house three doors down the street. He knocked. Twice. Harder than necessary.

The door swung open. A man with a doughy face and cheerful smile greeted him.

"Morning, Doug," Charlie said sheepishly.

"Well," Doug said, scratching his neck, "judging from watching that tow truck leave with your van, you're probably here for ours."

"If it's okay," Charlie replied. "I could sure use it right now."

"Of course! Keys are on the front seat waiting on you.

And remember, you and Bree can use it for as long as you want. Just bring her back with anything less than a dozen new dents."

A smile tugged at Charlie's mouth. "I can manage that."

He walked to the backyard. Sitting under the tired branches of an aging weeping willow was an equally tired van, more rust than paint. He climbed into the worn seat. The vinyl was cracked, the steering wheel rough, the musky scent of old oil thick enough to taste. He turned the ignition. The engine coughed twice before catching, causing the whole van to shudder. Charlie grumbled under his breath.

Fifteen minutes later, he was rattling along the Blue Ridge Parkway, the van's suspension complaining with every crack in the pavement. He missed the quiet hum of the Dashley and all the amenities, but for now none of that mattered. Now it was about confronting Peter and why he had chosen to invade his life and add to the stress that was strangling his spirit.

The van continued to chug its way up the winding curves of the Blue Ridge Parkway, coughing now and then, resenting the climb as much as Charlie did. Spring had just begun to touch the mountains—soft green hues blowing lightly through the trees, pastel wildflowers peeking up through the soil. The sky was a pale blue backdrop to the ridgelines that stretched out in gentle shades of blue and violet.

It was another spectacular day on one of the most scenic highways in the country. It should have been beautiful, but Charlie saw none of it.

Sweat from his palms had him gripping the steering wheel tight. Every turn brought him higher, closer to where the land dropped away into the kind of view people drove hours just to stand and marvel at. A postcard scene. A perfect overlook, the one that his older brother, Samuel, had always taken him to in hopes of catching a glimpse of the peregrine falcons that nested below the cliff's jagged edge.

His pulse quickened with his vision seeming to narrow, as though the world was shrinking into a single point he couldn't avoid, to a place he had vowed never to return to. He blinked, and an image of his brother climbing over the railing appeared before him. His hands were stretched wide, flapping like a bird. "Look," he called out, smiling. "I'm a falcon!" Behind him clouds had gathered and the wind howled. Samuel leaned his head back, his smile growing bigger. "I love this wind, don't you?" A white flash of light. His smile vanished.

Charlie shook his head, clearing the vision from his mind. The sky was again pristine, clear and pure. Ahead of him the sign came into view: *The Devil's Courthouse Overlook – One Mile*. He kept his eyes forward. He didn't look left where the ridgeline cut away into views of the four surrounding states. He didn't look right where the forest dipped into lush green valleys. He kept his gaze on the road. He wasn't here for the view. He was here for answers.

The van shuddered as he eased off the gas, the overlook's gravel parking lot coming into sight. He exhaled once, sharp and unsteady. "Alright," he murmured to no one, easing the van into the lot..

The parking lot held only two cars parked on opposite sides. He sat in the van, his heart pounding as he scanned the horizon. His gaze turned to the path that led up to the lookout's peak, a dark imposing mass of craggy rocks with a cave underneath. Legend said that the devil held court in that cave, lore that still rang true in Charlie's mind. Although the path to the summit was less than a half mile up, he remained clutching the wheel, choosing to confront Peter in the gravel lot.

For thirty minutes he waited. A father and son eventually came down and rode off in one of the cars with a young couple following shortly. For another hour he sat, his eyes continuing to dart back to the road, anticipating another car pulling in, knowing his demand for Bree to contact Peter would eventually bring him. A man so possessed with tormenting him would surely not miss such an opportunity.

As another hour came and went, his patience waned. In the distance, a wall of gray rose behind the peaks. His stomach wrenched as old images gathered with the approaching storm. All he could see now was that same dreadful sky that had rolled in so many years ago, the same dark mass appearing before stealing an idyllic childhood, replacing it with unforgiving remorse. Unwilling to revisit that day, he turned the ignition in an attempt to flee, but the van stalled. He tried again—nothing. He slammed his fist against the wheel when suddenly it caught his eye. At the top of the overlook stood Peter, his red poncho fluttering like a warning flag in the rising wind.

Chapter Twenty-Six

Charlie eased his door open and stepped out, gravel crunching underfoot as he drifted to the edge of the parking lot, his gaze fixed on the overlook above, puzzled at how Peter could have slipped past him unnoticed. He stopped at the corner of the lot where the path to the summit began. It would take him less than five minutes to make the climb, but it was an ascent he had sworn he would never make. He glanced back at the van, the road, anywhere but the path ahead. With a sharp breath, he crossed his arms and glared upward, silently demanding Peter to know he wasn't going anywhere near that ground.

The air shifted, clouds continuing to gather, folding over one another gray and black. Thunder rumbled in the distance.

Charlie stood resolute, jaw clenched, eyes fixed on the man on the ridge. The air thickened with the scent of rain. A drop fell, then another, causing him to blink. He wiped his face. When he opened his eyes, the overlook was vacant.

"I'm sorry to have kept you waiting," came a voice.

Charlie turned to the path. There was Peter in his red poncho, the same dingy backpack slung over his shoulder.

His gait was steady and unhurried; his head slightly bowed against the wind.

"I'm sorry, Charlie. I should have met you down here. I hope you'll forgive me."

"What're you doing?" Charlie blurted. His chest began to rise and fall in quick starts and stops as he somehow lost his train of thought—only wanting to get to an answer that he suddenly could not articulate. "Do you think what you're doing has had any effect on me?"

Peter's head tilted, his eyes crinkling at the edges. "I don't know. Have they?"

Charlie shook his head and stared at him, anger simmering—not just at what he hadn't gotten from Peter, but at his own failure to press the point. The frustration built until it finally spilled out in a rant he could no longer contain. "Why are you sending these cryptic messages? Why are you showing up, unwelcome, like some sort of stalker? And why have you dragged Bree into this? What do you have on her?" He glared into Peter's eyes. "You don't know what I'm going through…whatever you and Bree are up to isn't working. You're making things worse! You hear me? Worse!"

"That's not why I was sent."

"So, someone *has* sent you! Is it Sinclair? Are you working for Sinclair? Is that it?"

"No, Charlie," Peter said, smiling. "It's not Sinclair."

"Then who?"

Peter didn't answer at first. He just watched him—calm, steady and gentle. He took a step closer, the faintest warmth drifting off him, a presence that felt somehow familiar.

"Charlie," he said quietly, "the One who sent me doesn't play games. And He doesn't answer to men like Sinclair."

Charlie blinked, confused but caught by something in Peter's tone—an authority he couldn't explain, something old, weighty, something impossibly sure.

Peter's smile softened, almost sorrowful. "I wasn't sent to torment you. I was sent because you're not meant to carry this alone."

The wind shifted, gently swirling Peter's words around Charlie, begging the question… "Then who sent you?" he demanded again, but quieter this time.

Peter's eyes lifted—not to the trees, not to the path behind them, but higher. As though acknowledging someone just out of sight. Someone watching. Someone he deferred to.

When he looked back at Charlie, that quiet, unshakable certainty remained.

"Someone who's been watching over you far longer than I have," Peter said. "Someone who knows you need help…even when you refuse to ask for it."

Charlie lifted his eyes upward, where Peter had drawn them, his words ringing in Charlie's ears. Suddenly realizing the message, Charlie fell back into bitter denial. He shook his head. "No! I don't believe He sent you. If He sent you, why doesn't He come down and talk to me? Better yet, why didn't He catch Samuel when he fell off that cliff up there?" With his chest heaving, he gnashed his teeth, eyes burning. "And why would He choose to put a young girl who so openly adores him—to put her in a wheelchair only to turn around and take her life? Why? Tell me why!"

Peter didn't flinch at Charlie's fury. He stood, shoulders soft, eyes full of a sadness that seemed to have been shared before. When he finally spoke, his voice was low and steady.

"Charlie…I wasn't sent to argue with your pain."

He let the words settle, then continued, quieter still.

"I know what you're asking. I've heard those cries before—more times than you'd believe. And I don't blame you for shouting them." Peter took a breath, almost like he was drawing strength from somewhere beyond the overlook. "But I wasn't sent to rewrite the past or undo what's been done."

He stepped closer, gently, like approaching a wounded animal.

"I was sent to you because you're standing at the edge of a storm that could swallow you. Because your grief is dragging you toward a place you're not meant to go."

Charlie's jaw tightened, but he didn't pull away.

Peter's eyes softened even more. "I wasn't sent to answer every 'why.' I was sent to make sure the 'why' doesn't destroy what's left of you."

He paused, letting the weight of his words sit.

"And as for the One you're demanding to see…"

Peter glanced upward again, just enough to acknowledge the presence Charlie denied. When he spoke, his voice trembled with reverence.

"He's closer than you think. Closer than I am. But sometimes…He sends someone like me because He knows you wouldn't hear Him—not yet."

Peter lowered his gaze back to Charlie, his expression full of compassion, not rebuke.

"I'm here because He hasn't given up on you, Charlie. Not even a little."

Peter's words hung in the air like a quiet promise. Charlie blinked, trying to steady himself, trying to make sense of it all. But when he looked again…Peter was gone.

Not behind a tree, not along the path—he was simply gone. The warmth, the subtle pull of presence that had anchored Charlie moments before, vanished as if it had never been there at all. Along with it the gathering clouds had disappeared, leaving a pastel blue sky and a gentle wind that stirred through the branches, whisking past him, carrying a lingering trace of Peter's voice, "He hasn't given up on you…not even a little."

"No…no, this isn't real," Charlie muttered, shaking his head violently. "I-I must be imagining this!"

He spun in place, desperate, trying to find some logical explanation.

Charlie pressed his palms against his eyes. "I-I didn't see him. I didn't hear him. It—it wasn't real. None of this was real!"

But even as he said it, a soft chill lingered, gentle as Peter's voice brushing past his ear: *He hasn't given up on you…not even a little.*

That evening Charlie lay in bed, staring at the ceiling and running over his encounter with Peter at the foot of the Devil's Courthouse. He tossed and turned, continuing to struggle with whether any of it was real. Had Peter just been a figment of his imagination? Had he even been to the lookout? Sweat poured off him and soaked the sheets. Unable to sleep, he slipped out of bed so as not to wake Bree, then put on his robe, grabbed a small figurine of Jesus on the cross that had been on her bedside table since the day they were married, and headed to his office.

Along the way he stopped into the bathroom. His hands shaking, he dug through the cabinet under the sink, searching for his bottle of white pills hidden under a small pile of hand towels. He held it to his chest along with the figurine of Jesus.

A moment later he was sitting at his computer, the door locked behind him, lights off, only the soft glow of his monitor filtering lightly through the room. In front of him, next to his keyboard was the pill bottle and the figurine, his eyes flashing from the bottle to Jesus, then back again, then again. He grabbed the bottle and poured every pill into his palm. With his other hand he grabbed a half-empty can of soda. The grandfather clock outside his door ticked louder and louder. He remained frozen, his hand full of the white tablets held out in front of Jesus, the clock's ticking now clanging in his ears. His breath came in bursts as his heart pounded. He slowly raised the pills to his mouth, his eyes still on the cross before him, Jesus's eyes fixed back on him, sorrowful, calling to him.

Without looking, he grabbed the empty pill bottle and poured the pills back inside, then slammed it down beside the image of Jesus. He glared at it, then the words came rushing out.

"If you're real—if you actually care—then listen to me, Jesus of Nazareth." His voice shook. "Save Ashley, and I'll give you everything. I swear it." He swallowed, forcing the promises out through his tears. "I'll sell this house. I'll give it all to charity. I'll create tens of thousands of acts of kindness. I'll go to church. I'll be who you want me to be!" His sobs came in waves as he buried his head in his hands.

A message, accompanied by the simple ding of a new email, appeared on his screen. He wiped his eyes, squinting at the blank subject line. His eyes widened as he scanned to the sender's name—Peter.

He clicked the message open. His breath caught as he

read, "The Lord your God should not be tempted. It is not bargains to which he answers, but to hearts surrendered in faith."

Charlie's whole body trembled. He seized the pill bottle, twisting the cap off with a violent snap. His eyes slammed shut as he threw his head back, a ragged breath tearing loose from deep inside him—half sob, half scream, all anguish.

The house was too quiet.

Bree slipped out of the bedroom, her thin robe trailing behind her, the early morning light spilling gently across the hall. She called Charlie's name softly as she padded her way to the kitchen where she expected to find him starting the coffee. No answer. She craned her head down the hall. A dim glow leaked from beneath his office door—cold, bluish, unnatural in the pre-dawn light.

She hesitated; a pinch of dread caught in her chest. "Charlie?"

She nudged the door open.

In the glow of the monitor, he was slumped over his desk, shoulders caved inward, head bowed toward the keyboard. One arm hung limp at his side, the other curled near the dimmed monitor. The pill bottle lay toppled beside him, casting a long, crooked shadow in the screen's glow.

For a heartbeat, Bree forgot how to breathe.

Her hand flew to her mouth. The world shrank to the horrible stillness of him—silent, unmoving. Then the floor creaked beneath her.

Charlie stirred. His fingers twitched. His head lifted a fraction, heavy with sleep, drifting back from whatever dark place he'd slipped into.

Bree's legs nearly buckled with relief.

"Charlie," she said, nudging him to stay awake. "What did you do?"

"Wha…" he replied.

"How many of these did you take?"

He shook his head, forcing his eyelids to widen.

"Charlie! How many pills?"

"Um…one," he slurred.

"That's all? Are you sure?"

"Sure, I'm sure."

Piece by piece, clarity returned to him. Along with it came the shame of being outed by his drug dependency now spread out over his desk.

Bree picked up the bottle, her jaw grinding as she read the label. She turned toward him. "When were you going to tell me?"

"They're just to help me unwind," he said, reaching out for the bottle.

She pulled it away, snapping back. "No more." With one swift motion, she swept every pill into the fold of her robe. Charlie lunged after her as she bolted to the bathroom, threw up the toilet seat, and dumped them in.

"Noooo!" he shouted. "Why would you do that? I needed those!"

"Mom! Dad! What's going on?"

Both spun around at the same time to find Ashley sitting in the doorway. "Why're you guys yelling?"

"It's nothing, dear," Bree said, summoning a normal tone. "I'm sorry, did we wake you?"

Ashley studied them, a look of suspicion in her eyes. "No, it's all the people outside on the front lawn that woke me."

Charlie hurried past her into the living room, muttering

under his breath. "I swear, if those kids are pranking us again, I'll—" He yanked the front drapes aside and squinted through the blinds. "What the—"

"Is it them again?" Bree asked.

"No."

She leaned over his shoulder. Outside, half a dozen men and women stood clustered on the lawn, all sharply dressed, all holding microphones. Along the road, satellite trucks lined the curb, wrapped in station logos and call letters. Neighbors peeked from windows or wandered closer in pajamas; morning papers tucked under their arms or cups of coffee in hand.

"Why are they here?" Bree asked.

"Dad," Ashley called from behind them. "What's happening?"

Charlie didn't turn. "I have no idea. Maybe it's some publicity stunt Xander forgot to mention."

"Dad!" Ashley said louder. "It's Lydia. She needs to talk to you."

He finally spun around. Ashley held out her phone. "She tried you first, then me. She says it's urgent."

Charlie hesitated, his eyes flicking from the phone back to the window.

"What is it?" he said wedging the phone to his ear while still fixated on the commotion outside. Across from him, Bree glanced over, catching only the tension in his face as his voice dropped to a hush.

"Okay, but call me back," Charlie said, letting the phone fall onto the sofa. He turned to Bree; his face drained to a ghostly white. "Close the windows."

Before she could move, three sharp knocks thundered against the front door.

She snapped her head toward him. "Should I—"

"No. Don't answer it." He lunged toward the entryway.

Another three knocks—harder this time.

Charlie twisted the deadbolt until it clicked, then pressed his back firmly against the door as if holding something out. "We do *not* open this door. Not today. Is that understood?"

Chapter Twenty-Seven

Bree's voice broke with panic. "Charlie…why can't we answer the door?"

He stood frozen, his back still pressed against it. The knocks came again—three more heavy, deliberate thuds that seemed to shake the picture frames on the wall. Charlie flinched.

"It's not safe," he said finally. "Not until I know exactly what they want."

"Mr. Carraway!" came a determined voice from the other side of the door. "This is Ken Ellis of Channel 4. We'd like to talk with you about *Following the Love*."

Before Bree could speak, Charlie's phone lit up on the sofa. Then Ashley's buzzed. Then the house line rang.

A second later, Bree's own phone began vibrating in her robe pocket.

The calls rolled in one after another, overlapping in a rising electronic storm.

"Nobody answer these calls," Charlie barked.

Bree's eyes widened. "Charlie…what's going on? Is there some kind of promotion going on for the website? Why do these guys want to talk about *Following the Love*?"

"Please!" he pleaded, "just hold tight until I have more information."

A moment later he was back in his office with his door closed, pacing back and forth, his phone pressed to his ear. "Talk to me, Xander. What's going on? I spoke to Lydia about thirty minutes ago and she told me not to answer any calls or talk to any press and that she was sorry, but that was all. She sounded frightened and like she was in a rush. I just tried her back and she's not answering."

"I don't know anything either," he said, "but I got a text message from her about the same time she called you that just said to call her asap. I've been trying to reach her, and it keeps going straight to voicemail. Are you getting calls from the press?"

"Yeah! My phone's blowing up and so are Bree's and Ashley's and the front yard's crawling with reporters. This is insane. Do you think I should find out what they want?"

The phone went silent.

"Xander? Are you still there?"

"Hang on," his voice came back distracted.

A moment passed. Charlie could hear Xander's breathing growing heavier on the other end. "What's happening?"

"Go to the Channel 13 news page, quick."

Charlie pushed his mouse to the channel's live stream. Blazoned across the screen, just below the channel's logo, was the scrolling headline: *Breaking News: Founder and Owner of Popular Kindness Website to be Indicted.* Under it was a live image of their house, reporters circling about the yard like sharks.

"Charlie! Come quick!"

Charlie jolted upright at Bree's voice—high, sharp, threaded with alarm.

He shoved his chair back and bolted out of his office.

Bree stood in the living room, gripping the front door with shaking fingers. She had it open just an inch, just enough to see out.

"Keep it closed!" he yelled, slamming it shut.

A second later, the door boomed beneath a heavy fist—BANG! BANG! BANG!

A deep voice followed, firm and official. "Police! Charles Carraway, we need you to come to the door. We have a warrant for your arrest in connection with ongoing financial crimes."

Bree's hand flew to her chest. "Financial—Charlie, what are they talking about?"

Charlie felt the blood drain from his face.

Another pounding strike came through the door.

"Mr. Carraway! This is the Asheville Police Department. You're under investigation for fraud and embezzlement. Step outside with your hands visible."

Bree turned, horror dawning in her eyes. "Charlie…tell me this isn't real."

The door shook again under another thunderous knock.

"Mr. Carraway, this is your final notice. Come to the door now!"

Charlie's throat tightened, his heart hammering against his ribs.

Charlie sat stiff in the small, windowless interview room, the fluorescent light above buzzing with an irritating hum. Across from him, Ms. Jamison, his attorney, spread open a thick folder of papers.

"Charlie," she began, her voice almost clinical, "we need

to go over the situation clearly. Right now, the authorities believe you're the one committing fraud."

Charlie's stomach dropped. "I…I know. But I didn't do anything! I swear I never touched the donations for myself."

"That doesn't matter at the moment. You controlled the media fund. You approved transfers. Therefore, it looks like you're the one diverting donations to Bay Bridge Consulting and into an offshore account."

"But that's not true! I don't know anything about an offshore account. I've never even heard of Bay Bridge Consulting."

"Here's the thing…the offshore account was actually set up by Lydia Phelps. I'm assuming you know her, given she's listed as a co-programmer for your business."

"Of course I know her. She's been with me from day one."

"Unfortunately, from the authorities' perspective, she's been implicated. And frankly, I'm concerned she did this intentionally." Ms. Jamison leaned forward, tone sharpened. "From what we can see, the account was set up by an expert. Offshore, protected, with clean invoices. Someone did this knowing exactly how to hide the trail. If the investigators are correct, I'm afraid you'll be wanting to reconsider this friendship."

Charlie's head snapped up. "She couldn't have! She's my friend—she even wanted me in her wedding!"

Jamison shook her head. "Charlie, I can't say what she is, but she's vanished. No forwarding address, no recent bank activity, nothing. That disappearance only makes her look guilty, and it makes you look worse by association."

Charlie ran a hand through his hair, panic threatening to overwhelm him. "So…I'm arrested. Lydia's gone. And the donations—the money—it's in an offshore account. And they think we're both involved?"

Ms. Jamison's lips pressed into a thin line. "Exactly. You're stuck looking guilty. Right now, the best we can do is work on bail and start investigating independently. But I have to be honest—you're not in a good position. Until we figure out Lydia's role, you're the authorities' main target."

Charlie pressed his forehead against the cold plexiglass of the jail's visiting booth, the receiver digging into his palm as his fingers tightened around it. He lifted his hand to the glass, meeting Bree's trembling fingers on the other side.

"How're you holding up?" he asked.

She tried to smile, but it collapsed halfway, leaving her face twisted with exhaustion and fear. "I've been trying to reach Xander nonstop."

"And Lydia?"

"Nothing. I've texted and emailed. Nobody's responding."

He shook his head. "I don't understand. They were supposed to be our friends. Were we that wrong about them? Was this whole thing a setup?"

"I don't know. I don't know anything anymore. Everything's falling apart. And-and…"

"Bree…" His voice softened. "What aren't you telling me?"

In an instant her whole body caved. She pressed her forehead to the glass, shoulders shaking uncontrollably. "It's Ashley," she choked out. "Charlie…she's…"

His pulse hammered in his ears. "Bree, just say it."

She raised red, swollen, desperate eyes.

"They don't think…" She squeezed her eyes shut. "They don't think she'll survive the week."

All the wind sucked from Charlie's body. Time stood still as the room spun around him, screeching to a halt at her next words.

"They think it might be…days. Maybe not even that."

Charlie recoiled like he'd been stabbed. The receiver slipped from his hand and swung by its cord, thudding against the wall. A strangled sound tore from his throat as he slammed both palms against the plexiglass. "No—no, no, that's not—Bree, they said she was stable! They said she was holding on!"

"They said that before you got arrested!" Bree wailed. "She's terrified. She's cried for you for the past two nights until she can't breathe. And then today, her heart rate dropped so low the monitors were screaming. Charlie, she's fading. She's slipping right through my hands, and I can't—" She broke entirely, sobbing against the glass. "I can't pull her back. I can't…my baby…"

Charlie's knees buckled. He gripped his chair. "I have to get out of here. Bree. We have to find the bail money!"

"I'm trying!" she cried. "But the bills—the van being repossessed—everyone abandoning us—we're drowning, Charlie." Her voice crumbled. "And Ashley's about to…"

Charlie pressed his forehead back against the glass. "This can't be happening."

"Ma'am," the voice came dry and to the point.

Charlie looked up, past Bree to a stoic guard standing behind her.

"I'm afraid visitation hours are over. I have to ask you to leave."

"But—"

"Sorry, ma'am. One more minute and then you'll need to leave."

She turned back to Charlie.

"What can we do?" he pleaded. "Just tell me. What?"

Bree took a deep breath, a sudden calm coming over here. She clasped her hands together, bringing them to her lips. "Pray." Throughout their life together she had made the request, but somehow it had always landed as if it were a demand. Now it was softened into something filled with hope, founded in an unflinching faith that he had witnessed throughout their lives but railed against.

"Just pray, Charlie. Our only hope is in Him."

The guard moved up next to her, motioning her to the door.

Charlie watched as he ushered her out. For a moment he sat staring at the empty space where she had stood, her words still trembling in the air.

"Time's up, Mr. Carraway," another guard said from his side of the glass.

He hung up the receiver with a slow, unsteady hand. The guard led him back through the narrow hallway, past metal doors and flickering lights, Bree's plea still trailing after him.

Just pray…

The cell door opened just long enough for him to step inside, then closed behind him with a final, thud.

The room felt smaller now—four gray walls closing in, the stale air pressing against his chest. He collapsed to his knees, hands trembling as they clasped together, forehead pressed to the concrete. The world shrank to nothing—no sound, no light—just the jagged rhythm of his heart and the unbearable ache in his chest. Then, just above a whisper, humbled, exposed, voice shaking with fear and love and the weight of his own shame, he began to pray.

"God…please forgive me…please forgive me for turning away from you all these years. I've been proud, blind to all my faults, chasing control, thinking all I had to do were good deeds all while doing everything for myself. Forgive me for my arrogance, every selfish act, and every time I turned my back on you."

His voice cracked, spilling grief and repentance into the stillness. "I accept You, Jesus, as my Savior. Everything I am, I lay at Your feet. My heart, my mind, my body, my soul, my spirit…all that I am is Yours. Save me…please save me."

Tears slid down his cheeks as he pressed his forehead harder into his hands. "And my daughter…my sweet, innocent little girl is slipping away before her time. I beg You, heal her. Let Your mercy flow through her dying heart. Let her live, let her feel love, let her grow, and experience joy. I can't bear to lose her…not now, not like this."

His prayer shook with desperate faith, a raw offering from a man who had nothing left to give but himself. "If it is Your will, then take me…but not my Ashley."

His voice faltered, then softened into one final plea. "And if You must take her, then let me be with her. Let me hold and comfort her. Let me show her with every touch, every word, every heartbeat that I have loved her, that she has never been alone, and that she is cherished beyond measure."

He bowed further, shoulders shaking, tears soaking the concrete beneath him. The prayer had left him spent and silent. He remained laid bare, stripped of pride, holding fast to the only force stronger than death itself—faith, love, and desperate hope.

The morning light seeped through the narrow bars of Charlie's cell. A sharp knock rattled the door, jolting him awake.

"Mr. Carraway, wake up," the guard said. "You've had a friend post your bail. You're free to go."

Charlie blinked at the light as the door swung open. Xander stood there, his expression tight and serious, holding the paperwork that would release him.

"Let's get out of here," he said quietly. "We've got work to do."

A moment later, without conversation, Xander was leading him through a maze of cars in the county jail's underground parking deck. His head was on a swivel, scanning the dark corners of the lot, searching for something Charlie sensed he did not want to find.

"What're you looking for?" he asked.

"Not right now," Xander replied as they came upon a small blue sedan. The squeal of car tires making a hairpin turn up the ramp caused him to jerk his head down. He clicked the door unlocked. "Hurry! Get in!" Xander dove into the driver's seat while Charlie lunged into the back. "Stay outta sight!" The second the other car passed, he thrust the car into gear and shot down the ramp in the other direction.

Charlie remained hunkered down.

Xander whipped the car out of the deck and into the daylight. "Stay down until I tell you."

"Whose car's this?" Charlie said, his voice buried into the floorboard. "And what's going on?"

Xander, eyes locked on the road, his voice void of expression and tone. "It's a rental and we're trying to stay alive."

Chapter Twenty-Eight

A few minutes later Xander turned off the main road and rolled the car into a small alleyway between two dilapidated industrial buildings. Sun reflected in the rearview mirror, catching the dust in the air as the tires crunched to a stop.

"You can get up now," Xander said as he killed the engine.

Charlie peeked up from the back seat. "This looks like one of the service roads in the old paper mill. Wait…this *is* the mill! We're only a couple of miles from my house. Why'd didn't you just go there?"

"Because we can't."

"But I need to see Ashley!"

"She's not there."

"Oh no! Don't tell me. Please don't tell me—"

"It's not that, Charlie…she and Bree are at the hospital. They thought she should be admitted."

"Then take me there!"

"I can't."

Charlie jumped out of the car with Xander following. He paced randomly one way and then another, washed back and forth in a wave of confusion and despair. "I appreciate you putting up the bail money, but I need to see my daughter before it's too late!"

Xander grabbed him by the shoulder, spinning him back to him. "Just listen a minute!"

Charlie stood, the veins in his neck pulsing, his glare now demanding an explanation. "Why'd you and Lydia disappear? Did you guys set me up?"

"No! We'd never do that. I know what it may seem like but absolutely not! I had to go into hiding and Lydia…" He shook his head, his voice cracking. "I-I don't know where she is."

"Who're you hiding from?"

"The person who framed you!"

"Which is her!"

"No, Charlie! It's whoever created the account."

"Did you not talk to my lawyer?"

"No, why?"

"Because she would've told you it was Lydia who set it up. And with her disappearing, everything points to her. Did she con you too?"

Xander reared back swinging his head. "But…she couldn't have. She would never do anything against you and certainly not me!"

"If it wasn't her, then who?"

"The same person who manipulated us."

"Sinclair?"

"Yes. It makes perfect sense."

Charlie began nodding. His gaze wandered as his mind raced. "Maybe she's in on it with him."

"There's no way. She may have set it up, but she had to do it under duress. Just like he spun his web around us, he had to do the same with her. We just don't know what he had on her. All I know is that she went into hiding to evade him like I did or—"

"Someone took her?"

Xander cupped his hands under his chin, lost in thought, tracing his steps back in time. "I went into hiding because I thought he'd be sending someone to pry information out of me, to get me to tell him where she was."

"But you don't know either."

"But he doesn't know that."

Their eyes met at the same moment in the same revelation. Xander swallowed. "He has her already."

"You can't be sure."

"When she stopped calling, I went to her apartment. The key was still under the mat where she always kept it. When I went in, nothing was out of place, no bags out like she'd been preparing to go somewhere, all her clothes still in the closet. Everything was in perfect order. She's been taken. Charlie, he's got her! He's taken her and is going to—"

"Don't say it! If he has her, we'll get her back."

"It's already been two days." His voice broke. "You know what they say about kidnappings that go beyond three days!"

Charlie grabbed him by the shoulders. "They're wrong. Besides, we're going to find her. But first, can we please go to the hospital?"

"We really can't."

"Please, Xander, I'm begging you. I need to see Ashley."

"I'm sorry, I really am, but we can't. Sinclair is more connected than you can imagine—including the police department. I guarantee he found out as soon as I posted your bail."

"So?"

Xander drew in an uneasy breath and closed his eyes,

gathering himself. Whatever he was about to say had been weighed carefully. "Charlie, there's something I've been carrying with me that I should've told you about long ago. Sinclair's more than what you might think."

"I think I know exactly what he is."

"I don't think you do." Xander averted his eyes, hesitating one last moment before turning back to him. "Remember how I told you he helped me get out of that jam with those companies I owed money to and how he took me on to handle his marketing?"

"Yeah."

"Remember how I said those guys up and vanished?"

Charlie nodded.

"I think he had something to do with that."

"You think he—"

"I can't say for sure but there's something else I believe to be true and in my mind it's worse. It's about Lydia." His gaze lifted to the clouds, as if asking permission to go on. He shut his eyes, unable to look Charlie in the face. "I believe he had her father killed."

The words fell with a deafening silence and Charlie reeled back against the car.

"I'm sorry. I-I've carried this too long. And I know I should've gone to the police long ago, but I was too weak. He had so much on me I just kept it in and…and then after so much time passed and knowing what happened, I knew I'd be considered an accomplice."

"Why would he kill him?"

"Sinclair hired me soon after her father disappeared and gave me his office. When I moved in, I found a flash drive taped under the desk. It held emails from him to Sinclair about illegal initiatives he was running for him. Most of it was technical, but it felt dirty—and from the way it was organized, I think he was preparing to take it to the police."

"Did you keep the flash drive?"

"I was just about to copy it when two guys walked in and confiscated my computer, saying Sinclair had a new one for me and they needed mine to set up the compatibility with it. I tried to object but the bigger of the two—a huge, burly guy—grabbed it before the copy could download. Later that day, the other man came to see me with the new computer. He was a well-spoken Scottish guy, polite and respectful, even apologizing for having to take mine, but what he said, I'll never forget. He said, 'I'm sure you're very careful with other people's property, just as Mr. Sinclair is of his.' Then he paused, gave me this strange look, and said, 'Let's keep it that way, shall we?'"

"Why didn't you go to the police?" Charlie asked.

"I didn't have any evidence. Like I said, all the technical jargon was beyond me so there was no real way for me to convey it. All I had was a gut feeling, a rude computer grab and a cryptic warning from some Scottish guy I haven't seen since."

Charlie's gaze turned to the floor.

"What're you thinking?"

"I think I may have met the guy you're talking about… back on the day you invited me in to pitch *Following the Love*." He shook his head. "Anyway, I knew Sinclair was evil but never figured him for murder."

"This is why I had to go into hiding and why you can't go to the hospital."

"What about Ashley and Bree?"

"As long as they're in the hospital, they're protected."

"But Ashley's condition is worsening by the day."

"I was able to speak to Bree this morning. Ashley's stable right now and they've got around-the-clock care for her. Don't worry, you'll be able to see her soon. But we have to find Lydia and get her to the authorities to explain the account. We have to get Sinclair behind bars before he gets to us."

Charlie stared up at the worn-out buildings that loomed over them—rusted steel bones, shattered windows, and a silence that felt like the steady tick of a clock running out. The morning sun now hung low, hovering just above the tree line over the western mountain range.

Charlie paced in frantic circles, his heels grinding into the gravel.

Xander sat in the middle of the road as if his legs had finally given out, Lydia's *Following the Love* token cradled in both hands. His eyes were fixed on it, pleading. "Where are you?" he said, closing his fist around it.

Charlie stopped. "What did you say?"

Xander looked up, hollow-eyed. "We're running out of time."

"Then think." Charlie's voice cracked with urgency. "Where would they take her?"

"I don't know!" Xander's composure shattered. "Maybe we should go to the police after all. I'll give myself up. I'll tell them everything I know. I don't care what happens to me anymore." He pressed the token to his lips. "Where are you, my love?"

Charlie froze. Then his eyes widened. "Your laptop!" he shouted. "Xander—where's your computer?"

"In the trunk. Why?"

"Just open it!"

A moment later they were sitting in the car, Xander still clutching the token, Charlie hunched over his laptop, tapping away on the keys.

"What're you doing?" Xander asked.

Charlie's keystrokes continued at a frenzied pace, eyes locked on the screen, then nothing. He sat frozen.

"What is it? Tell me!"

Charlie slowly turned his head toward him, a realization coming to him like a light switching on.

"Sylva."

"What?"

His eyes sharpened, alive now with certainty.

"She's in Sylva!"

"How do you know?"

Charlie angled the computer to him and pointed at the screen.

Xander leaned forward, his eyes scrolling away from the header "Token Locations" down to the tip of Charlie's index finger to the line that read: "Token 8675309, current location: 35.3746° N, 83.2133° W." He looked down at the token in his hand then went back to the screen. "Is that—"

"Yep! The token you guys exchanged that night at the house."

"How do you know? It's just a random string of numbers."

"Believe it or not, its part of the lyrics to an old song she likes—trust me, it's hers."

"But it doesn't say Sylva."

"Yes it does." He clicked over to a Google Maps tab, 35.3746° N, 83.2133° W already in the address bar. Below it was a map showing the town of Sylva, North Carolina. Next to it was *drive time: 31 minutes.*

"Let's go!"

"But where in Sylva? The system defaults to the nearest city's central latitude and longitude."

Xander paced a tight circle, his eyes scanning the ground as if scratching the hard pan for the answer when suddenly he jerked his head up. "The cabin! Sinclair owns one on the Tuckasegee River. Or at least he did when I first came on board with him. He took me there once. It's only a couple minutes outside the city."

"Do you think you can get us there?"

"I think so," he said, hurrying to the trunk where he pulled out a small black bag and reached inside. What emerged looked, at first glance, like an old Wild West revolver, complete with a long, dark barrel.

Charlie tensed.

Then the light caught it—the plastic sheen, the bright orange tip, the hollow, weightless look of a cap gun trying to pass for the real thing. A toy. Nothing more. Just one made to look dangerously real.

Charlie's shoulders eased. "What's that for?"

"My nephew's birthday party…today, hopefully nothing…at worst, a distraction."

Half an hour later Xander eased the car down a narrow, rutted path, branches scraping the sides like fingernails across a chalkboard. Somewhere in the dark the Tuckasegee River ran, its rushing waters close enough that they could hear it. Up ahead, half-hidden by trees, Sinclair's cabin came into view.

A single light streamed from one of the windows out over the river just a few yards beyond a small back porch.

Charlie leaned forward, squinting. "Someone's definitely there. I can see the outline of a car next to the cabin and someone in the window."

He braked before the last bend, killing the headlights, then shut the engine off. He opened his door with care, making sure it wouldn't creak. "We walk from here."

They exchanged a look—part nerves, part resolve—then slipped onto the narrow trail, careful not to break the silence.

Charlie's heart pounded, each crunch of leaves and twigs underfoot making him flinch. Somehow the closer they got, the calmer he became. For the second time in his life, he spoke to God. Unlike his jail cell confession and plea for forgiveness, he uttered a simple prayer of thanks for the river's roaring waters, allowing them to make their way to the cabin unnoticed.

A man's voice, strong and authoritative, broke out from the porch. "Take your smoke outside!" A moment later the silhouette of a mountainous man appeared at the back porch railing, a tiny flicker of light hovering within his hand as if holding a firefly by its tail. The light followed to his mouth, a hazy halo seconds later encircling his head.

"Do you recognize him?" Charlie whispered.

"I can't tell."

Charlie scanned the cabin, spotting a large holly bush next to the window where the light was flowing from. "Come on," he said, scurrying up behind it. "Nobody will see us here." He arched his back against the wall, Xander following suit next to him. Ever so slowly, Charlie leaned to the window, one eye passing over the first pane, then past the curtain drawn back on the other side. He jerked back.

Xander held out his hands, begging for a response.

Charlie nodded. "She's here alright. They've got her tied up in the corner."

"Is she okay?"

"Appears to be but she's blindfolded."

"What do we do now?"

"We wait."

"For what?"

"Until whoever's in there goes to bed, then we sneak in and take her."

A moment passed in silence. "Is there anything else we should do?"

"Will you pray with me?"

Xander tilted his head. "Pray…with you?"

"I don't know any memorized ones, so if you've got one for all this…by all means."

Xander wrapped his arm over Charlie's shoulder and began, barely audible, "Yea, though I walk through the valley of the shadow of death, I will fear no evil…" In the background the Tuckasegee raged on, muting his words from those inside yet resounding within their hearts, strengthening them for the task ahead.

Chapter Twenty-Nine

Charlie pressed deeper into the holly bush, shuffling his stiffening legs to a better position while Xander crouched low, choosing to move closer to the window in order to monitor Lydia's situation inside.

"How long do you think we've been out here?" Charlie said.

Xander checked his cell phone. "Almost three hours."

Charlie glanced at the window. The warm light spilling out onto the lawn remained consistent with an occasional shadow passing through it. "How much longer do you think before they go to bed?"

"I don't know," Xander said, raising his camera to the corner of the window, "but I need to take advantage of the light inside while I can." He pulled the phone back and checked the screen.

"Did you get anything?"

"A little blurry but you can tell it's her."

"Any more evidence-gathering tricks?" Charlie said.

Xander's fingers danced across the screen. A second later he tilted his phone to him, the image of a red microphone pulsating against a dark background. "I'll leave it on. Just remember to speak clearly."

Charlie shook his head. "I forgot how good you are with that thing."

At that moment the window went black, the yard a blank canvas void of anything but silhouettes of trees, bushes and undergrowth, all reminders of how alone they were. The stars suddenly became visible, twinkling serenely, their light flickering wildly over the river's current.

"That's it," Charlie said, eyes locked on the darkened window. "They're down."

Xander put his phone into his breast pocket and picked up the toy gun that lay beside him.

Charlie shook his head. "Not yet. We need to wait another thirty minutes or so just to make sure they're all asleep."

Xander checked his phone. "It's been thirty-five minutes."

Charlie took a deep breath. "Okay, remember…stay behind me until I have her untied. Then take her to the car. I'll be right behind you."

Together they slipped along the side of the house to the back porch, the sound of the river growing louder with each step, giving them the perfect cover. Charlie's hand hovered over the door handle. He glanced back. "Ready?" he whispered. Xander nodded.

He gripped the knob, but it didn't budge. He took a breath and tried again. And again. It remained fixed. He arched his head back, letting out a silent groan, when suddenly the door crept open. On the other side, hunkered down, was Xander, his head tilted toward an open window six feet away.

Charlie managed a nervous smile and a pat on Xander's

shoulder before easing past him. He tiptoed to the threshold where the kitchen opened into the living room and to the chair where Lydia was bound. Across from her, sprawled on the sofa, a man lay with his face buried in the cushions, snoring like the grizzly bear that matched his stature.

He inched across the room until he stood behind Lydia.

Her head hung forward, her body too still. For one terrible second, he thought he was too late until her eyes fluttered.

"Lydia," he said nudging her arm.

No response.

He nudged again, careful at first, then harder.

"Lydia," his voice tight now. "Come on."

The blindfold slowly rose, her head turning side to side. "It's me, Charlie," he said, this time lifting the covering from her eyes. She gasped. Charlie threw his hand over her mouth, turning back to the man on the sofa. His snoring indicated he was far from being roused.

"Go," he mouthed, pointing to the back door where Xander was waiting with outstretched arms.

Outside, Charlie tapped Xander on the shoulder, interrupting their tearful embrace. "I need your camera."

"But we've got her now."

"I need more evidence."

With one armed wrapped around Lydia, Xander pulled out his phone and placed it in Charlie's palm. "See you at the car."

A moment later Charlie stood alone on the porch. He drew in a deep breath and with measured steps, slow and steady, entered the cabin.

Charlie glanced at the chair where Lydia had been tied,

then swung Xander's camera toward the sofa, expecting to capture the sleeping man's image for the jury's judgment.

He blinked.

The sofa was empty. Only the deep impression of a huge body remained—as if the room itself had failed to notice he'd gone. Somewhere outside the camera's lens the man lurked.

Charlie spun on his heel and raced to the back door. Just as he passed through it, a fist slammed across his temple, sending him crashing back into the cabin. White-hot pain lingered only a moment before everything went black. A second later he was being dragged across the kitchen floor into a corner. A pistol's razor-sharp barrel slashed across the soft palette of his mouth. The taste of gun metal and blood filled his senses as his head slammed into the wall. He gagged as his body wedged in beside a trash can. With a quick twist of his wrist, his assailant thrust the gun deeper into his throat while holding him pinned into the crevasse with his other arm.

From behind the silhouette of the hulking man holding him against the wall came a thick Scottish brogue. "Mr. Carraway, come to ruin our party."

Charlie's eyes, bloodshot and bulging with fear, darted back and forth. With a mouth full of blood and metal all he could muster was a muffled gargle that conveyed nothing but sheer panic.

Through the darkness, passing over the shoulder of the massive beast holding him captive came a shimmering light. A thin sliver of silver glistened, coming in from across the room. Charlie tried to blink but couldn't, realizing the approaching object was a switch blade. Closer it came. In a straight, steady line it continued toward his right eye. Five inches, four inches, three, then two. Sweat poured into his eyes. Suddenly it stopped. An inch from penetrating his cornea, the blade hung suspended in the darkness, waiting for one single blinding thrust.

The patrol car sat in the shadows of a quiet street, engine idling softly. Tanner, a former Navy SEAL now in blue, leaned back from the steering wheel, hands curled around a cup of coffee that had long since gone cold.

Reynolds, a skinny newcomer to the force, sat arms crossed, eyes flicking to the empty intersections as if expecting something to appear out of the shadows. "Did you hear that the King of Kindness posted bail earlier today?"

"You mean the King of Con," chuckled Tanner.

"Yeah, he's out." He shook his head, "I hope he serves the time for what he did. My mom donated tons to that *Following the Love* site."

"I'm sure he'll get what he deserves."

Reynold's phone buzzed against the console. He picked it up, staring at the screen longer than necessary. A flicker of something unspoken crossed his face.

"Hmmm, this is a rather odd one."

"What? Your wife texting you to stop off at the grocery store again?"

"No. It's random for sure. I don't know what to make of it." He held out his phone to him. "What do you think?"

"Wow, that *is* random."

"Could it be a lead?"

"I doubt it, especially since it didn't come through dispatch."

"I think you're right."

A minute passed. Tanner fidgeted in his seat then tossed the remainder of his stale coffee out the window. "What the heck? It's not like we'll be grabbing any collars sitting here all night. Let's check it out." He put the car in drive and made a quick U-turn. "But first, let's do a drive-by of Carraway's house."

Charlie's chin bounced off his chest, his head wobbling, half unconscious. Blood trickled from his mouth and nose. His right eye was a purple pulp, swollen almost shut. His hands were tied behind him in the same chair where Lydia had been. Looming over him was the huge man responsible for it all.

Charlie fought against passing out, stretching his eyes open as much as he could. He looked at the burly man. His focus, blurred as it was, landed on the side of his neck and the tattoo of Thor's hammer.

"I…I know you," Charlie muttered. "First day at Sinclair's…the lobby…you're Thor."

"Aren't you the canny one," came the voice of the man with the Scottish accent.

Charlie rolled his head to the side and found the man standing there, switchblade loose in his hand. A pale tail of hair hung over his shoulder, catching the dim light.

"And you…" The words dragged from Charlie's mouth like syrup. "I remember the ponytail."

The man's grip tightened around the knife.

"You're Murdock."

The man brushed past Thor. "I'll handle it from here." He pulled up a chair and sat in front of Charlie, their knees touching.

Murdock cleared his throat. "Let's make this quick. As it stands now, your friend is off in the woods with our house guest, backtracking to your getaway car. Does that sound accurate?"

Charlie shrugged.

"The wee problem is that you should be with them— except on your way out the door you got detained by my associate." He held up his knife in front of him. "So…we have options. One, you can lead us to them, or two, we can start extracting fingers until you do." The corners of his mouth curled up like snakes.

"Why do you need my friends? Aren't I enough?"

Murdock reared back. "You? You're nothing but a pawn, Mr. Carraway. A wee pawn duped by a higher intellect."

"Who, Lydia?"

Murdock gave a small, pitying laugh.

Blurry eyed and worn, Charlie could still make out Murdock's reaction knowing he only needed him to keep talking for a chance to get more evidence on Xander's phone recording in his pocket.

"Her father. He was the one who knew too much."

Murdock's eyes sharpened.

Charlie pushed harder. "Is that why you killed him?"

Murdock turned to Thor with a knowing nod. As if practiced, he cut one of Charlie's hands free then spread it onto a coffee table next to him.

Charlie's eyes bugged as he watched Murdock float his blade over it. "So…what's it going to be, digits or no digits?"

"Just-just wait. I'll take you to them but first just tell me. Did you kill Lydia's father?"

"Of course we did you idiot," Thor growled. Just like we're gonna do you!"

"Shut up!" Murdock snapped. "Are you really that soft? Just stand there being big and SHUT—YOUR—TRAP!"

Thor nodded apologetically.

Murdock spun back to Charlie, placing his hands on his knees as if the outburst had never happened. Then, in a flurry, he splayed out Charlie's fingers and in one fell swoop ground the switchblade down through his pinky. Charlie jerked back, howling in agony, rocking the chair side to side almost toppling over.

"See what you made me do, you thick-headed ox?" In an instant, Murdock's eyes went black. His voice slithered. "How much do you and your friend Xander know? And don't lie! The girl's already confessed she was planning to go to the cops." He snarled, "Like father like daughter."

"All I know…" Charlie said, each word ragged, "…is that…" His voice dropped, suddenly calm, almost reverent. "Yea, though I walk through the valley of the shadow of death…"

From behind him, two voices joined him, "…I will fear no evil, for thou art with me…"

Charlie craned his head back to the door, just enough to see Lydia standing next to Xander, her eyes wide, arms trembling, but steady. Xander's toy pistol, rigid in his grip, was locked on Murdock.

Their voices continued, wrapping the room in a moment of hope. "…thy rod and thy staff, they comfort me."

A breathless moment passed. Xander's plastic replica shaking, Lydia beside him, eyes red and swollen, Murdock and Thor motionless, glaring at them, aching to strike.

Charlie slowly rose and hobbled back to his friends, clutching his bloody stump.

Xander pulled Lydia to Charlie. "Take her! I'll be right behind you."

Charlie grabbed her around the waist, and together they stumbled outside, supporting each other as best they could.

Back inside, Xander narrowed his eyes into as menacing a look as he could muster. Just as he began to inch his way out the door, Murdock's eyes twitched, his focus sharpening on the gun's barrel, the orange tip now glaring like an absurd beacon. He chuckled, almost to himself, then louder until breaking into a full belly laugh. "Look, Thor, our lad's come back for a game of make-believe."

In a blind panic, Xander threw the plastic gun at him. It slammed against his face with a crack. Before Murdock could react, Xander was gone, barreling through the door and into the night.

"Get him!" Murdock shouted. "But take out the girl first!"

Charlie turned just in time to see Thor racing outside behind Xander. For a split second the world almost stopped as he watched him pull a real 9mm Luger from his waistband and level it on Lydia.

"NOOOO!" Xander screamed as he hurled himself in front of her.

The Luger exploded, the shot ringing out over the river's thunder. A second crack split the night—this one from somewhere deep in the shadows.

Thor's hands flew to his chest. He stared in shock at the blood welling in his palm. Then, like a great oak cut at the trunk, he pitched forward and dropped face first into the dirt.

Chapter Thirty

Charlie stood frozen over Thor's lifeless body.

"Noooo!" Lydia's scream shuddered through the trees.

Charlie spun. At her feet, Xander lay motionless.

He dropped beside him. The bullet meant for Lydia had found Xander's temple. With shaking hands, Charlie tore his sleeve in half and bound it around the wound, pressing hard.

Lydia collapsed at Xander's side.

"My dear... my dear, speak to me. Xander, please—my love."

"Asheville police! Don't anybody move!" The command cut through the moment, leaving no room for grief. From the darkness, the silhouette of a police officer emerged, his pistol used to bring down Thor still raised. As he walked to them, he lowered his weapon but kept it at the ready. "Shots fired," he spoke into his radio. "One suspect down." He turned in a circle, searching the woods then the house. "I'm Officer Reynolds. Anyone inside?" he said.

"One man, I think," Charlie replied, his voice thin and distant.

"Chief?" Reynolds shouted, glancing past Thor's body.

"Over here!" From around the corner of the house walked

Murdock, his hands cupped at the back of his head. Behind him stood Officer Tanner, his gun pressed between the man's shoulder blades. "Caught him trying to sneak off down by the river." Tanner surveyed the scene as Reynolds cuffed the man. "What's the situation?"

"The big man's dead," Reynolds said. He motioned to Xander. "This one's still alive. An ambulance and backup are en route." The distant sounds of sirens confirmed their arrival any minute.

"And her…" he said, motioning to Lydia, still sobbing as she continued to cradle Xander.

"Her name's Lydia Phelps," Charlie said. "She works for me. The man's her fiancé, Xander Whitman…my best friend."

"And your name?"

"Charlie Carraway."

The officers exchanged baffled looks as the first of two cop cars swung into the clearing, sirens blaring at full pitch. An ambulance followed right on the latter's bumper, its red lights tangled in the blue of the police cars glaring off the cabin windows in a dizzying blur. Within seconds a dozen cops and EMTs were swarming the front yard.

Charlie was guided toward the first cruiser, two offi-cers' hands firm on his shoulders, moving him along as if he were just part of the scenery, their actions practiced and quiet amid the chaos. Within moments he was seated inside, holding his bandaged hand against his chest, the door snapping shut behind him. He slumped down and looked away from the madness outside. The car peeled away, its blue lights flashing through the trees.

Murdock, pulled along by his cuffs, was taken by another policeman to the second cruiser, his eyes flickering back toward the cabin for a moment. He didn't struggle, but merely tilted his head, a quiet, unsettling acknowledgment of the chaos around him, before stepping into the back seat. The cruiser followed the first, sirens meshing in sync with it.

Meanwhile, beneath the ambulance's flashing red lights, the rear doors flew open. Inside, Xander lay on a gurney while the EMTs worked quickly, checking his vitals and securing lines.

Charlie stumbled into Mission Hospital just as the sun was rising, the previous night's horror still with him. His left eye was bloodshot and hollow; his right one still shut from Thor's right hook. The tip of the bandage wrapping his severed finger was now a crimson blotch. His clothes were wrinkled and stained and his hair matted with sweat and fear. Each step felt heavier than the last, as if the weight of the world was pressing down on him. His hands trembled from sheer exhaustion and the panic of having witnessed his best friend being shot and now racing to find a daughter teetering on the edge of death.

"May I help you?" a nurse coming down the hall asked.

"Can you tell me where the cardiac intensive care unit is?"

"Of course…straight down this hall, through the double metal doors, turn right and it's through the next set of doors."

A minute later he was through the second set of doors, his hands clasped together as he came upon the admittance desk and a robust man in scrubs staring at a computer. The man looked up, eyebrows raised in shock at Charlie's appearance. "May I help you?"

"I'm looking for Ashley Carraway's room."

The man's eyes fell back to his computer. "I'm sorry sir, she's no longer—"

"WHAT?"

"No, no, what I was about to say is…" He leaned forward, eyeing Charlie's name tag. "Are you her father?"

"I am."

"Mr. Carraway, I believe your wife has been trying to reach you since last night. Your daughter has been transferred to the Carolinas Medical Center in Charlotte."

"Why?"

The man's lips pressed into a thin line. "I'm afraid your daughter's condition started to become unstable. Unfortunately, our facility isn't equipped to handle…" He paused, searching for the words. "Well, the CMC is just the best place for her condition. They've got the equipment and most importantly some of the finest cardiologists in the country."

Charlie threw his hands over his face, shaking his head. "Lord," he muttered, "please help me."

"Maybe you should call her."

"I don't have my phone."

"Here, you can use mine," the man said.

After a dozen rings with no answer, Charlie handed it back. "How far is the CMC?"

"About three hours." The man handed him a card. "This is the address and the exact location she'll be at when you get there."

"Before I go, can you tell me if a Xander Whitman was admitted last night? They would've come in through the ER."

The man scanned his computer again. "No. I don't see anyone with that name."

Charlie dropped his head, standing motionless, eyes closed.

"Sir, are you okay?"

Charlie's eyes grew misty. "I-I'm fine. Thank you for everything." He turned and walked back down the hall, picking up his pace as he went. By the time he left the building, he was running to his car in hopes of making it to Charlotte before it was too late.

For the next three hours Charlie drove with his hands clamped down on the wheel, white-knuckling in and out of traffic, speeding most of the way. With his eyes locked on the road, he prayed. Fervently and without pause he prayed aloud, every moment crying out to God pleading for both Ashley and Xander.

By the time he pulled into the CMC parking deck, the despair and hopelessness that had a hold on him in Asheville was somehow gone. In its place was an unnatural calm, as if a loving hand had lifted the weight from his shoulders. He turned off the ignition. Then with both hands stretched out over the dash, palms up, he softly ended his journey's prayer. "If it is your will, dear Lord, may all these things be done. In your Son's holy and precious name, I pray. Amen."

The hall of the CMC's cardiac care unit smelled of antiseptic and metal tinged with a scent of worry. There was a quiet tension accented by the sterile walls and overhead fluorescent lights, the distant beeping of monitors and hum of medical technology seeping from the patient rooms, a harsh reminder of the fragile hearts within. Nurses moved in and out of them, their footsteps purposeful, carrying charts or wheeling equipment on small carts. Cracked doorways provided glimpses of controlled chaos inside.

As Charlie approached room 223, a nurse appeared, greeting him with the hint of a smile, the type produced out of polite obligation. He hesitated for a moment.

"You may go in," she said.

Slowly he entered.

Ashley lay still on the bed, pale, her eyes closed, tubes running from her mouth to a machine with a plunger that rose and fell with the rise and fall of her chest. IVs and wires tangled around her body. Bree was beside her, curled up asleep in a chair with her neck painfully wedged into the corner.

Charlie inched his way to her. He placed his hand on her shoulder. "Bree," he whispered.

Her eyes opened, and in an instant she was awake. She threw her arms around him. Tears flowed as her sobs came in waves.

For a moment they stood hugging, no words needing to be exchanged. They were together.

When they parted, Bree pulled back at the sight of his damaged face. "Oh no!" She reached down, taking his bandaged hand in hers. "What happened?"

"I'll explain later. What's her condition?"

Bree wiped her eyes, then began, her voice quivering. "She—she's in what the doctors called advanced, end-stage heart failure. That's why they transferred us here."

"What's that mean…end-stage failure? Is she…"

Bree threw her hands over her mouth and nodded as more tears welled. "They…"

Charlie cupped his hands to her cheeks. "Is she…"

Bree nodded again, her voice catching with each word. "They used the words… 'imminent death.'"

Charlie looked away, his throat tightening. "How long does she have?"

"Mr. Carraway?" came a warm voice from the doorway.

Charlie turned to find a middle-aged black man in a white lab coat with a stethoscope wrapped around his neck.

"Yes, I'm Mr. Carraway."

"I'm Dr. VanGilder, Ashley's cardiologist. If you'd care to join me, I'll be able to answer that for you." He smiled the same smile the nurse had upon entering the room.

The doctor led them to a secluded waiting room across the hallway. "Would you care to sit?" he asked.

"No, that's okay," Charlie replied.

"I understand." He took a deep breath. "Ashley's condition is indeed critical. The term 'imminent death,' as woeful as it sounds, unfortunately defines the inevitable condition that it is. Ashley is not there quite yet, but from all our tests and current monitoring, I'm afraid it's just a matter of time before she reaches that stage."

"What about medication? Surely there's something that can help."

"I'm afraid not. Everything that we've done up to this point is…well…all that we can do."

Charlie's eyes widened. "What about a transplant? She could get a transplant, couldn't she?"

The doctor pressed his fingertips together, pausing a moment before having to give a practiced response he had delivered to too many desperate family members of dying patients. "A transplant would indeed be a possibility, but there are multiple things that are out of our hands that make that unlikely. The first is that there are currently no donors.

The second is that even if a donor became available, there are already two people ahead of him on the waiting list—and both are stable enough to undergo a transplant more easily. As it stands now, Ashley most likely will be entering her final stage any day now, possibly within hours. When that happens, she won't be able to receive a transplant. Once the body begins shutting down, it's too late."

Charlie stood, hands hanging by his sides, palms out as if begging for another response—any alternative other than what he just had to endure.

"I truly wish I had something else I could offer you. At this point, medically I just don't." His eyes drifted to a coffee table beside him, his focus drawn to a red Gideon Bible. "I've been reprimanded for this before, but can I ask you about your faith?"

"Of course," Bree said softly.

"Are you believers…Christ followers, that is?"

Bree nodded and looked to Charlie.

"Mr. Carraway?"

Charlie lifted his head, looking the doctor directly in the eyes. "With all my heart, I am."

Bree wrapped her arm through his, pulling him closer than she had ever before. Her head rested on his shoulder.

Dr. VanGilder smiled. "That's good because the prayers of a righteous person are powerful and effective. Do you have a church family or other families and friends who are believers too?"

"Yes," Bree replied. "We belong to a church and are part of a connection group who are all strong Christians."

Charlie's head dropped. "Bree's your prayer warrior, Doctor. I just recently became a believer. My prayer group is rather thin."

The doctor shook his head. "Mr. Carraway, your recent acceptance of Christ doesn't preclude you from being important to Him. Your prayer will be heard just as clearly as everyone else's. My recommendation is to gather those closest to your daughter during these final days and to asks for prayers from all those that believe in Him."

"We will, won't we, Charlie?" Bree said.

A slight yet sincere smile crossed his lips. "Of course."

As Dr. VanGilder pulled the door open to leave, he stopped and turned back to them. "Charlie, regarding your prayer group, I beg to differ."

"Excuse me?"

"Your website. You might want to check it." Just then a nurse pulled him away from the door, citing an emergency down the hallway, leaving Charlie and Bree with puzzled looks on their faces.

Charlie angled his head back to the door, contemplating the parting words.

"Xander and Lydia should be here," Bree said, breaking through Charlie's thoughts.

Suddenly the memories of the last twenty-four hours came rushing back. He took Bree by the hand and gently led her to a sofa. "I'm afraid there's a lot to tell you. And most of it's not good."

Chapter Thirty-One

Bree sat bent over, on the sofa, her elbows on her knees, her face buried in her hands. Charlie sat patiently beside her as she grappled with the harrowing details of his ordeal, waiting to rescue her from the avalanche of emotions he knew was to come. She raised her head. Chin high, she looked upward, her lips moving in silent prayer, then pulled her cell phone from her pocket.

"I've got to call Lydia. You should go back and stay with Ashley. We can't leave her alone."

As soon as Charlie left, Bree speed-dialed Lydia. On the twelfth ring, just as she was about to hang up, a small broken voice came on the other end of the line.

"Lydia, it's Bree. I just spoke to Charlie. He told me everything that's happened. How are you doing? How's Xander?"

For the next several minutes Bree sat with her hand to her chest, Lydia's muffled sobs growing louder as she listened. A second later she was on her knees, crying out between broken prayers, her phone beside her.

"Bree! What's wrong?" Charlie said, rushing in. "Is that Lydia on the phone?" He picked it up. "Lydia? Lydia, are you there?" A dial tone beeped. He tossed it on the sofa and dropped down beside her. "What happened?"

"He's dead, Charlie." She grabbed his sleeve. "Xander died two hours ago!"

Charlie picked up a vase and reared back, ready to sling it.

"No!" Bree shouted, jumping up and grabbing his arm. "That won't solve anything."

Charlie lowered his hand. "This is all my fault—everything that's happened has been my fault."

Bree took him by the shoulders. "You didn't cause this. This is God's will."

Charlie jerked back and turned away from her. "Bree," his voice cracked, "I-I'm having a hard time with this. My faith—I've given everything to God, but suddenly I'm doubting again. How can this be justified? Help me! Please help me understand!"

Just then Bree's phone buzzed.

"It's Lydia!" she shouted as she snatched it off the sofa. For a long moment she stood silently scrolling through the text message.

"What's it say?" Charlie asked.

"It reads, 'Jesus said, 'I am the resurrection and the life. Whoever believes in me, though he die, yet shall he live.' Then it ends with, 'Charlie, know that Xander believed.'"

Charlie looked at her. "I never knew how strong a believer she was."

Bree smiled. "Yes, you weren't around enough to see how much, but Charlie, this message isn't from Lydia." She held up the screen to him. At the very bottom the signature read, *Peter, your brother in Christ.*

Just then the door swung open. "Mr. and Mrs. Carraway, you might want to come back in…hurry!"

Bree pushed the door to room 223 open with Charlie crowding in behind her. The monitors still hummed but the ventilator was no longer pumping. Instead of Ashley lying with closed eyes, she was now sitting up, wide-eyed and with a thin smile inching upward.

"Mom…Dad," she managed in a raw, breathy exhale.

Bree and Charlie rushed to her side. Bree fell across her lap as Charlie kissed her forehead. For a moment they wrapped their arms around her and pressed into her, neglecting all the wires and hoses, desperate to feel the warmth of her skin and the life she had suddenly regained.

Bree, wanting to share her joy, turned back to the nurse who remained standing against the wall, a sliver of a smile appearing beneath concerned eyes, reluctant to reciprocate. A moment later Dr. VanGilder walked in then immediately disappeared back outside with the nurse in tow.

Charlie stroked Ashley's hair. "How're you feeling, dear?"

"Tired, but somehow better. I've actually got some energy."

"You hear that, Doctor? She's regaining her strength!" Charlie spun back to the door, not aware of the doctor's absence.

A moment later, Dr. VanGilder returned with the nurse, who was pushing what looked like a large computer on wheels. "Would you mind escorting the Carraways to our new coffee counter down the hall while I run a few tests?"

Charlie and Bree blew Ashley kisses as they followed the nurse into the hall.

"What do you think?" Charlie said, holding out his hands to the nurse. "It's a miracle!" He grabbed Bree by the hands and spun her around. "It's a miracle, Bree! Our baby girl's going to live."

Bree clasped her hands in front of her mouth, a smile stretching wide from beneath them. She turned to the nurse. "She *is* going to be alright, isn't she?"

The nurse remained tight-lipped, her focus on the tiled floor.

"She is, isn't she?" Bree asked again.

"I'm sorry, Mrs. Carraway. I'm afraid I'm not allowed to offer my opinions or diagnosis. Dr. VanGilder, however, will let you know after he's run his tests. In the meantime," she said, holding out her hand to a sleek, polished stainless-steel device sitting next to the nurses' station, "may I interest you in some of the best coffee in the CMC? Trust me, it's much better than the cafeteria."

Bree glanced at Charlie. "I'm sure my husband could use some, but I'm fine."

"No ma'am, I'm okay too," he replied. "I just want to get back to see how those tests are coming."

"I understand, but they could take up to a half hour. In the meantime, the doctor told me that you might be interested in that prayer group of yours."

"I told him I didn't have one."

The nurse shrugged. "Evidently he thinks you do…" With her back turned to him, she pulled a laptop from behind the nurses' station and began clicking away. She stopped, gave him a curious look, then returned to the laptop. Stopping again, she turned back to him with a huge smile. "You wouldn't happen to be the guy who created this, would you?" She spun around, holding out the computer to him, the screen displaying the *Following the Love* website.

He gave her a sideways look. "Um…yes, that's mine."

She pushed the laptop to his chest. "I've got to run back to assist the doctor. In the meantime, you might want to consider some nice responses."

Charlie tilted the laptop and stared at the screen, his brow furrowed. His expression softened, piece by piece, as if a puzzle were coming together on its own right in front of him. He leaned back, his eyes roaming over it. "Wowww," he breathed, the word spilling out full of wonder.

"What is it?" Bree asked.

He turned the laptop to her. She blinked once, then reached up and with her finger scrolled the page down as Charlie held the computer, his smile growing larger as she moved from page to page.

"There must be a thousand prayers for her on here."

Charlie punched several keys. "Try five thousand, nine hundred and forty-seven…and they're from all over the country. In fact, from all over the world! This is going to make her feel even better!" He turned to Bree. "This truly is a miracle, isn't it? Dr. VanGilder was right! The prayers of the righteous truly are powerful."

Bree and Charlie sat side by side on the waiting room's sofa, eyes fixed on the computer in Charlie's lap. Bree stretched back, rubbing her eyes, while Charlie remained hunched over, reading all the prayers and well wishes that had poured into the *Following the Love* inbox.

Several minutes later the nurse entered carrying a box of Kleenex, which she placed on the coffee table. She glanced at Bree with the same unreadable smile she had when they first came in.

"How're the tests coming?" Bree asked.

"He's finishing up right now." Her response came short and direct, as if her obligation was only to deliver the tissues.

"Can we go back in?"

"Not just yet…" Before she could finish, the doctor entered the room, a clipboard in hand.

"Thank you, Becky," he said, smiling to the nurse as she slipped out the door.

Charlie shut the laptop and started to get up. The doctor motioned him to stay seated as he pulled up a chair in front of them.

Bree clutched Charlie by the arm. "Are you finished with the tests?"

"We are."

"And…" Charlie said.

The doctor's sigh had Bree digging her fingers into Charlie's arm.

"The tests indicate what is known as a terminal surge or terminal lucidity. It's where a patient becomes more alert, begins speaking clearly, and in general, shows signs of recovery."

"Which she is—right?"

"It appears as such…but medically it means the body is using its last reserves of energy."

Bree gasped.

"But…" Charlie began, unable to finish.

"In end-stage heart failure, these surges are common. I was hoping otherwise, but all the tests indicate her condition, other than the surge, remains the same."

Charlie pushed the computer away, arching his head back with a sorrowful moan that echoed out into the hall.

"Then how much more time does she have?" Bree asked.

"I'm afraid it's not an extension. Whatever time she

had remains in effect. It could be a day, maybe two…or it could be hours."

"So, all these prayers did nothing but give us false hope?" Charlie said.

Bree looked at him with pleading eyes. "Charlie, don't go there. Please…"

He shook his head. "I don't understand. We've prayed, our friends prayed, people we don't know have prayed… and now this. A sign of hope and then this cruel twist…I-I can't believe…"

Bree took his face in her hands. "Listen to me, Charlie. His will isn't for us to question. All those prayers didn't go unheard."

Dr. VanGilder placed his hand on Charlie's shoulder. "She's right. He heard every single one and whatever happens, just know there's a reason. Right now, he's given you a chance to at least spend some time with her during this stage. She's awake, alert and off the ventilator."

Charlie squeezed his eyes shut, fighting to steady himself. Then he opened them and nodded. "Okay… okay. Let's go. Let's go see our daughter."

Charlie and Bree entered Ashley's room to find her sitting up with a huge smile on her face.

"Hello, darling," Bree said, taking her by the hand.

Charlie leaned over and kissed her on the forehead.

Ashley's smile faded as she searched their faces. "Have you guys been crying?"

Bree mustered a warm smile. "A little."

"I wish you wouldn't." She turned to Charlie. "Dad, you guys can't be doing that, okay?"

Charlie stood, unable to answer.

"Seriously, you guys can't cry because I know something that I bet you don't know."

"What's that, dear?" Bree said.

"That I'm going to be okay."

Charlie bit his lip, forcing himself to hold back the tears. "Of course you are, honey."

"Show her the computer," Bree said.

Charlie brought out the laptop with the *Following the Love* site already open. "Take a look at the inbox number. Almost 6,000 of those new emails are for you. All prayers for you to get better."

For the next thirty minutes Ashley scrolled from message to message, occasionally stopping to read a particular prayer aloud. "I can't believe you did this," she said, glancing to Charlie.

"Did what, dear?"

"Created the *Following the Love* site."

"But I didn't create it."

"Well, you and Lydia, that is."

"No, we didn't…but you know who did?"

The corners of her mouth turned up in anticipation of receiving the punch line to one of his lame dad jokes. "So, who did?" she chuckled.

"God."

"God?" She turned to Bree with a questioning look. "Mom, did my father…your husband, just say *God*?"

Bree's smile stretched wide. "He did. My husband— your father—after all these years finally found his savior."

Ashley jerked her head back to him. "Really? You accepted Jesus as your Lord and savior?"

"I did."

Ashley's hands came together over her mouth, her eyes glistening.

Charlie bent down and wrapped his arms around her and whispered in her ear. "And it's amazing." He pulled back to find her eyes shut, the trace of smile on her face.

"Ashley?" he said.

The beeping of the heart monitor suddenly doubled.

"Ashley…dear?" he said again, his voice rising.

The door swung open. In rushed the nurse, followed a second later by two more along with Dr. VanGilder.

."Mr. and Mrs. Carraway," he said as he placed his stethoscope on Ashley's chest, "if you wouldn't mind stepping outside please." The nurse, without waiting for their reply, gently guided them into the hallway.

Charlie stood with his back to the wall, arms folded tight across his chest. Bree sat beside him, hands gripping the computer in her lap, her foot tapping the tile floor like a jackhammer. The door to room 223 remained closed, their eyes darting to it every other second.

Charlie checked the clock across the hall—12:41. Two minutes later he checked it again.

At 12:50 the door finally opened. They both stood at the same time.

Dr. VanGilder stepped into the hallway and closed the door gently behind him. His expression was flat. He didn't rush but walked to them in a measured way that held Charlie breathless.

"How is she?" Bree asked, the words coming out too quickly.

Dr. VanGilder drew a breath. "We're seeing changes,"

he said. "Unfortunately, they're what we anticipated." The doctor met their eyes, one and then the other, as if making sure they were both still there. "The terminal surge has passed. Ashley is back where she was before, progressing to the final stage…this time, I'm afraid, at an accelerated rate."

Bree's mouth opened, then closed.

Charlie swallowed. "You're saying—"

"I'm saying we need to prepare," the doctor said gently.

"How long are you thinking?" Charlie asked.

"Most likely she'll reach imminent death by this evening. After that, it's just a matter of an hour or two."

Chapter Thirty-Two

The late afternoon light crept through the hospital room's blinds, painting pale amber stripes across the tiled floor and climbing the side of the bed where Ashley lay, motionless except for the shallow movement of her chest, fading little by little with every beat.

Bree sat next to her, shoulders hunched, fingers laced tightly together, head down in continuous prayer, while Charlie stood at her bedside, rejecting a chair, refusing to add any distance between him and his daughter. Without realizing it, he counted her breaths, each one a silent plea for time to stand still.

For five long hours, nurses drifted in and out of the room, their movements hushed, their voices lowered. Even their footsteps seemed careful, as though the sound might disturb the fragile balance between life and death.

Then the door burst open.

Dr. VanGilder rushed in, urgency suddenly filling the space. His previous calm composure had been sharpened by something new and immediate. "Charlie, Bree, could you come with me?"

His steps quicker than usual, he led them to the nurses'

station where a young woman stood with several manila folders pressed to her chest.

"Bree, Charlie," the doctor said, "I'd like to introduce you to Catherine Hicks. Catherine is the CMC transplant coordinator."

Charlie's eyes flashed wide. "Transplant! As in heart transplant?"

Dr. VanGilder smiled. "That's right. I believe we've found a match."

Bree gasped and wrapped her arms around Charlie.

"Here's the thing. It does appear to be a match, but we won't be completely sure until it's here and the second thing is timing. Ashley is close to reaching total heart failure. If that happens, I'm afraid it will be too late, and we won't be able to do the procedure."

"Where do we sign?" Bree blurted.

The doctor chuckled. "Thank you, Bree. That's the other thing. You'll just need to sign the consent forms Catherine has for you."

"This is incredible! You've saved our daughter's life!"

"Not so fast, Charlie," Dr. VanGilder said, holding up his hands, attempting to temper his enthusiasm. "Remember, all this is contingent on us getting the heart in time and confirming it to be an exact match."

"When will it be here?"

"Approximately forty-five minutes."

"Didn't you say there were two potential recipients ahead of us?"

"Neither was a match."

Just then a hand caught his sleeve and a nurse tugged at him, her voice coming in an urgent burst. "It's Room 223!"

The doctor's professional calm snapped into motion. He squeezed Charlie's arm, firm and apologetic. "I have to go."

"I'm coming with you!"

"No! Stay here."

Before Charlie could answer, the doctor rushed into Ashley's room as alarms spilled into the hallway, their frantic beeping cutting through the air.

Charlie stood frozen, watching him disappear inside, nurses converging, a crash cart rattling forward, voices rising and overlapping.

The door to room 223 swung shut.

Bree sat across the hall from Ashley's room, praying silently with her head bowed, while Charlie paced back and forth. Sweat beaded across his forehead, his eyes jumping from Ashley's closed door up to the hallway clock. A drop of sweat rolled across his brow into his swollen eye, the sting suddenly reminding him—for only a second—of the horror of the previous night. Then back to the door his attention flew, back to the clock, again and again repeating the cycle, agonizing over the time that had elapsed. Five minutes, ten minutes, fifteen, twenty…his fingers curled into fists as he stared in contempt at the clock for every second that passed without any sign that Ashley was still in that room holding off the final stage of heart failure.

"I can't stand this, Bree. I have to find out what's happening."

Bree jumped up and grabbed him by the sleeve, pulling him back. "No, just wait. They can't be distracted."

Just then Ashley's door flung open with two nurses pulling on one end of a gurney. At the other end was another nurse with Dr. VanGilder close behind. On the gurney, still entangled in wires and hoses, was Ashley, a mask now over her face. A man in a surgical cap was leaning over her, frantically adjusting tubes running into her arms while a nurse wheeled a portable monitor beside them.

"Come on, team, let's move!" Dr. VanGilder shouted.

With military precision they all doubled their steps to the point of running. In a flurry another set of nurses and doctors came alongside, syncing up with them in their controlled, tense race against time.

Charlie ran along behind them in a panic, wanting to grab one of them for information but knowing that might jeopardize the immediacy of their task. Unable to control himself, he called out, "Dr. VanGilder, what's happening?"

Just as they pushed the gurney through a set of double metal doors, the doctor stopped and took two quick steps to him.

"What's happening?" Charlie said. "Is she in the final stage…is she—"

"No, not yet." His words were clipped, calm but immediate. "We're actually going into pre-op."

"For…"

"For the transplant." He placed his hand on Charlie's shoulder. "I'm sorry, I have to go."

Before Charlie could utter another word, Dr. VanGilder was already through the double doors.

A moment later Ms. Hicks walked out the same doors, her gait purposeful, her expression poised with an unnatural serenity that belied the chaos swirling around them.

"Mr. Carraway, I wanted to give you a quick update. As the transplant coordinator for Ashley's case, I'll be keeping you abreast of what's going on."

"Thank you," Charlie said.

"I'm sure you're probably worried about the urgency and the overall frenetic atmosphere."

"Yes, is that normal?" Bree asked.

"To a degree it is. But I have to be transparent. Ashley's case is atypical. Most transplants all have some issues, but in this case it's all about timing and the rapid onset of her final stage of heart failure. The reason the team had to rush in before was that there was an episode that advanced her to that stage. In short, her viability window for the transplant is all based on how quickly they can get her through pre-op and when the heart arrives."

Charlie nodded, turning to Bree with a forced smile. "They'll be quick…and that heart will be here soon, I know it."

"There's one other crucial element." She turned first to Bree then Charlie. "Dr. VanGilder told me that you're both believers. So, this goes without saying—pray. Pray for time to be merciful—swift when it needs to be, generous when it counts. In other words, pray that she receives the heart in time and handles the surgery."

"We understand," Charlie said.

"Thank you," she replied with a smile. "If you'll excuse me, I'll be going back in now to monitor the progress. I'll return shortly with more updates. In the meantime, keep your ears open for those angel wings."

"Excuse me?" Charlie said.

"The landing pad for the helicopter that's bringing the heart is right out this window."

Charlie's reflection in the window looking out to the helicopter pad was grim. The results of Thor's beating was still fresh, still brutal, but it didn't come close to the agony etched across his face from the relentless anxiety of watching his daughter's struggle against death.

The clock on the wall ticked away, each second pounding in his ears. He closed his eyes and prayed—praying for Ashley while hoping his words would drown out the clock's ruthless countdown.

Off in the distance came a low hum, morphing a few seconds later into a shallow rhythm of thumps each one growing heavier. The sound of metal connectors from outside clanked together. He jerked his head up and stared out onto the dark heliport. A split second later a wash of blinding white light filled the hallway. He stood in the harsh glare of the floodlights, yet all he could imagine was the angel's approach, his wings stretching up and down with the rhythm of the helicopter, just as Ms. Hicks had promised.

Twenty-Four Hours Later

Bree sat rigid in the plastic chair, a bouquet of white lilies clutched in her lap. She kept smoothing the ribbon absently, thumb tracing the edge where the card was tucked.

A nurse walked by, smiling without making eye contact.

The flowers looked wrong in her hands—too soft, too final for where they were in this journey.

Charlie stood beside the window, staring out at nothing. Neither of them spoke. They didn't need to. Everything had already been said. Every prayer had already been prayed.

At last, her fingers found the card. *Get well soon*, it read. *We're all praying for her*. Inside the envelope was a *Following the Love* token.

Bree stared into the flowers as a tear slipped free, landing softly on a petal.

"Mrs. Carraway, would you like me to put them with the others before we go in?"

She looked up to find Ms. Hicks standing with her clipboard in hand, a warm smile across her face. Bree handed the bouquet to her, then watched as she placed them in the corner where so many others were stacked and spilling into one another, stems crossing, cards tucked everywhere there was room. Ms. Hicks plucked the *Following the Love* token from the envelope and placed it on a pile of several hundred others. She walked back and reached out to take Bree's hand. "Ready to go see her?"

Bree nodded.

Ms. Hicks led Bree and Charlie down the halls of the transplant ICU, stopping short of going into Ashley's room. She pulled out two surgical masks.

"Here, you'll always need these whenever you're around her or anywhere else in the ICU. And remember, she's going to be exhausted, and her voice is still hoarse from being intubated for so long."

"Is it okay for her to speak?" Charlie asked.

"Yes but just take it slow." She gently eased the door open.

Bree and Charlie carefully made their way inside, tiptoeing to her bedside where she lay, eyes closed. Tubes, wires and hoses still engulfed her, multiple monitors beeping and humming, following her vitals.

Charlie bent over to kiss her forehead, but Ms. Hicks waved him off. "Sorry, Mr. Carraway, remember—no germ passing."

"Oh, I'm sorry!"

"Who's sorry?" The voice came rusty, dry and fragile. Ashley's eyes opened, her eyebrows struggling to arch upward.

"Hey, sunshine," Charlie said softly, his eyes glistening.

Bree stood behind him, hands over her mask, tears streaming down behind it.

"Mom, would you stop it—I made it."

Bree nodded. "Yes! You did, honey…you told us you would."

"How do you feel?" Charlie asked.

She blinked up at him. "Like an ole smoopy britches."

Charlie glanced at Bree. Their eyes crinkled at the edges.

"Smoopy britches," Charlie said. "Hmmm, I'll have to confer with Dr. VanGilder about that particular condition."

Ms. Hicks chuckled. "She's on some heavy painkillers right now so her responses may seem a little wacky."

"Hey, Dad!" she said. "Didja know Dusty's here?"

"What's that, hon?"

With a raspy swoon, she replied, "Dusty…my Dusty. Love of my life, my sweet Dusty."

Charlie shook his head. "Dusty who?"

"The Dashley Dusty."

Charlie looked at Bree and shrugged.

"She must be talking about Dusty Harmon," Ms. Hicks said.

"That's him, sister!" she said, rolling her head to Charlie like a drunken sailor. "He's a patient too."

Ms. Hicks shook her head toward Charlie. "She evidently overheard some of the nurses talking about him." She turned to Ashley. "And when you're all well again, you might want to send him one of your dad's tokens."

"Why's that, Ms. Hicks?" Bree asked.
"It was his helicopter that delivered Ashley's heart."

Chapter Thirty-Three

Four Weeks Later
(Two days before Easter)

The Dashley eased into the Carraways' driveway. For a moment, it idled beside the junker Charlie had been driving since the luxury van was repossessed—until Dusty Harmon came to the rescue by buying it back for them.

The side door slid open. Inside, Ashley sat upright in her wheelchair—smaller and frailer than she had been a month before but alive in a way she had never quite been.

Charlie jumped out of the driver's seat and rushed to the ramp, his hands steady as he guided the chair to the ground. Bree came running out the front door, Lydia following behind and smiling broadly. For a second no one spoke. This was new ground. It was the same home with a new beginning.

Moments later they were gathered around the kitchen table. A long banner with *Welcome Home Ashley* written across it stretched above them. In the middle of the table was a cake with a big purple heart scrolled in icing on top of it. Surrounding it were all the *Following the Love* tokens that had been sent to her while she was in the hospital.

"Good gosh," she said. "How many do you think there are?"

"A lot!" said Charlie.

Lydia stretched her arms wide, bending down for a hug. "I bet you're happy to be home!"

"You wouldn't believe how much!" she said.

Just then the doorbell rang. Bree ran off to answer it.

Ashley gave Lydia a knowing look. "I bet I know who that is!"

"Just a solicitor," Bree said, walking back in.

Ashley frowned. "Shoot, I was hoping it was Xander. By the way, can someone tell me where my favorite X-man's been? Every time I've asked, you all change the subject. Don't tell me he's been friend-shunned."

Lydia looked away, hiding the building tears. The room went quiet.

Charlie took her by the hands. "We didn't want to tell you while you were in the hospital for fear of it affecting your recovery."

Ashley's eyes darted to Bree then landed on Lydia, who sat with her hands between her knees, her eyes on the floor. "What is it? Is something wrong?"

Charlie sat at the kitchen table with Bree next to him, her hand gripping his forearm while he continued holding on to Ashley's. Lydia occupied the chair beside her, her head still lowered.

Ashley stared down into the piles of tokens as if summoning all the prayers that had accompanied them to somehow be redirected back in time to Xander, shielding him from the bullet that took his life.

Charlie could still hear his own words hanging in the air—careful, steady, cruel in their honesty. Lydia's fiancé. Ashley's friend. Gone.

No one rushed to fill the silence.

"I'm sorry," Charlie said finally, his voice even lower now. "I wish there was some other way to tell you."

Ashley didn't look up. She nodded once, small and mechanical. She turned to Lydia. "You said his heart was donated. Do you know to who?"

Lydia shook her head. "They don't tell you who it goes to."

Bree sighed. "It's their policy. It was part of the paperwork we signed as well."

"That doesn't make sense."

"I agree," Lydia said. "All I know is they used Dusty Harmon's helicopter to transport it to wherever it was being transplanted."

Bree and Charlie turned to Ashley, their eyes following her hand as it moved over her chest.

Charlie was halfway out the door when Bree called after him. "Wait," she said, hurrying toward him with a folded card in her hand. "You almost forgot this."

Charlie took it, turning the card over once, a chuckle slipping out. "Doesn't quite seem like enough, does it?"

Bree smiled. "I'm pretty sure he already knows how we feel."

"You think he'll be there?"

"I've got a good feeling about that too."

A moment later, he stood on his neighbor's front step, idly twirling the keys to the van he'd borrowed weeks earlier. The morning sun warmed his back as birds chirped nearby, and with a full heart he drew in an easy breath and smiled to himself. Behind him, the van waited at the curb, gleaming beneath its fresh coat of paint.

"Top of the morning to you, Sir King of Kindness," came Doug's sunny welcome from inside the house. The screen door opened. "Don't tell me you've had enough of my dumpster on wheels?"

Charlie held out the keys to him. "Bree and I want to thank you from the bottom of our hearts for letting us use it. And I hope you don't mind, but as much as I know you enjoyed the original rustic finish on the old gal, I thought you wouldn't mind if I gave her a new coat."

Doug looked over Charlie's shoulder, bug-eyed. "A new paint job! Are you serious?" He squinted. "And where're all the dents?"

"It's the least we could do," Charlie said, handing him the keys.

"You're too much, Carraway." He shook his head. "Can't wait for Doris to see her." He swung his head again. "Wow, that's all I can say…just wow, and thank you."

"I also wanted to give you something." He reached in his pocket and pulled out a *Following the Love* token. "You're one of the first to get a new one. Notice anything different?"

Doug cupped it in his hands and stared down at the logo, his eyes turning up at the edges as he traced the image of the cross that had been added next to the heart. "I love it, Charlie—absolutely love it!" He slapped him on the shoulder. "Well done, mister!" He hesitated just long enough to soften his voice. "Charlie…you can't imagine how happy we all were when we found out you weren't involved in that fraud case. And…I'm so sorry about your friend Xander. I-I just don't have the words."

"That's okay. I appreciate it. He was truly special."

"I'm just glad they've got that Sinclair guy behind bars now."

Charlie nodded. "Yeah…well, I better get going. I've got a special trip to make."

"Will you be back for Easter sunrise service tomorrow?"

"Absolutely! I'm not going far." He turned and trotted off to the Dashley.

The Blue Ridge Parkway unfurled ahead of Charlie as he guided the Dashley through the curves, the road lifting him higher with each mile. What rose with it was no longer dread, but something gentler, something welcoming. He hummed to the van's quiet rhythm, a small, unguarded smile finding him by surprise. He glanced at his hand on the wheel, noticing how much the tremors had faded to residual traces of something that now belonged to his past.

His thoughts drifted to the meeting ahead; not certain it would come to pass yet holding to the hope that it might. There was a calm in the thought now, a steady knowing that answers rarely announced themselves with thunder. More often, they arrived on clear days, in beautiful places, when the heart was finally open—ready to listen, ready to be humbled.

The Devil's Courthouse overlook sign appeared, modest and weathered as before, but now surrounded with a fringe of wildflowers—delicate purples, yellows, and whites swaying gently in the breeze. Charlie turned in, the van settling onto the loose stones as it came to rest. He shut off the engine and lingered for a moment, listening to it tick as it cooled, sunlight glinting across the hood. Stepping out he scanned the empty parking lot then lifted his eyes toward the overlook. It too was deserted.

For several minutes, he leaned against the Dashley, head tilted back, eyes fixed on the railing of the overlook. It was a sharp reminder of that day decades ago—the day that had carved fear so deeply into him he had avoided this place ever since. He could still feel the panic and the gut-wrenching horror of how his brother had lost his footing and fell to his death, leaving him with the guilt of not being able to save him.

And yet now, as the spring wind brushed his face and sunlight warmed his shoulders, something unnamable stirred within him, reaching down and untangling the grip that terror had on him for all those years. The dread loosened, unraveling so suddenly it felt miraculous, leaving him empty of fear. He moved forward without thought, drawn almost instinctively to the path leading to the summit.

A few minutes later he was standing at the top, the overlook unfolding before him. He turned, expecting— hoping—to see the man he had come to meet, but found only a clear blue sky, clouds billowing lazily above the vast panorama of mountains stretching out into infinity.

"Charlie." The voice, warm and familiar, drifted to him. He turned to find Peter clad in his same red poncho, only this time he was free of his backpack. "I'm glad to see you." His smile stretched wide, his eyes bright and welcoming.

"I didn't know if you'd be here," Charlie said, "but somehow I did. I-I just had to come."

Peter remained smiling, letting him go on uninterrupted.

"After everything that's happened and how you've been there for us…well…I mean, your messages and all. I'm not sure how to tell you how much it meant to us." He looked down for a moment, staring into the huge granite beneath his feet. "I'm just sorry for not appreciating it like I should have or understanding it as Bree did." He reached into his pocket and pulled out the folded card she had given him. "This is for you. To be honest, Bree wrote most of it but…"

"What? No token?" Peter said with a grin.

"No tokens, not anymore—not from me anyway. The site is all Lydia's now. I'm on to something else, something with Bree and Ashley."

Peter returned a knowing smile. "Mission work suits the Carraways well, I do believe."

"How'd you know it was…" He shook his head. "Never mind."

Peter looked down on the card, his eyes crinkling up at the edges as he scanned it. "You're married to a special lady," Peter said.

"I don't deserve her," Charlie replied, his eyes beginning to glisten.

"Of course you do," Peter said. "And she's blessed to have you as well. You now stand equally yoked in a bond that our Father has always intended. Bree has helped you along the way, but in your heart it has always been your journey. The storms you've weathered are ones that I've seen break other men, driving them away, but through it all…you've chosen Him."

"He was always there," Charlie said. "Just like you said. He never left me."

Peter placed a hand on his shoulder. "And he never will." His smile grew bigger, his eyes warmer. Slowly he turned to the side, allowing Charlie to see beyond him.

At the edge of the overlook, at the abyss where Samuel fell to his death, was a bright light, a magnificent glowing white light, greater and more brilliant than Charlie had ever seen or could ever imagine. From within its center, across the overlook, came a force so powerful, so wonderful it dropped him to his knees. Time stopped, the earth stood still, and all sound drifted away as the feeling embraced him. He squeezed his eyes and let the warmth and beauty of the moment radiate throughout him. Without words being spoken, he heard from within his soul how much he was loved. As he opened his eyes, the light had expanded around him, spanning beyond all horizons into infinity. In front of him, a figure stood, translucent yet with the subtle details of a man with long flowing hair, a beard and robe, his hands held out to his sides and holding those of two others. One was Xander, the other Samuel. Both were smiling, both happy. In that moment Charlie knew they were at home with their Father, the figure who remained standing before him in all his glory now reaching out to him as they faded away. With his head lowered, Charlie stepped forward as the loving arms of his Creator embraced him. His breath left him as the love enveloped him. He didn't know where he was anymore, only that he didn't want it to end. This was where he was meant to be.

Then, from below the cliff, the raspy cry of a peregrine falcon rose through the distance as a gentle breeze whispered over his skin. Below, car doors shut and the faint laughter of sightseers floated up to him. The moment he wanted to hold on to dissolved when he opened his eyes to a vacant overlook.

He turned in place, searching for Peter, hoping—almost pleading—for the moment to unfold again. But he stood alone now. And yet there was no sense of loss. What remained was peace and an understanding that what he had been given could not be taken away.

He stepped to the edge of the overlook and lifted his eyes to the horizon. The mountains stretched before him, vast and silent, and into that stillness came the image of *Manfred on the Jungfrau*—the painting beneath which he had first met Bree. But the vision had changed. Where once a man rushed forward in desperate rescue, now stood Christ—the cross rising behind Him. From it poured the same love that had found him when all his good deeds had still been about himself. The same love that had reached past his pride and his need to be admired. No longer did he need to be seen. He only needed to follow.

The End

A Personal Note from the Author

If you read *Following the Love* I would like to say a heartfelt thank you for sharing your time with me. If you enjoyed it and have time to post an honest review, I would greatly appreciate it. And if you'd like to contact me directly, feel free to email me through my website below.

I love making new friends!

For more info and a list of my other books visit:
LewisPennington.com

www.ingramcontent.com/pod-product-compliance
Lightning Source LLC
Chambersburg PA
CBHW032001150726

47990CB00005B/1791